MORTAL MAYHEM

A Gloam HOLLOW

COZY WITCH MYSTERY

BOOK TWO

JANE LENORE

For more information, address: jlvampa@jlvampa.com.

First edition October 2024

Cover by J.L. Vampa — www.jlvampa.com
Character Art by Yulia Volska
Gloam Hollow Square by Anastasiia K

TikTok: @jlvampa

Paperback ISBN 979-8-3304-8432-4
Ebook AISN B0D47TF2Z2

*For all the reading familiars out there,
and mine: Manon & Moira—the greatest kitties*

Stone
wood
Brews

Zar's
Gelato

THE SPECTRE CAFE
GLOAM HOLLOW CANDY SHOPPE
Broom & Blossom Florist
Gloam Hollow

ENJOY

Gloam HOLLOW

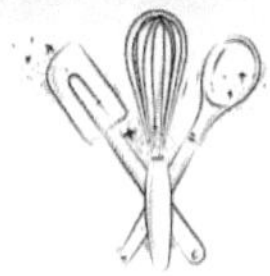

RECIPES

in the back of the book

MORTAL MAYHEM

A Gloam HOLLOW

COZY WITCH MYSTERY

BOOK TWO

SAMHAIN NIGHT

Samhain Night

I can't hear anything over the roar of blood in my ears and my heavy breaths rushing out like bellows blowing into a hearth.

If I could think clearly, I would cast a spell to discern if they were still behind me. But I can't think beyond: *run.*

Tree branches slice at my face, my arms, bramble cutting at my bare feet as I rush through the woods, slipping and sliding on the slick leaves.

I risk a look backward—just one. I can still see the glow of the Samhain bonfire between the naked trees, but nothing else. Only dark shadows looming.

I don't see anyone, hear anyone, but I can't trust my ears.

And I've made a fatal error.

At my glance backward, I missed seeing the branch hanging low ahead of me.

With a slap, my face crashes into it. I fall to the forest floor, realizing with blood-chilling terror that my glasses have fallen off in the mayhem. On my knees, I scramble for them through the leaves. But it's no use. My hands are too cold. Trembling too much. I can't find them.

Maybe this was a mistake.

No. I can't think like that. Forward. I have to keep going.

I stand, but then I sense someone behind me.

Instantly, I freeze.

I have to keep moving. But now I can't trust my eyes, either.

CHAPTER 1

Six Days Earlier

"**T**he floor is *sticky*."

I didn't have to see Hamish's face to know it looked like he'd been sucking on a lemon. In his defense, the floor *was* incredibly goopy. Like a bunch of teenagers had unanimously decided to dump all their soda over their shoes and trudge about for three days. But no amount of goo would hamper my joy when the lights were dimmed, the air smelled of popcorn, soda bubbles tickled my nose, and the screen too big for the tiny theater began to glow, a crackle coming over the speakers.

"Hush!" I whispered sharply at my cousin, snatching the popcorn from him. "It's starting."

Maggie reached across Hamish to grab a handful of popcorn, but at the same time, I stole the bucket, resulting in her lightly slapping Hamish's leg by accident. He yowled at her and this time the shushing came from everyone in the theater.

A deep chuckle came from my left as Aramis dunked his hand into the popcorn bucket. "Told you we should have gotten two," he whispered in my ear, causing a shiver to run up my arms.

We still hadn't been on an *actual* first date, Aramis and I. *Spectre Café* had officially been cleared as a crime scene and opened a couple of weeks ago, and he'd been swamped ever since. I knew his food was phenomenal, and now the entirety of Gloam Hollow did too. Most days, the wait to get in was ridiculous, so I'd only been there twice to eat—once on opening day and once for dinner with Mags and Hamish as promised before all the *murder* occurred in our sleepy mountainside town.

No other crimes had been reported in the few weeks since the last murder, and nothing suspicious had happened, but we were all sort of living in a state of expectancy. We knew for a fact that someone wanted Aramis dead, and that, most likely, someone had attempted to frame him for the murder of his employee, Steven Littlebottom. Our working theory was that at least three people had been present in Gloam Hollow in connection with the vendetta against Aramis and there was a possibility the attack on Anon a few weeks ago was also connected.

It was all we had to go on at the moment, but life has this funny way of just continuing, no matter what travesty has happened or how anxious you are for something to be solved.

Aramis and his handler/friend, Kenny, compiled a list of those Aramis had put away during his time as a detective and private investigator who might wish him harm. Sheriff Corbin Oliphant and I, however, had yet to see this list because Aramis refused to put either of us in danger by having it in our possession. I didn't see how having a list of people would put us in danger, but Sheriff had seen his point, so I assumed my naivety had been apparent in that argument.

Tonight, Aramis had managed to slip away from the café just before closing time to meet my cousins and me for a late movie, but he didn't know Oliphant planned to ambush him when it was over. Corbin's agreement about the infamous *list* could only last so long. There was a killer on the loose, after all.

Maybe I should feel bad about the ambush, but I don't. Aramis gave up the detective life and his badge when he moved to The Hollow, and now he was too busy at the café to save himself, so Sheriff and I were on the case. (Perhaps my involvement came a little reluctantly on Oliphant's side, but we don't need to talk about that.)

Mags only jumped at the (completely predictable) scary parts of the movie five times, and before we knew it, the credits were rolling. Aramis stretched beside me, a stifled yawn pulling at his mouth.

"Don't you dare tell me you were bored!" Maggie accused Aramis. "That movie was terrifying. I'm going to have nightmares for a moon!"

Hamish rolled his eyes. "You realize we've already seen that movie twice, right? This theater only has about ten films."

I stood from my seat and Aramis did the same. "We have to figure out how to get newer movies here," he said, headed for the end of our row of seats. "From the posters I saw in the lobby, they're all at least a decade old. Some were closer to five."

"Hey, I like the classics," I pouted as we all filed out, my platform boots sticking to the ground with each step, a little *skritch, skritch, skritch* sound following all of us until we reached the blood-red carpet of the tiny lobby.

"The classics are, arguably, the pinnacle of film," Aramis said, falling back to walk beside me. "I'll give you that, but —" He stopped mid-sentence and halted. "Hm. Why is Oliphant here and looking like he's about to arrest me again?" Aramis looked down at me with a raised brow and I grimaced.

"That's our cue," Hamish sang, and whisked Maggie out the side door and into the cool night.

Aramis stood perfectly still, his mouth set in a bemused grin while he waited for Sheriff Oliphant to approach.

"Blair." Corbin dipped his chin. "Hawthorne."

"Oliphant." Aramis cut to the chase. "To what do we owe the pleasure? You don't seem like the late-night horror flick type."

Obviously Aramis already had at least *some* semblance of an idea why the sheriff was there. He was, after all, a good enough detective to make enemies...

"We need the list, Aramis," I spoke first, pulling at his sleeve. "We've waited long enough and Steven's killer is probably already long gone. We don't have much of a chance of finding them unless we track down who's after you or they come back, and—"

"They *are* going to come back," Oliphant finished for me. "Or the entire thing will repeat itself at the very least. Someone on that list wants you dead. I'm not willing to let any more harm come to Gloam Hollow while we wait around."

Aramis's jaw tightened. "I don't want that any more than

you do. Kenny and I have been looking into the cretins on that list. We haven't just been sitting on the information."

"You're not a detective anymore, son. You need to hand the list over and let me do my job."

"Nobody needs that list in their possession but me," Aramis shot back. "I'm not risking anybody else over this. Come to the café for breakfast in the morning and I will *show* you the list."

Oliphant gave one of his long, famous sighs. "Son, I'll still have to write the names down. That's how this works."

I had a sudden, brilliantly Witchy idea. "What if I make a memory potion for you?" Both men looked at me. "It could help you retain the information you read after you've taken it."

"That could work..." Aramis rubbed at his beard, considering.

"If I make it last long enough, we could even destroy the list so no one has it."

Oliphant was shaking his head in a manner that most would see as dismay, but I knew him better than I knew my own father and I suspected there was pride in the gesture too. "You'd better get to brewing then, darlin'. I'll see you both bright and early."

Aramis helped me wrangle myself into my gorgeous deep olive trench-style peacoat from Aunt Moira's new Dark Academia clothing line. Technically, my entire ensemble was from her new line set to debut in a couple of weeks. A pair of darkest-chocolate wool trousers, a black turtleneck made of such a soft, airy cashmere that Moira *had* to have spelled the material, and a pair of platform lace-up boots just a shade lighter than the trousers. I'd opted for a long braid over one shoulder and, of course, the wire-rimmed glasses I was helpless without.

"Walk you to the apothecary?" Aramis asked, holding out his elbow like a gentleman.

I looped my arm through and said with exaggerated gusto, "To *The Copper Cauldron!*"

Aramis chuckled, deep and throaty, and I felt it in my toes. In general, I enjoyed being the one to make anyone laugh or smile, but Aramis? It was like orbiting the moon.

Outside the theater, the crisp air of autumn had begun to dip lower, headed toward frigid. This meant the entirety of Gloam Hollow was preparing for Samhain. I, for one, was positively giddy. Our seasons follow no predictable order, and we're just as likely to be thrust into spring rain or back into the heat of summer without warning as we are to remain in autumn perpetually. Why our seasons do this, we aren't exactly sure, but legend has it that four witch sisters dubbed *The Sisters Solstice* preside over the magic in our realm, and they select our season based on their fancy. Or, as Grandma Wardwell insists, their foul tempers. That would certainly explain why we have spring one day and winter the next sometimes. But they *never* miss Samhain— that is if the legends are to be believed.

I snuggled into my coat as Aramis and I walked around the square to my apothecary. I smiled at the cheery plastic skeleton inside the bank's front window, and my handsome Dread Monster escort pointed at the decoration.

"Someone told me there's a walking skeleton in Gloam Hollow." His breath clouded the air in front of his mouth just a little more now than it had on our way into the theater. "Why haven't I seen him?"

"Balthazar," I chirped. "But he goes by *Zar*. He pushes

around Art's candy cart during the spring and summer, offering taffy and things like that. He usually takes a break during fall and winter. He says the cold makes his bones ache, but he always pops up for Samhain."

Aramis regarded me with his brow furrowed. "He takes a break? For moons at a time? As in he hibernates somewhere?"

I laughed. "If you call holing up in his apartment above Art's shop playing video games *hibernating*."

"Wait." Aramis stopped walking, so I did as well. "Now, hear me when I say I don't mean to be insensitive, but..."

"But he doesn't have eyes or a brain or muscles." I shrugged. "It's best not to question it."

He blew out a breath and laughed. "I'm definitely looking forward to Samhain now. I need to meet this skeleton."

"Zar prefers the term '*Unbodied*.'"

"Right. Of course." Aramis gave me a wry smile and we continued walking.

The *Spectre Café* stood next to the bank, and I was pleased to see Aramis had also hung Samhain decorations. "Little Witch hat lights," I breathed, my eyes lighting up like most creatures' do looking at a Yule tree.

Aramis shrugged and strode onward, his hands in his pockets as he left me gawking. When I didn't follow, he turned back with a half-smile. "Come on, Wardwell."

Blessed be those Solstice Witches for their seasonal selection because I *live* for Samhain. What Witch wouldn't? The honoring of the dead, the celebration of colder moons, and, of course, the festivities. With the Harvest Festival behind us and the trees going bare, Gloam Hollow had put away hay bales and apple-bobbing. Instead, most of the shops boasted festive lights in the shape of little plastic skulls, pumpkins, or bats. All the colorful leaves still littered the ground, and all the pumpkins around town would soon be carved into Jack-o'-Lanterns to scare away bad spirits.

In reality, it sounds a lot spookier than it is. For Witches, Samhain is a night for letting go of the past and negativity to embrace the future. And no one throws a better Samhain Night bonfire than Grandma Wardwell at *Moonrise Manor Inn*, so all the mythical creatures of The Hollow love to join in.

I hadn't yet decorated *The Copper Cauldron* for Samhain because I'd had very little time between my sleuthing and Grandma's long list of bonfire preparation demands to do so. Thus, *The Cauldron* was just its usual Witchy mix of gloom and cozy, all dark shades and warm candlelight, colorful potion bottles, and resident spiderwebs. I spelled open the lock, turning to Aramis, and realized I wasn't yet ready to say goodnight, despite how terribly late it was.

"Would you like to keep me company while I brew the potion?"

The look that crossed his face was one I couldn't decipher. His moss-colored eyes seemed to glow, his jaw going tight and his shoulders just a bit rigid. He stepped closer, his lips parting like he was about to say something, but then he closed his mouth again. My coat was suddenly feeling far too hot. With the back of his knuckle, he gently traced the curve of my face. When he reached my chin, he took it in his fingers and brushed his thumb along my jawline. I watched with increasingly uneven breaths as his gaze dropped to my lips before sliding back up with what seemed like quite a lot of forced effort.

"I don't think that's a very good idea, Wardwell," he said

quietly, a rasp to his voice I hadn't yet heard from him, but really, *really* wanted to hear more often. "I'll wait up for you next door, though. Come knock when you're finished brewing and I'll walk you home."

His hand dropped from my chin and he slowly strode to the café.

CHAPTER 2

I walked into my apothecary, carelessly flinging my magic out to light the gas lamps before I tore off my coat and sank against the door. I needed to get it together. I couldn't brew a complicated potion with an addled brain. But there was one thing for sure, I would be able to live off the way Aramis had just said my name for at least the next moon.

Fanning myself, I grabbed one of the wicker hand baskets meant for customers and perused my shelves for any bottled ingredients I might need. I'd not cast this particular spell before, but I'd jotted its page number down when I was researching tracking potions after the first murder. It had seemed useful at the time, along with a handful of other spells, and I was grateful I'd marked them.

With the items I could recall in hand, I let my magic pluck the correct grimoire from the shelf. Delicately, it floated down onto the counter and flipped open to the intended spell. I scanned the list of ingredients.

- Rosemary

- Thyme
- Sage
- Bay Leaf
- Coffee Beans

"Ah, the coffee is what I forgot," I murmured to myself, darting to the back room for a bag of my *Stonewood* coffee beans and two fresh vials—one for Aramis, one for Sheriff. With my hand clasped around the vials, the pair of them clinking together, I lifted my chin and decided to grab a third. One for me. I was in this whether the *boys* liked it or not.

Once I had those sitting with my basket of other ingredients, I retrieved a large glass jar of moonwater and my mortar and pestle. Carefully, I placed each ingredient into the mortar, keeping my intention clear and concise in my mind's eye: *Recall with a photographic memory,* and crushed the ingredients one at a time. When each was sufficiently pulverized, I deposited them into my copper cauldron over the ever-lit fire.

Stirring in the moonwater slowly, I had to be careful to tailor the spell and my intention correctly. It would be dangerous to cause someone to remember *everything* with a photographic memory—a brain isn't meant to handle so much, it would drive them mad. And it wouldn't do to remember too little either or have the timing wrong. Say someone remembers everything they saw an hour after taking the potion rather than what they're immediately seeing after consumption. It would also be useless to recall something with photographic memory if it only lasted ten seconds.

Pleased I'd managed what was necessary and that I'd

been quite careful, I let my intention fall away. The potion immediately began to glow a buttery yellow color, and my spellwork was finished.

Yawning repeatedly, I poured three vials of the potion and stoppered them. I let my magic melt yellow wax over the corks—this part is very important—and I left the rest of the potion in the cauldron to bottle at work tomorrow after I'd gotten some sleep. Leaving my mess for the morning as well, I deposited the three vials into my bag and lazily threw a spell to lock the apothecary behind me for the night.

Half-asleep, I walked next door to the café and peered in the glowing window to find a Dread Monster also barely clinging to consciousness. Aramis had a book open in his lap where he sat on a stool at the bar, angled so he could also see out the front windows. Well, he could have if his eyes weren't nearly closed. I knocked on the window and he jerked upright, almost falling off his stool. I couldn't help but giggle and, though he couldn't hear me, he immediately smiled, albeit looking a little embarrassed.

Feet dropping down from the stool, he closed the book and set it on the counter. I watched him flick off a couple of light switches and he was outside in the chilly air with me in no time. "How'd it go?" he asked me as he locked up with a key—the poor non-magic-wielding creature.

"It went well. Hey, who spelled your locks when you bought the café? Wardwell or Tuttle?"

One of the Wardwell or Tuttle Witches—the strongest two Witch families in Gloam Hollow—usually spelled every lock in town to only answer to those the owner intends. Sometimes this is a simple procedure, and sometimes it's ridiculously complicated. Like the time Mom sent me to spell Ms. Cooper's *Cards and Paper Store*. Though she looks like a sweet elderly lady about the size of a thimble with a halo of white hair, she's actually a terrifying Banshee. This, coupled with the fact that she's Gloam Hollow's resident Gossip Princess (only second to Queen Lilly Tuttle), meant it was a nightmare. The list of people she wanted to allow through the spell was mind-boggling. So-and-so, but only if they have gossip, so-and-so, but only if they have bad news, *never* so-and-so unless she has pie, and so on and so on. Two hours into the weaving of a complicated spell, I told her I had to take a break and came back with Mags. We got it done, but Ms. Cooper had shifted into her Banshee form by the end, reminded of all the people in The Hollow she was angry with for one reason or another. She chased Mags and me out, screaming until I thought our ears would bleed.

Aramis shoved his keys into his pockets and held out his arm for me to take. It was funny how such a small gesture had become a custom for us as we walked these last couple of weeks. "I wasn't here for the spelling of my locks, but I remember the phone call." He chuckled, his eyes crinkling at the corners. "Kenny had been here overseeing the remodeling for only a few days when Ms. Lilly came in like a wrecking ball, demanding it was time to spell the locks."

This struck me as odd, considering Ms. Lilly was the one who was pestering everyone about café details before Aramis took down the paper covering the windows from prying eyes, but I didn't say as much.

"Ken called me a few hours later to say she'd finally left and I thought he was going to have to sleep for a week after dealing with her."

Kenny was a new friend of mine, but I'd certainly gathered he didn't enjoy being around people for long stretches of time. The introvert in me *definitely* understood that.

"That must have been a sight to see. Ms. Lilly is a force to be reckoned with, that's for sure."

Exhaustion clung to us both like fog to the leaves, but every second with Aramis was more and more precious to me every day. I wanted to know every detail about him, everything that happened in the hours between our stolen moments together. The conversation always flowed so easily that I'd eventually given in to the idea that maybe, just maybe, he felt the same way about me. We moved from subject to subject seamlessly without ever having to ask the boring get-to-know-you type questions. It was this easy, uncomplicated thing despite how complicated our lives actually were.

It dawned on me then that the beauty of life resides in those places—the in-between where we're safe to be seen, to enjoy a reprieve from the storms that will never cease no matter what our walk of life.

Though I said none of this aloud, the corner of Aramis's mouth tipped up as if I had, and he dropped his arm, catching my hand in his and twining our fingers together. "Coffee for your thoughts?"

A laugh bubbled up out of me. "That isn't the phrase."

"Anyone who shoves you into a cliché phrase is dead to me." He smirked down at me and shrugged. "Coffee, on the other hand, you respond well to."

I tipped my head back and laughed full and free, spying the waning moon shining down on us as we left the square. "I do enjoy coffee— Oh, hey!" With a little hop, I sped up and pulled Aramis along. Turning around to see his face, my heart flipped at the spark in his eyes. "It's closed, but I want to show you something."

He listened earnestly while we walked as I told him about a concert Mags and I had dragged Hamish to one summer, his tired face perking up when he realized the band I was talking about.

Dropping my hand, he stopped walking and stepped back. "Was this in Dornwich, three years ago?"

I nodded, cheeks hurting from smiling so much.

"I was there!" he crowed.

"You were not."

"I swear it," he laughed, lifting his palms in a show of honesty. "That year was awful. I'd just quit the police force and started private investigation, but it was tough." His enthusiasm dropped a fraction, and his eyes filled with too many emotions for me to decipher. "Anyway, I took off after a particularly heinous case. I just needed a break, so a road trip out of the city sounded perfect. I spent ten days going to every show I could find on the East Coast. The one in Dornwich was undoubtedly my favorite."

And I'd been there. To think, what would have happened if I'd met him that night?

Maybe I did see him. Maybe he passed right by me.

Life is so peculiarly beautiful sometimes.

"C'mon," I eventually said, and pulled him along down Pecan St. until we stopped in front of the record shop I'd promised to show him weeks ago.

The red paint around the exterior separated it vividly from the handyman store on its left and cell phone and computer shop on its right. *RECORDS* in giant neon letters glared down on us, bathing us in red light. Two lonely security lights shown on the records spinning from fishing wire in the large windows, one on each side of the door plastered with band posters—mostly shows in New Haven and Dornwich. I watched with a deep sense of joy as Aramis cupped his hands around his eyes against the window, peering in, his breath fogging the glass.

"It's too dark to see much," I said. "We'll have to come back when it's open."

Aramis removed his face from the window and turned around. "I've seen enough to know I'll be lost in there for hours."

"If you don't already have too many records," I teased.

"There is no such thing. One can never have too much music or too many books."

"Agreed." I dipped my chin once, very diplomatically and Aramis laughed. "They have CD's, tapes, and even 8-tracks as well."

His jaw went slack. "They do not."

I chuckled and we ventured back toward Wardwell Cottage in no rush, despite how tired we were. When we eventually reached the tree tunnel road that leads to the cottage, I pulled Aramis to a stop. Staring up at the twisted branches and their remaining few leaves above cocooning us in, I inhaled the coming promise of winter. "It won't be long," I said softly.

"Until what?" I could feel Aramis's attention on my face instead of the trees, and my cheeks flushed.

"Snow."

"And how do you know that?" He'd taken a step closer.

I moved my attention to Aramis and smiled. "I can feel it."

For the second time tonight, Aramis's gaze dropped to

my lips, then crawled back up to my eyes. "Let's get you home, Wardwell."

CHAPTER 3

Turns out my alarm was useless. As was the misguided thought that I might be able to soak up the last few minutes of blessed sleep before the alarm was to beep at me.

Instead, I was awoken by a smudge stick shoved under my nose and a very terse, "B, get up. We need to cleanse the workshop."

I shoved Hamish's hand away and hid under my duvet, groaning. He threw the smudge stick onto the comforter, claiming it was staining, so I '*better hurry*.'

Most likely, the shriek emanating from me was far more dramatic than was strictly necessary, but you must understand how much I *love* my comforter. After clawing my way out from under it to inspect the damage, I realized it was all just a ploy. I promptly threw the smudge stick at Hamish's head—ten points—and Grandma-Wardwell-Cursed him all the while putting on my glasses, robe, and slippers and following him down to the workshop.

Mags and Aunt Millie were already there, waving their

smudge sticks around and swaying in the tendrils of smoke, chanting.

"What's going on?" I asked Hamish in a whisper. "I can't help cleanse if I don't know what's happened."

His voice low, Hamish explained in a rush, "Grandma came by last night to retrieve her little experimental paste made out of Aunt Millie's cross-bred herbs. When she got here, she felt the tell-tale tingle of a hex."

Immediately, I shut out everything natural around me and listened with my Witch sense. The hair on my arms stood up, and a chill ran up my back, almost like a little spider had just skittered up my spine. "I can sense it, too."

Hamish nodded grimly. "No one can get in the cottage without Wardwell permission, so Grandma thinks the hex was on something one of us brought in."

We'd all been in the workshop countless times lately, even Mom who has her own secret brewing room in her private wing of *Moonrise Manor Inn*.

"Who would want to hex us?" I asked Hamish, conjuring a flame to light my smudge stick and promptly shaking it out. My tendril of smoke joined the others in the room.

"Beats me." Hamish lit his stick as well and began waving it around methodically.

We chanted and waved for several moments before Grandma stopped us. "That'll do, for now, darlings."

She set her smudge stick on a ceramic mushroom plate in the middle of the work table and we all did the same, the last of the smoke twining through the bundles of hanging herbs and curling up into the plant-strewn rafters.

"The hex will not be broken by what we've just done alone," Grandma explained, "but it will hold off the effects until I can decipher what in a crow's tomato foot is going on."

I pursed my lips together so as not to chuckle at Grandma's *bananas* version of cursing. Hamish coughed into his fist and I could only guess he was having similar thoughts.

"Have you three brought anything or anyone out of the ordinary into this cottage as of late? Or made another Witch in this town angry?" Grandma was about half my size, but at least thrice as fierce. She squinted at us all, her hands on her hips. "And don't you lie to me. I will make a batch of truth serum as quick as you can kiss a toad."

"Gross," Maggie muttered, her face twisting in a pucker that led me to believe she'd had personal experience kissing a toad.

"I'm certain none of you have forgotten the last time." Grandma looked meaningfully at each of us as our attention dropped to our toes and I suddenly felt thirteen again.

There was absolutely zero chance any of us would ever forget the last time we were dosed with truth serum by Grandma. Or *why* we'd been dosed. Three little Witchlings were having a lovely picnic behind *Moonrise Manor,* when *someone* dared *someone* to spell Grandma's beloved hen, Betty, to lay glitter eggs. Now, this spell wouldn't be advisable for even the most seasoned of Witches, but when you're a Witchling, magic is as wonky as hormones, and... Betty was spelled into fried chicken.

"I still can't eat fried chicken!" Grandma scowled.*

---

* Please Note: this statement is entirely false. Penelope Wardwell was seen eating fried chicken last Starday, and Blair Wardwell would bet her entire apothecary that poor Betty hadn't even been spared a thought.

Regardless, no one lied to Grandma Wardwell.

"If we've made someone angry or brought something into the cottage," Mags spoke up, "it was unintentional."

We stood fidgeting beneath her scrutiny for another moment before Grandma softened back into her warm chocolate chip cookie self. "Alright. Think on it today and let me know if you recall anything strange or if something peculiar happens here at the cottage." She kissed each of us on the cheek and bustled out the back door.

I glanced at the owl cuckoo clock on the wall and ran upstairs to get dressed. I didn't know what to expect from my day past breakfast at the café with Aramis and Corbin, so I settled for practical chic (that's a thing, right?) Cropped black denim jeans, a flowy pewter turtleneck sweater—tucked in just at the front—and my trusty, chunky boots. I threw on a little makeup, a dark lip, a few beaded bracelets, and what Mags refers to as my '*pants necklace*' (a delicate chain, thank you very much), and shoved on my headphones over arguably frizzy hair. I'd braid it on the way while I listened to the audiobook of this month's book club read: **LIES AND OTHER VOWS**, a thriller I'd been sucked into irrevocably.

When I told my cousin I had no time for a coffee pre-game, Mags tossed me my peacoat as she sipped her delicious-smelling brew, and I rushed out the door.

The mornings had already begun to feel on the frosty side until the sun cleared the mountains, and I purposefully puffed little clouds of air in front of me as many times as I stopped in the middle of the tree tunnel road, fingers tangled in my hair, to gape at what was happening in my audiobook.

"A *cult*?" I screeched, startling a starling from a low-hanging branch. "There was a cult under the apartment building? Everyone was in it but her?" I all but screamed in excitement. This book's twists were *too* good.

It had been Andrew's pick, the Centaur new to Gloam Hollow. Tina, a friend and employee of Grandma's at the inn, had invited him to book club to try and pawn one of us ladies off on the poor guy. I'd worried about his presence in town on several occasions when the first murder occurred, and several times since Steven Littlebottom's murder, but I'd mostly scratched him off as a suspect. He had been with us at book club when Anon was attacked, and he was allegedly still with Grandma and the other club members around the time when the first murder occurred outside *Toil & Truffle*.

From what I'd been able to gather, Andrew was in town to shoot his new indie film in the forest and surrounding mountains. *Moonrise Manor* was the perfect place for him to stay because the forest began, quite literally, at the inn's back door. Not to mention Aunt Millie often led nature hikes up into the mountains from the inn, and she'd given Andrew the lay of the land. Millie was precisely how we knew what little we did about Andrew, seeing as the Centaur was fairly reserved when it came to sharing about himself, unlike when sharing his book opinions. He'd been an absolute joy to have at book club. We always have great book discussions, but they'd hit a new level since Andrew had joined.

Recovering from my book high, I continued my walk to the square, only stopping to speak with Mr. Pedigrew about the three new frogs he was hoping to purchase this week, and Betty Tuttle, who was still showing off her engagement ring from Cory Tennenbaum like he'd just proposed days ago instead of weeks ago.

Kitty-corner across the square, I just spotted Aunt

Millie's outline as she watered some of her plants in the greenhouse above her floral shop and I waved. I was probably too far away for her to see me, but polite is polite.

One glance into *Spectre Café*'s windows and I could already tell how loud it was going to be inside, so I was prepared when I removed my headphones.

CHAPTER 4

Sure enough, the din of voices and cacophony of clattering plates and silverware drowned out the tinkling of the bell above the door. Still, Aramis immediately noticed me and waved me over as he poured coffee at a table.

"Been waiting for you to finally show up," he said with a faux glower when I reached him.

"Hey, it's only"—I checked my watch—7:30."

"That's a long morning when you're waiting to see someone." He couldn't hold the frown any longer and it slipped into a sideways grin.

I wanted to offer a witty or flirty response, but I was too busy trying to get my mouth to work.

Ms. Lilly waved for Aramis to come over and I followed, picking up a pot of coffee to top off some mugs as we made our way.

"You don't have to do that," Aramis said out the side of his mouth when he saw me stop off to fill Luther Cornick's mug.

"I don't mind. You could use the help with Steven gone, and I know coffee pretty well."

Aramis snorted. "You can say that again."

I stopped to fill up a few more mugs and met Aramis at Ms. Lilly's table just as she requested a type of falafel that wasn't on the menu.

Aramis sighed but eventually gave in. "I'll see what I can do, Ms. Lilly."

"Sit, dear," the elder Witch commanded me, and I plopped down in the chair across from her.

"Your table is over there in the corner," Aramis pointed out, but Ms. Lilly glared at him and he relented. "When you're done here that is." He grinned at her, but his smile was all teeth.

Lilly tapped the rim of her mug like she was the queen and I the servant, but I dutifully filled it for her, then turned to consider getting a mug of my own. Aramis was already there, handing me my favorite cup from his eclectic collection: a deep orange stoneware mug with dark speckles scattered all over it.

"That boy is smitten," Ms. Lilly said between sips when he walked away.

"Aramis?" I asked dumbly and Lilly nodded. "With who?"

"With you, dear. Plain as day."

Part of me wanted to press her to explain why she thought that, but the larger part wanted to avoid the subject completely. "So what's new, hm?" I poured my cup of coffee and took a sip, relishing the bold bitterness and the warmth spreading through my chilled fingertips from the mug.

Ms. Lilly spent the next few moments talking my ear off about town gossip I usually would have been very interested to hear and pass on to Maggie and Hamish, but I found myself tuning her out as I watched Aramis work. He had his shirt sleeves rolled up his forearms and I was learning it was my favorite look.

Did I have a thing for forearms?

"Dear?" Ms. Lucy's voice finally broke through my infatuation.

"Oh, yes?" I took a drink of coffee to cover my blush.

"I asked if you've been reading Katarina's news blog lately."

I tried not to let my confusion show. "I didn't know you read her blog. I thought you preferred *The Hollow Herald*."

Ms. Lilly adjusted the fork sitting on her napkin. "You know I'll take news and gossip any way I can get it." She waved a hand flippantly, her many rings twinking in the café lights.

Sheriff Oliphant strolled in then, and I jumped up. "That's very interesting. I have to get going, Ms. Lilly. You have a lovely day."

"You too, dear."

Grabbing my mug, I caught Corbin's attention and motioned to the table Aramis had set aside for us. Goddess bless the Dread Monster's sweet soul because he already had a carafe of piping hot coffee sitting there, and a little mini pumpkin pie *in* the shape of a pumpkin. *Freaking adorable.*

Corbin grunted. "I take it that's your seat." He sounded mildly dismayed and I wanted to laugh.

Quite cheerfully, I slid into my seat, setting my coffee mug next to the adorable pie and taking the tiniest moment to enjoy not only the aesthetic pleasure of perfectly complimentary colors in my dessert and mug but also the obnoxious, squealy voice in my head singing: *I have a boy who bakes me* pies.

Sheriff grunted as he took his spot in the booth across from me, and I noticed for the first time how much older he was beginning to look these days. Some of my elation faded. "How have you been?" I inquired carefully. Men like Corbin Oliphant don't take kindly to being fussed over.

"I'd be doin' a lot better if I felt like our little hamlet was safe." He poured himself a steaming cup of joe.

"Has something else happened?" I hated to cut into the little cute pie but, c'mon, it's pie—so I did.

"No," he said, almost grumpily, "but it's going to."

The words landed in my chest like a bad omen. As I've probably mentioned before, Witchcraft is performed in as many different ways as there are Witches and Warlocks who perform it. It's not until you really get to know one that you can begin to understand how their version works, and even then it's only a slight understanding. I did, however, know that Sheriff Oliphant was a very powerful Warlock just shy of Wardwell-level, and he had an affinity for scrying. This is almost an archaic form of magic nowadays that most of us no longer practice very often, but it does have its uses, like predicting bad events. But it has its limitations as well. Just because one scries and sees a bad omen in the dark depths of the water or black mirror glass, it doesn't often reveal *what* the event will be, or *when*. To me, it just leads to anxiety.

And that would explain the look on Corbin's face.

I, for one, don't need any help in the anxiety department. I load up on that well enough alone, so I was relieved when Aramis strode over before we could discuss *omens.*

"Sorry about that, guys." He slid into the booth next to me, a towel on his shoulder and a smile spread across his handsome face. He smelled like maple syrup and cinnamon. *Intoxicating.*

"Business is booming, eh?" Corbin said in lieu of a greeting. "Good for you, Hawthorne."

"Aw, shucks, Oliphant. You're gonna make a guy blush."

We all chuckled but sobered quickly and appropriately when Aramis leaned back into the booth's seat to pull a piece of crumpled paper out of his jeans pocket. He spread it out in one of the menus and flipped the thing around to face Corbin. Without missing a beat, Sheriff held one end of the menu open and up to shield the list from prying eyes— just a man putting on his cheater glasses and perusing his food choices.

In reality, I didn't think most of the people in Gloam Hollow would even remotely guess that we were anything but an odd trio of people having breakfast together. That, in itself, was typical for our small town. If you walk into a coffee shop or restaurant and see someone you haven't chatted with in a couple of days, you pop in for a hello and before you know it, you're enjoying the establishment's products together.

I also didn't think anyone would guess we had a list of super-bad people who wanted to see harm come to Aramis. But, in my overly cautious companions' defense, we'd recently had an unknown Golem morph to look like others we *did* know.

I decided three mumbled *'hmms'* into Sheriff's reaction to the list that their caution was founded and I'd respect it.

"Is this some sort of joke, son?" Corbin hissed abruptly, looking at Aramis over the rim of his readers.

"Unfortunately, it is not." Aramis looked both grim and slightly amused. Kind of his go-to look, honestly.

"You've got Alfred Hughes on here." The skepticism on Corbin's face was unabashed. "He runs one of the most sinister mafias in New Haven. Everyone on this side of the country knows what he's up to, but no one can pin him. No one can catch anyone from his crew."

"Except one," Aramis interjected, his hands clasped in front of him on the table. "One guy has been caught in connection to Alfred Hughes."

Sheriff gave Aramis a level stare. "You want me to believe *you're* the one who put away the driver of Alfred Hughes three years ago?"

"Four years ago," Aramis corrected. "And yes. What most don't know is that Alfred's driver is also his illegitimate son."

I gasped and Sheriff ripped his glasses off. I didn't know anything about who they were talking about, but I was *invested*.

Aramis shrugged. "I truly don't think it's Hughes, though. He's sent thugs after me before, but it's not his MO to employ Golems or Mimics. He keeps things in-house."

"In-house?" I asked, leaning in, engrossed.

"Other Werewolves," Aramis explained.

"Like Tom." The words were out of my mouth before I realized I'd even been thinking them.

Sheriff squinted at me. "There's an entire pack of 'Weres in Gloam Hollow, darlin'. Don't single out Tom just because you're angry with him right now."

"I'm not," I spat defensively. "I'm not angry with him or singling him out. There is still something off about the night Anon was attacked. What if Tom was with him? There were three trails in the park."

"But the two that led into the trees most likely weren't connected," Aramis countered.

My pulse spiked with the excitement of a lively debate about to begin. "*However,*" I said slowly, "one trail disappeared in the woods. Like they'd shifted into their true form. Like a Werewolf."

"Or any other creature," Aramis shot back.

Sheriff's eyes were following us back and forth, his brow low.

"I'm not disagreeing that it might have been Tom," Aramis amended. "In fact, I've thought about it quite a lot and..." He grimaced. "Brace yourself, Wardwell."

I frowned at him and rolled my eyes. "Braced."

"I'm not convinced Anon was attacked at all."

Evidently, I had *not* been braced. "Come again?" I said as Sheriff *hmm'd* thoughtfully into his coffee mug.

"Think about it. He wasn't mugged, and his wallet wasn't taken. He fell on his face, but his glasses weren't even smudged. All things *you* pointed out, Wardwell. And according to reports—"

"Hey now," Sheriff interrupted. "How'd you get reports?"

One corner of Aramis's mouth tipped up. "You wanted me to consult on some cases and Mrs. Cobblepot has taken a liking to me."

Sheriff frowned so deeply he resembled a trout with a mustache. "Go on, then." He waved a hand dismissively. "Let's hear it. "

Aramis leaned forward on the table, his face animated in a way I hadn't seen before. A detective at work. "Anon didn't shift, either." He turned to me and I was quite proud I'd already deduced everything he'd said so far on my own. "He's a squirrelly kind of guy. You said he almost shifted just because Katarina left some Pixie dust on the floor of *Stonewood*. I get very tired of cleaning up her sister's Pixie dust here, too, but I'm not in danger of my vipers getting out of control over it."

All very valid points that had my mind whirling again. Judging by Corbin's silence, his mind was at it, too.

"What do you think happened?" I asked Aramis.

"I'm not sure, but we all suspect it has to do with Anon and Tom's new mysterious friend, right?"

Sheriff and I nodded.

"My hunch is it also has to do with—"

"The ink!" I nearly shouted and clapped a hand over my mouth. "*The ink*," I whispered, remembering how excited Lacuna and Tom were about the new glowing tattoo ink provided by the anonymous friend.

"My thoughts exactly," Aramis said. "If you want to know what happened to Anon, I say you follow the ink trail."

"I don't believe Anon's attack, or non-attack, had anything to do with the murders, either," Sheriff interjected. "I just can't see the connection. I've not written it off though, of course." He put his cheaters back on and looked at the list again. A few seconds later, he let out a low whistle. "You have Carmine Fortin on here, too." He watched Aramis over the rims of his glasses.

"Same thing, though," Aramis swatted at the air. "He always employs other Vamps. Neither he nor Hughes would have any sort of frail bird as a symbol, either."

He was probably right. The bird tattoo both the John Doe Golem and the Mimic murderer had didn't exactly scream mafia.

"You've got a point there," Sheriff said, and I was inclined to agree, even though I had no idea who Carmine

Fortin was. My guess was another gang leader and it was comical to picture a scary gang with a sparrow for a mascot. I chuckled at the thought and they both looked at me funny.

Eventually, Sheriff sighed and set the list down. "Alright, darlin'. Let's get this potion taken."

I briefly scanned the café. The crowd had somewhat thinned out but Katarina's sister, Kendall, looked like she was getting overwhelmed serving the few tables she had left. "You'd better go first," I told Aramis as I slid the potion discreetly to him. "Kendall looks like she might panic soon."

Without a word, Aramis cracked the yellow wax sealing the vial, uncorked it, and downed the contents. He took the menu concealing the list and carefully looked at the names. As I watched his eyes slowly scan each one, I peeled off the wax on my potion vial under the table in secret. When he reached the bottom of the surprisingly long list, Aramis nodded once and flipped the menu around, sliding it back in front of Sheriff Oliphant.

"Now what?" Aramis addressed me. He gave an almost imperceptible shiver, and I knew the spell had done its work.

"That's it," I said, but...my pulse was kicking up speed. Neither of them knew what I was about to do. I popped the cork out of my vial of potion, downed it before they could stop me, and snatched the list from Corbin.

Both men started to say something, but I shushed them, studying the list. When I reached the bottom, a little shiver ran down my spine and I smiled at the two men watching me with wide eyes—one bemused, the other quite perturbed. To the latter, I returned the list of names and slid him a vial.

Shaking his head and muttering under his breath,

Sheriff uncorked, tossed the contents back, and began his study of the list.

While he did this, Aramis turned to me, nodding toward my menu. "What am I making for you, hm?" His smile sent a little moth fluttering in my belly.

"Hmm..." I looked over my menu. "Your eggs benedict is amazing..." I started chewing on my bottom lip until I felt Aramis's attention go there.

I saw Sheriff move out of the corner of my eye and I looked up, watching in abject horror as he slid the list off his menu and started looking at the food options instead. "Corbin, no!"

A little shiver went through him, and I panicked. "*Lock the spell, hold no more.*" The words flew out of my mouth, the only magical solution I could think of fast enough.

"What?" Aramis asked anxiously. "What's happened?"

"Corbin..." My Witch sense was souring my stomach. "Did you finish the list?"

"Pancakes," he said, then looked confused, like he had no idea what just came out of his mouth. "*Pancakes,*" he tried again. "Orange juice. Coffee. Bacon!" The pitch of his voice rose with each word, and he looked around frantically, then at me with wide eyes. "*Eggs!*"

"Wardwell..." There was much caution in Aramis's tone as he reached across the table and quickly folded the list of names, depositing it in his pocket. "Did we break the sheriff?"

I winced. "Um. Yup."

CHAPTER 5

"Cordon Bleu Quesadillas," Oliphant grumbled in my ear as we pulled him along through the busy kitchen of *Spectre Café* and out the back door into the alley. "Blackberry cobbler," he spat at me when the door closed, and I had the distinct feeling I didn't need a translator for that one.

"Maybe just stop talking for now, Corbin."

"Chicken pot pie!"

Aramis let out a deep, throaty laugh from where he was leaning against the back door, arms folded over his chest. "Got a good look at that menu, didn't he?"

"This is not funny!" I insisted, trying and failing to keep my lips from twitching.

"*Sliders and slaw!*" Sheriff cut in.

Aramis and I both lost it, sputtering with laughter while Corbin grew more and more frustrated, gesticulating wildly and spouting food and drink items.

"Too bad this didn't happen to Bill," I chuckled.

"I don't know," Aramis argued. "Winslow might have been worse, considering how much he talks."

I sagged, and Corbin went to sit on the curb. "I hope I can reverse this."

"Of course you can, Wardwell." Aramis pointed a thumb at the back door. "Unfortunately, I have to get back in there. Will you two be okay?"

"Yeah, sure," I said with more confidence than I felt.

"Pickles," Sheriff grunted, glaring at me.

"I'll come by the apothecary the first lull we get."

"Hey, what are you going to do with the list?" I asked just before he opened the door.

"Headed to burn it right now."

I nodded, ignoring Corbin's protests via food names. "Come on, Sheriff." I motioned for him to follow me and he did, albeit reluctantly.

We stopped in front of the apothecary's rear door, but... on second thought... I kept walking and Corbin trailed along, still determined to question my motives in his new language that I continued to ignore.

On one hand, it was my potion and my accidental spell that created this mess, but I'd decided to see it as an opportunity, and my sinister plan was three-fold.

1. Drop poor, pitiful Corbin off at *Toil & Truffle Bakery* to Mom, enacting a daring little forced romance for the two mid-life cuties.

2. If I pawn this problem off on someone else (hey, just for a little while), I can do some sleuthing without Sheriff Oliphant breathing down my neck.

3. Okay, so between parts one and two and Corbin shouting the drink menu at me, I forgot part three. It'll come to me.

I paused behind Art's *Gloam Hollow Candy* and turned to Corbin. "Hang on. Did you just say, '*Bat's Brew*'?" I thought I knew Aramis's menu pretty well, but I wasn't familiar with that one.

Corbin heaved an epic sigh and rolled his eyes. "*Wine mulled with spices for Samhain,*" he quoted the menu.

"And remind me what comes with the burger?"

"*Choice of two sides,*" Corbin gritted out.

"Hm." I popped my lips to myself cheerily. The potion's spell might have gone a tad haywire, but he had remembered *everything*. So had it really gone *that* haywire?

We stopped at the back door of *Toil & Truffle* and I found it was unlocked. I didn't love that, seeing as we'd had multiple murders of late, but there was trash in the bin and I had to assume—or hope—someone had just been to throw it out recently. Stepping inside, Corbin fair shoved past me and barged into the kitchen.

"Oh, hi!" I heard my mom greet him, a smile in her voice.

By the time I made it in, Corbin had two fingers up. "Cheese, tomato..." And he was ticking off a third. "*Lettuce...*" That last one was rather emphatically stated.

Mom stood there with dough in her hands looking between me and Corbin, her eyebrows high and her mouth half-open. "Are we discussing...hamburger toppings?" The dough began to slide down her fingers and she sloughed it off onto her worktable.

I cleared my throat and pulled my shoulders back. "I do believe he's angry with you for not locking your back door."

"Pie!" Corbin pointed at me with gusto.

I had to stifle another laugh. Until Mom's eyes narrowed and she sniffed the air. "Pray tell," she murmured as she approached us methodically, "why do I smell a spell that has run amok?"

I risked a glance at Corbin and his eyes were as wide as mine. "Pickles," he said in a hushed tone.

Maybe, *maybe* I hadn't thought this through. Quickly and with a tumbling vocabulary that reminded me of being a Witchling caught out too late, I explained the situation to my mother. "I was hoping you could keep him here." I attempted a smile, but it felt as cringey as it probably looked.

"He's not a stray puppy, Blair." She said this as she filled a plate with cookies and a cup with milk, setting them in front of Corbin and making her statement feel fairly contrary.

I wanted to say, '*You sure about that?*' But I went with, "I know. But I need to figure out how to correct this without him shouting menu items at me."

Mom turned from frowning at me to Corbin, her face softening. "He is a bit of a grump, isn't he?"

"Peach cobbler," he directed at Mom. That one I didn't know how to translate into words, but his tone told me it was something grouchily sweet.

This was adorable and all, but I had to go. "I'll come back for him later."

"With a cure!" Mom shouted after me as I dashed out of the kitchen toward the front door.

Out on the square, I almost wanted to rub my hands

together maniacally. I had a list of hardened criminals magically embedded in my brain. And I'd recently learned how to use the Interweb.

(Yes, I still hate it. Don't think for one second I've given up on my convictions. But a useful tool is a useful tool.)

I didn't even bother going to the apothecary. The mess of potion from late last night would still be waiting for me when I returned, and it wasn't like I'd seen more than a handful of customers in the last moon, anyway— a depressing thought, but I digress. Instead, I marched across the green toward *Stonewood Coffee*. The kerfuffle at *Spectre* had cost me my breakfast and who could function on only one cup of coffee? (The answer is many people. Possibly even *most*. But I am not most people.)

Aha! That was the forgotten third part of my three-fold plan:

3. Talk to Lacuna about the glowing tattoo ink.

Lacuna

"See you later, Lacuna!"

"Later, babe!" I waved farewell to Katarina as she left *Stonewood* and leaned over the counter resting my chin in my hand. The coffee shop had officially hit its first lull of the day, and I welcomed a small moment to lose myself in my mind. I took every spare moment to dive into my thoughts, mostly because they weren't mere thoughts at all. I'm not certain if their visions or memories that aren't my own, but I feel as if they *are* mine.

I've always been fascinated with the Mortal Lands. Their realm isn't so different from our own when it comes down to it, but the Mortals themselves take my breath away. They have such a tragic melancholy about them that never seems to subside, yet that very thing makes them love harder and live fearlessly. I hate to see them suffer, and Anon—the only person who knows my secret—often tells me I'm so focused on *them* that I miss what's happening to *us*.

He's probably right, and I do feel a tinge of guilt for it, but it's like this addiction I can't break away from. Those confounding souls in the Mortal Lands captured my heart from the first moment I saw one of them. They're even why I ink my body with delicate tattoos. One for every tragic, resplendent soul I've seen during my clandestine visits into the fog between Gloam Hollow and the Mortal Lands. The fog no one here knows exists, save for me and Anon. The fog I lovingly call the Inbetween.

One tattoo apiece, to capture what I see in each Mortal, individually.

The first time was an accident. As children, Anon and I had snuck away one day after school to explore the mountains. Every kid in Gloam Hollow knows the trails closest to town like the back of their hand. Without much else to do around our town, many a field trip is taken there and we'd all been on countless hikes behind *Moonrise Manor* with Mildred Wardwell.

On a day like so many others, when the weather had just turned unexpectedly from sweltering summer back to the crisp, lively green of early spring, our little group of friends was out behind the inn running wild—free. I remember almost every moment of that afternoon, a day I'll never forget—the one that changed my life forever. Maggie and Hamish ran inside to fetch us all some of Grandma Wardwell's famous strawberry lemonade, and Maeve dared Blair to climb the side of the inn. Anon and I watched as Blair achieved this, jumping off the balcony and letting her magic float her back down barefoot to the grass.

What happened next changed everything.

Hamish came running out the back door. He said Maggie had cut herself trying to slice lemons and Blair's magic was the strongest. Maeve, still a young Vamp, knew she needed to leave before she did something she might regret. She was gone in a flash, Blair was rushing in after Hamish, and so was I. But Anon pulled me back.

'I can't see the blood. I'll pass out.'

He was already so pale, his eyes wide behind the spectacles too big for his head, and he was starting to shift into his Wendigo form. Anon hates being in his other form. So I smiled at my friend and led him off into the woods. If he was going to shift, he would be more comfortable hidden in the trees.

Anon gained control of himself, and we ventured on and on along the trails until we came to a cave that didn't look familiar. It was almost dark by then and Anon was terrified, but...I heard voices. It was like something pulled me forward by an invisible string attached to my heart. Venturing in, I saw it. *We* saw it. The fog. So thick it was almost inky.

'Let's go, Lac,' Anon begged me over and over. But I'd already seen them. The Mortals.

Ever since that day, a wisp of that fog has followed me, revealing itself every time I focus on it.

Lost in my moment of silence, I let everything in the coffee shop fade away. The hum and whir of the machines in back as Anon cleaned them out. The brilliant blue couch sitting amongst tables and cozy spots. The shelves of books patrons borrow from...

A little gasp left me. There it was. The shimmer. It danced along the edges of my vision as it always does when I'm deep in my own wonderings, waiting for it. With the shimmer came the vignette of thoughts. Thoughts that weren't mine. Not truly cognitive thinking itself, but a vague sense of a place I wasn't standing in—of a perception that didn't belong to me.

Not a reading of thoughts, either—that wouldn't explain it correctly. There was no distinction of words or images. Just a hazy hue of someone else's awareness. One that had been with me since that very first day.

The bell above the door of *Stonewood* jingled, shaking the mist, warbling the vignette.

"Hey, Lac!" Blair's cheerful voice pulled me the rest of the way out, severing the connection.

CHAPTER 6

Blair

I paused at the look on Lacuna's face, barely even inside *Stonewood*. "Woah, are you okay?"

"Absolutely!" She smiled wide, the strange aura around her shifting.

Though I was excited to be more attuned to others' auras as of late, I didn't know what to make of Lacuna's. The bright, effervescent lilac made sense, but there was something else, almost like a brooding gray—like a storm about to break across the velvet indigo of night sky. In a way, it all melded beautifully together, but it didn't seem like Lacuna.

Abruptly, the storm around her receded, leaving only a clear night as bright as her smile. "I have the Samhain menu up!" She spun a quarter turn, lifting her arm to point out the chalkboard menu of late fall goodies.

"Oh my." I was practically drooling already. She still had all of her pumpkin and maple perfection listed, but we'd moved past the lightness of autumn, and it was time for the darker, Witchy shades.

Goddess, I love my town.

After what was most likely a painfully long time for Lacuna's patience, I settled on the brown sugar pecan latté with oat milk and an apple strudel. I scooted down the counter as Lacuna set to brewing the espresso and steaming milk. We were alone in the shop and I decided it was now or never to *'follow the ink trail,'* as Aramis had put it.

"Have you set a date for your new tattoo?" I tried to sound nonchalant, but realistically, Lacuna had no reason to think I was prying.

"Yes!" Some of the steamed milk sloshed over the rim of her little steel pitcher as she frothed. "Day after tomorrow. I'm *so* excited."

"That's great! So I guess Tom finally got the glowing ink in, yeah?"

"Yep, he texted me yesterday that Anon *finally* got it from the supplier. I'm going to be his first tattoo with it."

I thought furiously as Lacuna poured the milk over espresso and syrups, then popped the black plastic lid on the cup. *Follow the ink trail.*

"Thanks. This smells delicious," I told her when she slid it across the counter to me and moved to pull my strudel from the bakery case. "Would it be okay if I joined you? I'd love to see how it turns out to decide if I want to be his next client with that ink."

The lie was smooth as silk because I was overdue for a new tattoo and glowing ink did sound almost too good to pass up. My ulterior motives could be kept to myself. With only a smidgen of guilt...

Crackers on a monkey. Was I really trying to implicate my friends in a crime?

No, I chastised myself firmly. I was trying to absolve them of one.

"I'd love for you to come!" Lac exclaimed. "My appointment is at 8 pm. Want to make a date of it? We can grab some dinner and then head over?"

Okay, I was legitimately in now. "You have yourself a date, Lac."

She gave a little squeal of excitement. "We haven't done this in what feels like ages."

We truly hadn't.

I pondered the passage of time as I left *Stonewood* and walked through the square—how it slips by without notice until things look different and you'd never even realized the good old days were already over.

Growing up, Lacuna, Maeve, and Anon were always with Hamish, Mags, and me every free second. Even when we'd all gone off to separate universities split between Hamish and Lacuna in New Haven and Mags, Anon, and I in Dornwich (Maeve stayed in town to work at the inn), we still met at least once a week for coffee and a late-night study session. Once we all moved back to The Hollow, things picked up right where they'd left off.

Sure, we all had our lives and some of us had dated here and there, opened businesses, etc, but it hadn't been until very recently that we'd begun to grow apart. Lacuna had always been the closest with Anon. He was so quiet with the rest of us, but the strain between the two of them and between Maeve and Tom—still the newest in our friend group—was felt by all. Now we were all so busy with our lives that I was beginning to consider the possibility that we may never again be what we once were.

The thought put a sour taste in my mouth. So, I pushed it away. Very healthy behavior.

By the time I'd successfully driven the gloomies away and sipped some of my latté between sweet, tart bites of strudel, I realized I had not headed in the direction of *Copper Cauldron* or *Toil & Truffle.*

I stopped in front of Aunt Moira's *Spellbound Boutique,* looking in the window at her Samhain display. She had dozens of black floating candles dispersed amongst a luscious, cascading black-bough chandelier that *must* be the creation of Aunt Millie. The moment the last Samhain bonfire spark floated up into the night sky, Moira would undoubtedly slip holly and frost into the boughs.

She also had one mannequin on display with a teaser of her Dark Academia line: *Blair,* set to debut before Yule. My fingers curled around my cup, itching to go inside and touch the fabric of that tweed coat. Instead, I sighed, turning to look across the square at the apothecary and bakery (might have snuck a little look at the café, too). Obviously, I needed to check on Corbin. And I also needed to go clean up the potion mess in the apothecary.

But...

I took another sip of coffee, relishing the flavor of sweet brown sugar mixed with the sharp bitterness of espresso and a nutty, buttery hint of pecan, and considered my options. Everything was calm in The Hollow. No attacks, no more murders, and we'd laid Steven to rest a couple of weeks ago. In my subjective reasoning, that meant two things.

1. The town could do without their sheriff being of
    right mind for a *little* longer
2. Steven's murderer still needed to be found

I turned on my heel and headed down Lotus Street toward the library, ticking through clues and hypotheses in my mind like sifting through a Rolodex.

We knew that the Mimic arrested for the first murder in town (carted off to a prison in New Haven to await trial) had been hired by someone to kill Aramis. He had accidentally killed a Golem walking around with Aramis's face, who had also been in Art's candy shop asking questions about Aramis.

I paused mid-step, a passing Faerie eyeing me strangely.

Art had said something else, hadn't he? That the Golem was questioning him about. What was it? I wracked my brain but couldn't recall what it was. It would come to me eventually, so I kept walking.

The Mimic admitted to being here to kill Aramis, but he didn't know who'd sent him—fact. He was likely hired by someone outside of Gloam Hollow, from Aramis's time as an investigator and detective—hypothesis. The Mimic did not admit to killing Steven, nor Anon's attack in the park just before the murder—possible fact, but we'll stick it in the hypothesis column.

If this was true, the second murderer either mistook Steven for Aramis—highly unlikely as one was a short, round troll and the other a tall, dark Dread Monster (I promptly ignored the moths gathering in my stomach at that thought)—or, the murderer was trying to frame Aramis.

Another running hypothesis: Anon's attack was not directly related to the murders.

If all of the hypotheses are true, Steven's murderer is at large, he (or she) attempted to frame Aramis and/or wishes him harm. Either way, I couldn't see a possibility that Steven's murder wasn't absolutely connected to who was after Aramis—hired hand or not. And since Anon's attack did not seem related any longer and I had a way to look into its connection with the mysterious glowing tattoo ink, I only had one option: solve Steven's murder.

I'D NEVER HEARD a library so loud and quiet all at the same time. There were students everywhere, ranging in age from *little* to *acne-prone*. (Listen, I haven't been that young in a long time. I can no longer tell a difference beyond the aforementioned categories.) All of the computers were occupied in the visible two nests of them, so I wandered to the back only to find all of those occupied as well.

Frowning, I climbed the steps to the second floor huffing elegantly. There, I was met with the same issue. One of the librarians waved to me from the help desk and said hello, but I couldn't for the life of me recall her name. Halfway over to her, I remembered—Angela! She was a Witch I had gone to Gloam Hollow Primary with, but she'd moved away for many years and had only recently returned. She smiled prettily at me, her face as bright as her blonde hair, such an infectious joy about her that I couldn't help but return it.

"Hey, Angela. How are you enjoying being back in The Hollow?"

"I'm having the best time." She hugged a book to her chest that she was re-binding. "Big cities are just not for me. Almost every day at the library in New Haven was busy like this." She gestured toward all the kids whisper-shouting as they milled about.

"Yeah, what's with that? It's usually dead in here during the day."

Angela set her book project down on the desk space in front of her. "I guess the computer labs at the schools went down, so a few classes had to come here."

That struck me as odd. Maybe one lab going down at one campus made sense, but multiple? I shrugged it off. "Do you happen to know where Hamish is? I didn't see him at the front desk."

Angela chewed on her bottom lip. "I believe he went down to the basement for his break." She pointed toward a door in the back corner. "If you go down there, just please keep the door to the stairwell closed." Angela grimaced apologetically. "Sometimes Hamish's snacks are a little..."

"Gross?" I finished for her. "I'm so sorry. I told him he has to stop bringing things like boiled eggs and kimchi."

Angela giggled and I bid her farewell. Before I even opened the door to the basement stairwell I could smell Hamish's snack two flights of stairs down.

The basement houses countless nooks and crannies, but I had no trouble finding the breakroom because it nearly fogged green with the smell.

"*Hamish Wardwell*," I censured when I entered the atrociously lit room and he looked over his shoulder at me, holding a fork aloft. "How many times have we talked about —" I stopped mid-sentence. There was steam rising from the boiled egg on a plate in front of him and the microwave door was still open. "Hamish, *don't!*"

But I was too late with my warning for the second time today. Hamish poked the microwaved egg and it exploded into tiny, hot pieces of white and yellow all over him. He cried out, swiping the steaming bits off his hands before he jumped and batted at his chest, smearing the creamy yolk across his vest.

"Argh! This was a new waistcoat!" he groused, turning and looking at me like it was my fault.

"I tried to warn you." I walked over and ripped off a paper towel from a roll next to the sink and handed it to him. Crossing my arms, I leaned a hip against the counter while he rubbed furiously at the mess on his *waistcoat*. "Do you have your laptop here?"

Hamish stopped his swiping and looked at me with nothing short of contempt. "Why would I bring my laptop to work?"

"Um. In case you need it..."

"There are computers here."

"Fine. And on days like today when they're overrun with young folk?"

Hamish eyed me with disdain, his face contorted. "*Young folk*? Are you six hundred years old? The problem here is not the students or my laptop, it's your aversion to owning your own. You need to get with the times, B."

Irritated with both his logic and lack of success with his waistcoat, I sent magic out to clean the vest. The magic gave off a blue gleam just before all the stains disappeared and it swirled off to clean up the egg bits splattered across the counter, too.

"Thank you," he mumbled. "You can use my laptop at home. Just go grab it."

I lifted my glasses and ran my fingers over my tired eyes. "I don't have time to go all the way to the cottage. I need to get back to the bakery to check on Mom and Sheriff—" I realized my mistake after it was too late, my eyes going wide and giving me away even more, and Hamish stilled.

"B... What did you do?"

"Nothing."

"Liar!" He was grinning now though, that glitter in his eye that comes when he's about to learn a secret. "Tell me."

"I sort of broke Corbin." I winced.

"You *what*?"

I recounted the morning's events and Sheriff's new food-only vocabulary, and Hamish was howling by the end.

"Yeah, yeah. Hilarious. So I wanted to get as much investigating done as I can before I have a stick-in-the-mud partner again."

Hamish snorted. "Does Corbin know you think of him as your partner?"

"Eh. He'll come around. I just need to look more into Steven's murder while I can." An idea struck me then. Something Aramis had said at breakfast. A brilliant, brilliant idea...

"Uh oh."

"What?" I snapped at Hamish.

"You have that look."

"What look?"

"The one you get when you've just come up with a *really* dumb idea."

"Fine, you twerp. Then I won't tell you what my *brilliant* idea is." I turned on my heel and left, Hamish calling out apologies after me. Not because he was sorry at all, but because Hamish hated being out of the loop.

CHAPTER 7

Lacuna

Q*uantum entanglement.*

It was the closest thing I'd found to describe the shimmer. The essence of someone else reaching my own consciousness. I have a living, breathing connection with someone from the Mortal Lands. I have since I was a child. It still shocks me at times. I can *almost* make out enough of them to formulate a tattoo to capture their essence—almost, but not quite.

The aura is gloomy, lonely. It's a shade of silver akin to the moon when out beyond the lights of Gloam Hollow, lost to nature near Molten Lake. There's a depth to that aura, too. Knowledge spilling out like an overfilled cup of tea. That's another thing. My entangled soul distinctly prefers tea. I can just feel it. Almost smell it, despite Anon making espresso down the counter from me.

"*Lac,*" Anon said my name for probably at least the second time because his tone was clipped. He's been irritable since he was attacked in the park, but this was different. "Can you please focus?"

"Yeah." I straightened out of my dreamy state. "Yeah. Sorry, hun. What did you need?"

Anon blinked at me, a crease forming between his brows nearly hidden by his thick, black glasses. "Ms. Lilly asked for a scone." He pointed to where the Elder Witch was reading a magazine at a corner table.

Ms. Lilly always wanted a cinnamon scone, so I didn't bother asking which kind she'd requested—she probably hadn't even specified. I might be lost in my own head most of the time, but I know my regulars' orders by heart, and they know that I do. I heated up the scone and used tongs to set it on a plate, walking it over to her. She thanked me and returned to her celebrity gossip magazine. That reminded me that Kat has asked me to proofread her newest article. She was trying to branch out a little from town gossip. I thought she should ask Blair, but Kat and Blair had been... frosty toward one another since the night of Anon's attack, though I didn't know why.

Near the bookshelf at the back of the shop, I paused on my way back to the counter, running my hand over the spines of the books. As always, my thoughts of the here and now slipped away to a place not my own and a person I don't know, yet do.

Once, I'd caught a glimpse of a book cover flitting by in the foggy essence of my entangled soul. It took me three years of carefully watching the gloom, but I finally discovered it was titled *The Catcher in the Rye.*

Without thinking, I reached into my apron pocket to run my fingers along the worn pages of my contraband copy of that very book from the Mortal Lands.

Blair

I tossed my empty coffee cup in the trash bin outside the library, and by the time I made it the two blocks to the Sheriff's Department, I already wished I had more. Perhaps cider. Anything warm to drink. *The Sisters Solstice*—if they are who decides our weather as legend states—had never let another season befall us without Samhain in autumn, but they *had* been known to let another season slip in for a day or two before correcting for the end of autumn celebration. Judging by the chill in my fingers and the chap of my cheeks, they were letting winter in for a moment, or it would *very* soon follow Samhain.

Rubbing my hands together furiously, I narrowly escaped a very insistent starling singing for my attention and stepped into the Sheriff's Department, not bothering to discard my coat. Thankfully, Deputy Pete's cruiser wasn't outside, but Mrs. Cobblepot was at her desk. I approached, opening my mouth with a prepared excuse as to why I was there to look at case files without Sheriff Oliphant present, but the elderly woman was dozing in her desk chair.

Clamping my mouth shut, I tiptoed past her and slipped into Corbin's office, reminding myself to ask why he felt it was fine to leave boxes of case files out in the open. If I could sneak past sweet Mrs. Cobblepot, couldn't anyone else? It seemed highly irresponsible. Nevertheless, it was serving me quite well at present.

Apparently, Mrs. Cobblepot had felt the chill creeping in before she'd nodded off because the heater was *heating* back here. I removed my coat, slung it over the back of a chair, and dropped my bag onto the floor. There were a few scattered files across Corbin's desk, but only one box, marked with a case number. Sure enough, it contained the files on Steven's murder. My objective was clear enough: see if anything stood out, make some notes, and then when I could get my hands on a computer, I could look into the list of Aramis's enemies magically burned into my memory and see if there was a connection.

I sank into the chair, two file folders in hand. They were dismally filled. One of them only had three pieces of paper —Steven's obituary, the autopsy report, and a copy of his birth certificate. Discouraged but not willing to let it drag me down, I flipped to the autopsy and began to read it. A few words in, a message began scrawling itself out in sparkling purple cursive above Sheriff's desk.

Don't worry about Corbin. I've got it covered
xoxo

To say I was relieved would be accurate, but I was also confused by Mom's message. I dug around in my bag until I found my notepad and pen used for the specific purpose of our secret magical communication.

How? I cast the spell, don't I have to be
the one to fix it? xx

I went back to the autopsy report while I waited for her answer, but there wasn't anything I didn't already know. I'd been just across the room when Steven was killed, after all. Granted, the café had been set up as a haunted house and it was nearly pitch black *anddd* I might have been about to canoodle with a Dread Monster behind a curtain of gauze when it happened but...I was still one of the first people to see the body. I knew well that Steven Littlebottom, the sweet Troll employee of Aramis's, had been stabbed in the back with a kitchen knife belonging to Aramis. A knife from the same set that had been used to stab the John Doe Golem several days prior to Steven's murder.

The rest of the information simply detailed Steven's height, weight, race, and physical features. I did note that the physical attributes were listed in both Troll and his 'other' form, the one most creatures walk around in so that we're all more cohesive yet still wildly different.

Mom's return message came in, dropping little specks of glitter onto the autopsy report before they disappeared.

Send me your potion recipe xo

I jotted down:

I'm not at the apothecary, but there is extra still in the cauldron and the spellbook is open on the counter.

I started to spell the message to send but then added:

P.S. Don't clean up the mess in there. Not your job! xx

My message left in a flurry of wispy green, and I heard footsteps down the hall. I turned around just as none other than Aramis Hawthorne walked through the door of the office.

"Thought I might find you here," he said with a hint of a smile, but there were worry lines etched on his forehead.

"How's that, Hawthorne?" I cocked my head to the side, eyes narrowed.

He took a seat in the chair next to mine, the old faux leather upholstery protesting under his weight. "Well, I went by *Copper Cauldron* to check on you as promised after the sheriff debacle this morning, but you weren't there or at *Stonewood*. Lacuna told me you'd left there quite a while ago with no sheriff in tow. I thought about checking at the cottage, but then I got smart and phoned Hamish."

"Intriguing," I said very seriously. "Do go on."

"*Hamish*," he put emphasis on my cousin's name, "said he did not know where you were, but that you'd been spouting off about '*breaking Oliphant*,' and then got '*that look on your face you get when you've had a dumb idea.*' His words, not mine." Aramis put a hand to his chest to drive that particular point home. "I've seen that look a time or two and I'd call it one of dubious inspiration."

I laughed. I couldn't help it. "I like that description better. And you assumed that idea was to come here and steal police files?"

He lolled his head from side to side, mouth quirked in thought. "Police file perusal," he corrected. "No sheriff breathing down your neck? It's the most logical Wardwell thing to do."

"Wow, Hawthorne. You really do know your stuff." I looked up at him with mock approval and those eyes of his glimmered. He was going to *have* to stop looking at me like that or I'd become one of those doe-eyed girls. "Excellent detective skills."

"Dreamy, too." We both turned to see Mrs. Cobblepot in the doorway.

"Now, now, Mrs. C," Aramis censured teasingly. "What would Mr. C have to say about that?"

"Oh, dear, he's a dinosaur." She waved her gnarled hand at him. "Would you two like some tea?"

"Please and thank you," I answered cheerily.

She hobbled off down the hall and Aramis leaned in, his breath tickling my ear. "Did you know she's a Dragonborn?"

"A *what*?" I had to keep from shouting, but the end of my sentence still hit a high pitch.

"Shh," he laughed. "She doesn't realize I know, so I wouldn't tell anyone."

I sat back hard in my chair, flabbergasted. "Dragonborn are so rare! I guess it explains why Corbin feels free to leave files out everywhere." I gestured to the mess.

"Sure does." He clapped his hands together lightly and pushed himself up out of the chair. "I have to get going."

"Already?" I looked up at him.

"Spent my entire lunch looking for a missing Witch who likes to land herself in trouble." He smiled, but I could hear the truth in his words and felt a little thrill at the idea of him quite possibly worrying about me. "I have to get back to the café. But I did want to ask if you'd like to go on that date tonight—a real one. Kendall is getting the hang of closing up. I think she can handle it tonight and what she can't manage I'll just go in early to do. Maybe 7:30?"

I made a valiant attempt to keep my excitement in check.

"I'd love that. I could meet you somewhere so you don't have to leave the café too early."

Aramis frowned. "That's not very gentlemanly."

"I promise I'll let you walk me home afterward."

He studied me for a long moment, then sighed. "Alright. Meet me at the record shop, then. I'm not telling you anything else or meeting me would ruin it."

My stomach did a little flip. "Deal."

One corner of Aramis's mouth quirked up. "Wardwell and Hawthorne strike another deal," he said in his best reporter's voice.

"What *will* they come up with next?" I mimicked his tone and he laughed.

"You won't find much in those files you don't already know." He pointed toward the manila folders on my lap. "But let me know if something sticks out."

I put four fingers to my forehead and saluted him. "Got it, Chief."

He rolled his eyes with a barely concealed smirk and strode out just as Mrs. Cobblepot was bringing in my tea.

By my third cuppa, I was pretty much through the entire box of evidence and still hadn't seen anything that stood out. Blowing hair out of my face, I took off my glasses and cleaned all the smudges off with the hem of my sweater. The effort was ineffective because all the soft fabric had managed to do was create a haze over the lenses. *Bah.* I magicked them clean and stood, rifling through the contents of Corbin's desk.

Obviously, this was not something he would approve of me doing, but he was presumably still shouting food obscenities. I needed to intake as much information as I could before our kindly grump of a sheriff was right with the world again and bent on making me follow protocol.

One of the manila envelopes caught my eye. I didn't recognize the name scrawled across it, *Boris Leek*, but I did recognize the date. It was the day Hamish and I had found the real Art locked in his pantry, and Sheriff had arrested the Mimic *mimicking* Art. The man who confessed to killing the John Doe Golem.

Careful not to rip the envelope in my excitement, I removed the contents. Quite a lot of information stared up at me. The Mimic's photo—a mugshot—in his true form, plus three other mugshots in various faces not his own, a lengthy arrest record, a long fact sheet with things like known aliases, addresses, etc, but it was the transcript of his questioning that excited me. Sitting down with the papers, I made to pour more tea, only to find the pot was empty. Minorly disappointed, I resigned myself to locating coffee when I was done here, and dove into reading the transcript.

Most of it was just a lengthier version of what Corbin and Aramis had both already told me, but my attention snagged on some things toward the end.

OLIPHANT: *And you stand by the statement that you had never met the victim prior to the incident, or known anything about him?*

LEEK: *I said it already, bub. I didn't know the guy. Never seen him. But how can you ever really know with a Golem, ay?*

. . .

OLIPHANT: *Could he have been the one who sent you after Mr. Hawthorne? Checking in on how well you were doing your job?*

LEEK: *Nah. I've worked for a lot of these type'a guys and they never do nothin' themselves.*

I COULD ALMOST HEAR Corbin ignoring the implication that Leek might have killed others while working for 'those types of guys.' I supposed he was thinking the same thing I was: Leek was at least off the streets. Once he was convicted of this crime, perhaps we could look into some other unsolved cases he might be connected to and get some closure for victims' families. Or, maybe he'd just confess his backlog of criminal activity if we were lucky.

LEEK: *This joker made me get a tattoo though. *snort like a barnyard animal**

OLIPHANT: *Your contracted employer required that you… be tattooed?*

CORBIN HAD MENTIONED as much to me after questioning the Mimic, but it was still such a peculiar fact.

. . .

LEEK: *Sure did. He's a weird one, this guy.*

OLIPHANT: And where did this tattooing take place?

LEEK: *Beats me. There was a knock on my door the night I took the job. Masked guy.*

OLIPHANT: And you opened the door for this person?

LEEK: **shrug* I got a call that he was coming.*

OLIPHANT: Okay. Guy shows up. Then what?

LEEK: *He blindfolds me and says, 'this is gonna sting.' I was freaked at first, but I got other tattoos and I figured out the sound and sting pretty quick.*

OLIPHANT: Did you ask any questions during this?

LEEK: Nah. Wouldn't have done any good. I've been working for guys like this since I was a kid.

OLIPHANT: Your employer is different each time you're hired?

LEEK: *shrug* Best I can figure, yeah. It's the sorta career where the contractors do the contacting and you say yes no questions asked or you end up in a world a hurt way worse than a dumb bird tattoo you didn't want.

I HONESTLY HAD SO many questions about this process...

OLIPHANT: You're certain the one who hired you to kill Aramis Hawthorne was a man? You've spoken to him?

I THOUGHT this might be a trap, because earlier in the 'interview' Sheriff had asked the same question in different words.

LEEK: I already said all I know. I get a call about a job, I do the job. I don't know who I'm talkin' to. The number is always blocked. Sometimes the voice on the other end is female, sometimes it's male, but the boss is always referred to as 'he,' and no name's ever been given.

Oliphant: Remind me how that phone call went. The one hiring you to murder Mr. Hawthorne.

Leek: *laugh* That old crone in the corner don't got it in her notes? Woah! Did smoke just come out her nose? What the he—

Oliphant: Mr. Leek, refrain from using foul language in my precinct or insulting my staff. What happened on this phone call?

Leek: Take it easy, bub. I was eatin' my burrito on the couch and watching some old soaps, my ma loved those ya' know, and I get a call from a blocked number. A lady tells me, 'Be outside your apartment in fifteen minutes.' I go down in ten. I've learned not to make these people mad. A black sedan pulls up, all fancy-like, and the window rolls down just enough for a

slip of paper to stick out. I take the
paper, the car drives off.

OLIPHANT: And this is that piece of paper.

. . .

MR. LEEK, the transcript can't see a nod.

LEEK: Yeah, yes. That's it.

I STOOD UP, rifling through all the documents, but there was
no slip of paper. Then it dawned on me that it would be
better suited to go in the evidence box for John Doe's
murder. *There*, along the back wall. I pulled off the lid and
paused. *Salt on a turtle*. I needed gloves, didn't I? Better safe
than sorry. Pulling open the drawers of Corbin's desk too
roughly, I found a box of latex gloves and slipped on a pair.
My hands were much smaller than his, and the gloves
flopped at the tips of my fingers, but I rifled through the
plastic bags of evidence anyway.

Bingpot! I held up a bag with a tiny scrap of paper in it.
Aramis Hawthorne, PI
1724 Town Square
Gloam Hollow
I turned and rifled through the John Doe case file

looking for any other similar scraps of paper. There wasn't anything like it, but someone had to have told the now-deceased Golem to come to Gloam Hollow, too.

If we were right and it was the same person...

"Personal effects!" I jumped back over to the boxes lining the wall, carelessly lifting off the lids. Finally, I found a box with clothes that looked familiar. The shirt was in a plastic bag, heavily discolored by dark, rusty blood stains. In another bag was a pair of jeans. Had anyone checked the pockets? Surely they had... But this is a small town with a small-town police duo, not even a force.

I had gloves on, after all...

Gloves or not, I settled on letting my magic do the job for me. It might leave a signature another Witch could see later, but probably not—not for such a mundane spell. Carefully, a tendril of magic slithered out, my gloved finger directing it to unzip the evidence baggie and slip into the pockets of the jeans. In one of the back pockets, so small that a quick check might have missed it, was a tiny scrap of paper.

Almost squealing, I directed my magic to pull it out. While it hovered in the air, I Grandma-Wardwell-Cursed. It needed another evidence bag. And now that I'd actually found something, I'd have to tell Corbin. Eventually.

I looked frantically around the room, realizing this probably wasn't where they bagged evidence. We had baggies at home. What could it hurt to use a regular old plastic sandwich bag rather than police grade? Was there even a difference? I summoned a bag right from the kitchen drawer at Wardwell Cottage, smiling to myself as it appeared in mid-air next to the scrap of paper.

The problem was that the paper was rolled up like a tiny

croissant. Carefully, I directed my magic to unroll it, straighten it (that's fine, right? Who knows...), and slip it into the baggie. My hands were gloved and I'd taken extra precautions already, so I sealed the bag the old-fashioned way and rushed to put it side-by-side with the other scrap from Boris Leek.

Aramis Hawthorne, PI

1724 Town Square

Gloam Hollow

Same exact handwriting.

I tapped my finger over the plastic. On both notes, the ink was slightly smudged on the left side of the words. That could easily happen on one of the notes for any number of reasons. But on both? There was a high possibility we were looking at a left-handed person.

Really, there was nothing else significant here. But it did tell me two things:

1. The person after Aramis knew *exactly* where he was despite Kenny 'erasing' him, and likely had for some time. That meant they'd been watching longer than we'd thought.
2. The same person had sent both the Golem and the Mimic—a hypothesis almost confirmed.

If these two were definitely sent by the same person, then whoever killed Steven probably was, too. *And* I had a new lead: The person who wrote these notes was most likely left-handed. Now I just needed to know if Steven's killer was as well.

Looking through the autopsy and other case notes, I

hadn't seen anything that suggested so, but I'd ask Aramis about it.

In the meantime, if anyone could use magic to figure out more about who wrote these notes, it was Grandma Wardwell.

CHAPTER 8

Locating Grandma at the inn was always tricky. Tina and Maeve usually (wo)manned the front desk and the rest of the small staff cleaned and served in the tiny restaurant. More often than not, Grandma milled about chatting with guests, which meant she was hard to pin down. Sometimes she was performing little tricks of magic for guests' children, sometimes she was on the porch sipping iced tea and talking someone's ear off, or, one time, she was gone for hours and we finally found her on the roof showing a guest '*a unique perspective of The Hollow.*'

Many years ago, Grandma grew so tired of us complaining about never being able to find her that she made a neat little magical invention that told her where all of us were, whenever she wanted to know.

Now, one might ask why she didn't share this particular divination with us or, better yet, produce and sell many of these devices. But, Grandma simply said that was ridiculous and no one needed that much power. Except her, evidently.

When we had a family meeting and declared this didn't

solve our problem of never being able to find Grandma, she'd installed a lovely little call button in a secret hiding place.

As I headed for this call button, I said a cordial hello to the two guests I happened upon in the library. One guest was reading what looked to be a bodice ripper of a book and the other was competing against an imaginary opponent at the chess set. My quarry sat on the mantel above the hearth, a miniature troll statue, prosaic amongst the little sea of other figurines—carousels, Faeries, cats, birds, basically any cute thing Grandma had ever seen at a fair or festival. The troll, however, had a very important pinky toe on its left foot. Feigning special (or was it peculiar) interest in said troll, I tapped its toe three times.

Grandma bopped into the library just as I was beginning to peruse the shelves so I didn't look like a strange figurine-obsessed weirdo.

"Pumpkin Pie!" Grandma said so loudly that she startled both guests from their quiet activities. "Oh, *flower pots*. I'm so sorry." With an exaggerated tip-toe like a cartoon villain, she came across the room to me. "Is everything okay? Your mother came by earlier with Corbin."

I winced. "How did he seem?"

"Like he was a glitching fast food kiosk."

I stifled a laugh and Grandma smiled, gesturing for me to follow her. "Come on. Cory just made lunch."

My stomach grumbled in response and I realized all I'd had to eat today was a strudel with my latté and the one bite of pumpkin pie Aramis made. "Ooo what's on the menu today?"

"I do believe it's a garden vegetable and beef stew with freshly baked bread."

The scent of that bread wafted up the main stairs as we descended, sending my stomach into a grumbling fit.

In all its quaintness, the inn's small restaurant was nearly empty, much to my surprise. Only one of the six tables had anyone sitting at it, and it was only Tina, filling out some paperwork. She half-heartedly waved at us and returned to her work.

"None of the guests are around today?" I questioned as we sat at the table closest to the stone fireplace, its glow casting the room in such warmth I began to long for winter. You'd never experienced cozy until you came down from the snowy mountains and had cocoa by one of the inn's many hearths.

"I think Andrew is around somewhere," Grandma answered, checking off soup and salad on her menu card. "He eats here most days for breakfast and lunch, running in between scenes he's filming for his documentary." She looked up at me from her card. "What are you drinking, dear? Is it too early for wine?"

I chuckled. "Water for me." I checked off soup and salad, plus dessert on the card one of the employees would retrieve soon to give to the chef, Cory. "Andrew's film is a documentary?" I asked Grandma. "I wasn't sure what it was about."

Grandma heartily checked off *red wine* on her card and set it on top of mine. "Never too early for wine for a wizened Witch." She winked at me and pulled in a deep breath. "I don't know much about Andrew's film. I think Mildred has spoken with him at length, though. From what I gather, he's interested in the caves. Particularly ones not often explored."

"I would think Aunt Millie had personally explored all the caves in The Hollow. This side of Molten Lake, anyway."

Unfolding her napkin, Grandma set it in her lap and straightened her silverware. She was always one for demure table manners, even if she was just as likely to spit peas at you through a straw. Penelope Wardwell, our matriarch, our conundrum. Goddess bless her.

"Oh, Millie's done her fair share of exploration to be sure, but I think she and Andrew might have found something new. Something peculiar out there."

Louis, one of the inn's restaurant staff, brought us some glasses of ice water and took our menu cards, chatting only long enough to ask how I was doing and tell me his wife was going to have another baby. I'd provided her with a fertility potion recently after their friend Laura had such success with the one I'd brewed for her. I might not see much business at the apothecary these days, but the customers I do have are lovely.

Once Louis rushed off to put in our order, I ran my finger down the condensation already beading on my water glass due to the fire's warmth. "What do you think Millie and Andrew have found?"

Grandma took a sip of her water. "I'm not sure. She mentioned it off the cuff a couple of days ago. But you know Mills goes out there every Samhain. Now that it's drawing close, she's been out in the woods often, sometimes showing Andrew around as he films and sometimes just..." Her words trailed off and she shrugged, sadness washing over us both.

We didn't talk about Phillip Wardwell often. He was a wonderful, beautiful soul, my Uncle Phillip. He loved Millie and Mags more than anything in all the realms. But he'd disappeared in the woods on Samhain when Mags was three and Hamish and I were four. Millie had spent so long combing the forest and caves for him that it became her second home. Still, she wanders the trails and takes tourists out for hikes between her duties at her florist shop. She insists it's just her hobby now, and I believe it is for a nature Witch like her, but part of me thinks she still looks for Phillip behind every rock and tree.

His disappearance is one of the reasons Grandma goes all out for Samhain every year. Before that dark day in our lives, it was already one of the biggest days of the year for Wardwell Witches, but since then, Grandma has made an even bigger to-do about it, inviting the whole of Gloam Hollow to a massive bonfire with a feast, dancing, and pumpkin carving. Aunt Millie has never come. She's always lost to the world, to the woods that night. But the bonfire helps Mags.

Louis brought out Grandma's wine and the salads and we dug in. "Not that I'm complaining you're here, Pumpkin Pie, but I have a feeling it's not just for lunch," she said between the crunch of lettuce bites.

"Mm." I wiped my mouth and chewed as I dug around in my bag for the two pieces of evidence I'd—*ahem*—borrowed and placed them on the table between us.

"Blair Coraline Wardwell." Grandma regarded me with wide, suspicious eyes as she reached for the evidence. "Tell me you didn't put a charm on poor Corbin so you could rifle through crime evidence."

Affronted, I scoffed. "I did no such thing! He is the one who farted around during a spell and muddled the whole thing up."

Grandma's lips pursed like she didn't believe a word I'd

said, but she didn't respond, summoning a pair of cat-eye reading glasses onto her nose instead. "What am I looking at here?"

"These are the pieces of paper found, one each, with the Golem who was murdered and with the Mimic who did the murdering." I spent a few moments catching her up on any case details Mom had not already told her.

Grandma compared the two pieces of paper in their separate baggies for quite some time before handing them back to me. "They're nearly identical."

"Exactly," I said as I shoved them back into my bag with probably less care than I should have, but Louis was bringing out our soups. When he walked away with our salad plates, I leaned in closer, feeling the heat wafting up from my soup. "I think the same person sent both the Golem and the Mimic to Gloam Hollow to kill Aramis. That leads me to believe they're also the same person that sent whoever killed Steven Littlebottom."

Grandma blew on her soup spoon. "That's a logical leap to make, I suppose. And what does our Dread Monster think about all of this?"

"I haven't told him yet what I found." I felt my cheeks blush and I tried to hide it behind bringing a spoonful of soup up to my mouth and blowing on it.

Alas, Grandma chuckled. "I see that look. Tell me."

"We have our first date tonight," I confessed.

She regarded me strangely. "I've seen or heard about you being with that boy every day for weeks. You mean to tell me he has yet to properly take you out?"

"There have been a couple of dead bodies in the way, Grandma," I sassed. "And the opening of his business."

Grandma laughed, a tinkling sound I never grow tired

of. Mom has the same laugh and it warms my soul every time. "Alright then. Go on, finish your story."

"I also noticed that both notes say *Aramis Hawthorne PI.* So, the person hiring assassins knows Aramis moved into private investigating after his detective days. It makes me think they've been watching him for a long time. I also think the person who wrote the notes might be left-handed."

Grandma dabbed her cloth napkin daintily to the edges of her mouth. "What is it you want me to do about all this, dear?"

"I want you to see if you can divine anything about the notes that would lead us in the right direction."

Grandma watched me for a few moments, then began eating her soup again without a word while I waited. Outwardly, I was patient. I knew how Grandma ticked. She would draw out the moment for far too long, but it was because she was considering it deeply and because she wanted *me* to consider what I was asking—have time to retract the request if I wanted.

I did not want to.

When her soup was nearly gone and the table was littered with bread crumbs from us both, Louis brought out my dessert—a generous slice of tiramisu that gave me the distinct impression Mom had made it, not the inn chef. The swinging door closed behind Louis and Grandma said, "Very well. Eat your treat, dear, and we'll head up to do some divination."

~

Lacuna

Massaging my temples, I listed off the duties I needed Anon to accomplish before the late afternoon rush hit. Normally, I wouldn't have to micromanage him, and normally I didn't have a pounding headache, but this day had gotten weirder and weirder.

The foggy essence tangled up in my mind had gone wonky—so askew that I found myself lilting to one side at times. It almost felt as if I'd had three too many glasses of wine or something much stronger, like Moira Wardwell's 'punch'.

There was a din of voices in my head sometimes, too. Like the café or even *Stonewood* when there's a rush, all the voices clambering to be heard. But this sounded more like thoughts, erratic and depressed. Then the haze would go all psychedelic and the thoughts with it.

Anon was still as sullen as he had been for a moon, so at least that was one constant, even if it was annoying. I'd tried everything I could think of to help him, but it seemed he didn't want help. It had gotten so bad that a woman walked out in the middle of him making her drink this morning.

"I know to take the trash out, Lac," he snipped at me.

I dropped my hands, sliding one of them into my apron to run my thumb over the comforting pages hidden there. "Anon, I've about had it with your attitude lately. If you don't want to let me in then fine, but I'm not going to sit here and let you run customers off or backtalk me. If you can't hang, then there's the door, babe." I thrust my hand out toward it and stormed to my office, slamming the door behind me. Let him prepare for the rush all on his own, or let him walk out.

CHAPTER 9

Blair

Grandma's workshop sounds much more mundane than it is. While most Witches' workrooms are littered with potions and cauldrons, hanging herbs and crystals galore, Grandma Wardwell made hers into what is best described as her aerie. And that is exactly what we call it.

The aerie resides in the tallest turret of *Moonrise Manor*, so high at the top of a winding staircase that it overlooks the forest, offering a truly majestic view of the mountains. When the clouds are high and the sky clear, you can just make out the Dragon asleep on her summit from the window above Grandma's potions table.

Penelope Wardwell is skilled in too many areas of Witchery to count, but her strongest areas are divination, augury, and tarot. She also enjoys experimenting with various potions and poultices, and the evidence of her wild genius is always on display within the aerie.

There were potion bottles anywhere they'd fit, two different cauldrons gurgling over magical fires, herbs and crystals scattered across every flat surface, and at least thirteen ritual candles floating unlit above the worktables with the drying flora, presumably because there was no room for them elsewhere.

My heart sang every time I set foot in Grandma's aerie. Sophistication and poise on the outside, untamed brilliance on the inside. *That* is our Matron Penelope Wardwell.

"What did you have in mind?" I asked Grandma, stirring the bubbling purple liquid in one of the cauldrons and sniffing it. Sleep potion. Who was having trouble sleeping?

Grandma was at the window, watching a flock of birds, the afternoon light emphasizing every worry and cackle line etched into her face. "Starlings." She turned to me with a frown, her black dress snagging on a piece of the sill's splintered wood. I moved to help her, but she freed herself with a wisp of magic and her frown deepened. "It's usually magpies on my grounds. Something is afoot."

Grandma was already at work, the tell-tale signs in her drawn face and her glazed eyes. Thus, I kept my mouth shut and followed her to a table reasonably free of clutter. We sat across from one another and a tin of cards appeared in her outstretched hand.

"Ah, the oldest of my decks," Grandma mused, offering me a gentle smile. "This deck has always reminded me of you."

That would explain why it was the deck of hers that I'd always been most drawn to, with its muted colors, beautiful florals, and heavy usage of night creatures.

"The goddess is already speaking if magic selected this deck for you, Pumpkin Pie."

Grandma set the aged tin down and I reached out to touch a finger to it. "What do you mean?"

"You came here seeking answers about the scraps of paper you have in your bag concerning Aramis Hawthorne and Steven Littlebottom, and yet the deck selection points to you and your involvement in this."

I didn't know what that meant, but I already knew about half of what Grandma would say during this endeavor would be mostly lost on me.

With practiced precision, Grandma shuffled the tarot cards and fanned them out in front of me. "Five."

I knew what she meant, and I tapped my long fingernail to five cards, letting my magic guide me. As I did, Grandma laid them out in a five-card spread.

"Don't you need the scraps of paper?" I asked, not seeing the connection.

"No." She flipped the first card over. The Tower. "This is about you and your involvement in the case first." She *hmm'd* and breathed deeply as I watched her flip over the next three cards, trying not to bounce my leg.

Tower—upright

Three of Pentacles—upright

Page of Cups—reversed

Moon—upright

The fifth card turned over onto the table with a faint *thwip*. Grandma's eyes shot to mine and I fought the urge to balk. "Five of Swords," she said in a hushed tone. "Reversed."

I was not one to use tarot cards myself. Though Grandma has pulled cards for me on many occasions, I much prefer oracle cards, where the meaning is more open to interpretation and more positive. Grandma has insisted time and again that tarot is all about how you view things, but—and I've said this before—I don't need help in the anxiety department. I appreciate a lighthearted look at things and my Witch sense was already tingling...

Grandma took her time, running her fingers over the cards and, I assume, choosing her words carefully. "My darling girl." She stretched across the table and took my hands. "This journey you have embarked upon will bring you fulfillment like you've never dreamed of, but it will be rife with struggles. There is a great awakening happening within you, trifold."

She gently pulled one hand free and pointed at my forehead. "In your mind: new challenges and utilization of skills you didn't know you possessed." Her finger moved trajectory toward my chest. "In your heart: new relationships and all the complexities of such things, whether manners of the heart or platonic." She took my hand again. "And in your powers as a Witch. It is important that you realize you cannot embark further on this journey alone. No one"—her gaze grew intense—"and hear me when I say this, *no one* succeeds alone. *Ever*."

I swallowed down the emotion lumping in my throat and nodded.

Grandma's hands squeezed mine tighter. "This path will grow very dark at times, but you are never alone, even when you think you are. And you must keep going. At all costs. Keep running forward. And when you grow weary, lean on those who love you and rest, but never quit."

Grandma let go and stood to retrieve something from her many vials and vases. She returned with a single moonflower blossom, the petals closed, save just for the tips as the flower considered how close the sun was to setting.

"Not everyone can bloom even in the dark. But you can." She handed me the flower and I spun its stem between my fingers, watching the petals gleam in the gaslights of Grandma's aerie. "Sometimes we bloom, sometimes we gloom." She smiled at me, that warm grandmotherly kind that reminds you of freshly baked cookies. "Remember that, Pumpkin Pie." She rested her palm against my cheek for a second before she pulled her hand back and clapped. "Now," she said brightly, turning to another corner of the aerie. "Where did I put my crystal ball?"

While she bustled around on her quest, I continued to spin the little moonflower she'd given me, contemplating her words. I knew the Moon card meant mysteries and often foreboding, and Grandma's divination of my current reality and coming path had a hint of darkness in it. Like a cloud of ink dropped in crystalline water. But I didn't feel fear or any sense of dread.

A crystal ball materialized in front of me on its shiny silver stand and an indigo cloth (neither of which was present before). Grandma sat down again and rubbed her hands together. "Alright, dear. Get those scraps of paper and let's find out what we can see."

I did as I was told, slightly surprised by how excited I was to learn what Grandma would divine. She began her whispered spells of divination, the air growing so thick with powerful magic that I could almost taste it—like cinnamon and spice. Grandma's eyes were closed, but I kept mine open, another way that our magic differed. I often needed sight to keep my thoughts in line, while Grandma found the outside world distracting.

The second before Grandma's eye flew open, I saw the shift in the crystal ball.

A fog rolled over the blown glass sphere, much like that dot of ink in the crystalline water of my life I mentioned earlier, blooming out until it colored the ball a murky gray.

"*Dilatare*," Grandma whispered, pinching the air above the crystal ball in her fingers and tossing the invisible divination into the aerie. Fog rolled through the room, clearing enough to show us a vision akin to a black-and-white movie projected onto a gritty screen.

It was the forest behind the inn, that much was certain. But I couldn't make sense of what else we were seeing. There were the sounds of night creature songs and the hooting of owls, but I couldn't translate the owls' language without being in their physical presence. I glanced at Grandma, and she looked as confused as I was when the scene became fast-changing clips of the woods, caves, mountains, a shadowed figure... It was almost like unedited clips of a nature film taken back to back to be spliced later.

The divination folded in on itself, leaving only fog until that quickly dissipated.

Grandma sat back in her chair looking bewildered. "I'm sorry, dear. My intention must have been misplaced." She shook her head and tucked a strand of silver hair behind her ear. "I've been so worried about Millie. She hasn't been sleeping."

Well, that was one low-level mystery solved: who Grandma was brewing sleep potion for.

"I must have let that worry seep in. I apologize."

I reached out and put my hand on Grandma's. "You have nothing to apologize for." I thanked her and gave her a quick peck on the cheek, then shoved the scraps of evidence back into my bag.

Hustling to Wardwell Cottage, I couldn't shake the idea that we'd just seen clips of Andrew's film.

CHAPTER 10

Tell her if she doesn't feed me that mac & cheese we are no longer friends.

"Hello to you too, Beetle." I closed the door to the cottage behind me. "I take it Mags is making food and not sharing?"

Beetle stuck her kitty nose in the air haughtily. *Aren't you supposed to be the detective around here?*

Beetle is easily the smartest of our three-and-a-half cats, but she is also the sassiest. I slipped off my boots and lined them up on the shoe rack in the foyer just how Hamish likes them. I was getting enough attitude from his cat, I didn't need to add a disgruntled Warlock to the mix.

"It never occurred to you to be nice to the Witch you're asking to con someone out of mac & cheese?" One brow raised at Beetle, I bent to scratch her behind the ears.

Unfortunately for me, Maggie can only communicate with owls and Hamish with bats. That means I'm often the liaison for three-and-a-half very particular cats. Yes, that includes Chester the ghost cat.

Beetle sighed through her nose and turned round, sad eyes on me. *Please, Blair. I would beg from my Hamish, but he's too busy for me.*

I fought the powerful urge to roll my eyes. It was well past closing time for the library, so Hamish should have been home by now. He wasn't one to dilly-dally after work or make many plans to socialize. "Come on then, you little heathen."

Beetle trotted right along next to me into the kitchen, where Mags was standing over the stove, stirring methodically as her magic sprinkled cheese into a steaming pot.

"Hey, B!" she called to me cheerily over her shoulder, but then her eyes narrowed on Beetle. "Don't you even think about it, missy."

Beetle meowed. I dropped my bag onto the floor and sat in one of the chairs at the table, curling one leg underneath me. "She wants some mac & cheese," I translated.

"Yeah, well, that was obvious even if I can't understand *cat*." The last word was a hiss directed at said cat. "Tell her to stay off the counters and I might be inclined to give her more treats."

I gasped a little too dramatically. "Beetle Louise Wardwell. Have you been on the kitchen counters?"

She huffed and hightailed it out of there.

"You only have *one* rule!" I called after her, then turned to Maggie shaking my head.

She chuckled, turned off the fire, and lifted the pot. "Want some?"

"Sure." I hopped up to grab two ceramic bowls in a lovely cinnamon color and set them on the table. Mags spooned two heaping portions into them before discarding the pot on the butcher block island and sitting opposite me.

We chatted about work and day-to-day things as I purposefully avoided the case and the scraps of paper. There was one thing I couldn't help but bring up, though.

"Hey, have you chatted with your mom much lately?"

Maggie shoveled her last bite of creamy, cheesy pasta shells into her mouth. The spoon clinked against her empty bowl and she sat back against her chair, chewing and considering my question. Finally, she swallowed and said, "Yeah. I don't think I've talked to her today, but she came over yesterday afternoon after my last hair appointment. Why? Is something up? Something besides you hexing Sheriff Oliphant?" She gave me a conspiratorial waggle of her eyebrows.

I sighed. "Hamish?"

"Hamish. He texted me when you left the library." She laughed and stood, gesturing toward my bowl with hers. "Done?"

"Yeah, thanks." I handed her the bowl, thinking that, for some reason, I shouldn't have eaten all that food, but I couldn't for the life of me recall why. "And I didn't *hex* Oliphant. Mom said she was handling Corbin, so I went to see Grandma this afternoon for a late lunch and she mentioned Millie might have found something strange in the woods."

A horrible clatter echoed through the kitchen as Maggie dropped the bowls in the sink and spun around. "In the woods behind the inn? What do you mean *'strange'*?"

I could have kicked myself. Of course the woods and their contents this close to Samhain would trigger Maggie. I stood in a rush and crossed over to the island. "Mags, I'm so sorry. I didn't think about your da—"

She held up a hand to stop me, her tawny face pale. "As long as she didn't find...him, we're good."

Him. I knew she meant her father's remains. My heart broke for her. Maggie had moved on—as much as one can from such a thing—more quickly than Millie because she was convinced only a couple weeks in that her father was either dead or—worse—left of his own volition like my own father. Only Hamish had a relationship with his dad out of the three of us, and even it wasn't anything to envy. He traveled so often when Hamish was younger that they still hardly knew one another.

Todd Wardwell had an apartment in Dornwich where he worked as a journalist. Despite still being technically married to my Aunt Moira, he hardly came to Gloam Hollow and both Moira and Hamish had all but stopped visiting him in the city.

"I don't think it's anything like that," I clarified to Mags. "Millie's just been out in the woods a lot with Andrew while he shoots his documentary and Grandma mentioned they seem to have found something she hadn't seen before."

Color slowly returned to Maggie's face and she tilted her head to the side, all those silvery curls swaying. "Mom knows the trails better than she knows her own house."

"My thoughts exactly."

A *tap, tap, tap* sounded at the window and we both looked over. A starling sat on the sill, its speckled feathers nearly glittering in the last remaining rays of sunlight. I went over to let him in and took the rolled-up parchment from his beak.

Pumpkin Pie,

Have your mother read your tea leaves.

Not today. Day after tomorrow. In the morning.

Goddess Blessings.

Grandma

Normally, this would be a very typical thing for Grandma, but she rarely sent starlings. They are my symbol, showing up repeatedly when I need to pay particular attention to something.

Come to think of it, I'd seen starlings all day...

"Doesn't Grandma usually send ravens?" Mags asked, reading the note over my shoulder. My cousin and I were very much of like mind today.

"She does." I bent to inspect the starling, watching as he fluttered his wings, the movement making his speckles ripple. He had something else stuck in his beak. I tried to pinch at it but he squawked at me. He made to fly away, but not before that squawk revealed a dark raven feather stuck in his mouth. "That little stink confiscated the note from Grandma's raven."

Maggie tittered. "It's a starling, too."

"I've seen several today..." I said quietly, more to myself than Mags.

She looked at me pointedly. "It's a full moon soon. I'd be out there scrying when it is if I were you."

"No one scries anymore, Mags."

"Archaic doesn't always mean ineffective."

My chin propped up in my hand, I leaned over the counter, watching Mags scrub at the macaroni pot. She had a point. Starlings weren't rare around Gloam Hollow, but I'd seen enough of them today to think scrying under the next full moon was likely a good idea. I'd just have to deal with the anxiety that usually accompanies it.

"Do you think I should call Mom?" Mags asked, turning off the water and drying the pot with a hand towel decorated with fall leaves. "She's so touchy when Samhain is approaching..."

I stood straight and leaned my hip against the island. "I don't know. Maybe it's nothing. Grandma would have stepped in if it was something serious." That thought jogged my memory. "Has anyone figured out what's going on with the hex on the cottage?"

Mags sent her magic to hang the freshly cleaned pot on its hook along the dangling pots and pans rack above the island. "We contained it to the workshop this morning. Things have been falling over in there, like a little ghost run wild." As if on cue, a loud crash came from the back of the house and we both winced. "I didn't find any traces of it anywhere else in the cottage."

"If it was an object, I suppose someone could have carried it through to the workshop and left it there..." I shook my head, dismissing the thought. "You still would have sensed a trail of it through the house if that were the case. Whoever cast the hex or carried it in only entered through the exterior workshop door."

Mags shrugged. "Fair assumption, if you ask me."

I chewed on my lip. "It couldn't have been one of us, then. Who all was here yesterday?"

Taking a bright purple hair band from the many on her wrist, Maggie tied her hair back in what would be a ponytail for most, but for Mags, it was what I call her *puff*. "I haven't had anyone over in ages." She frowned like it was a sudden realization. "You know Hamish didn't have anyone over." Then she looked pointedly at me.

"Aramis walked me home, but he didn't go anywhere near the back of the cottage or the workshop."

"Mom came by." Her thoughtful expression turned incredulous and she straightened. "She came in through the workshop. I was at the greenhouse when she arrived."

Drumming my fingers on the counter, I prodded her, "Okay, did she come further into the house?"

"Yes. We came in here to grab some cheese and wine and went out to the porch. She didn't stay long, she kept getting distracted."

Despite the way my heart ached for Aunt Millie, my newfound love of collecting clues bounded in and focused on the workshop hex. Was it tied to what Millie found in the woods? To Andrew? And what about Grandma's vision? Her intent was supposed to be focused on the notes I'd found detailing where assassins could find Aramis, and yet the crystal ball had shown us forest trails and caves... Perhaps Grandma was right, and she'd just been too distracted by her daughter's recent emotional plights.

"If Millie brought something in that was hexed, it was left in the workshop," I deduced matter-of-factly.

Mags thought about my assessment for a moment and nodded. "Yeah, that makes sense. But Mom wouldn't do something like that."

My Witch sense was tingling up into my scalp, making me shiver. "No, but she would if she didn't know what she was carrying. Did she have anything with her that she left in the workshop?"

Maggie thought hard, coming around the island and

sinking onto a stool. "She had a few herbs for me and I didn't really pay attention past that." She looked ashamed of herself and I reached out to fiddle with her dangly peace-sign earrings—the perfect touch to her boho outfit of flowing green top with bell sleeves and high-waisted black trouser pants.

"You didn't know your mom might be carrying around something hexed, Mags."

She nodded too many times, those earrings swaying. "Yeah, you're right. I already used the herbs, though, and they made a perfect pain relief poultice, so it must have been something else."

I squeezed her arm. "We'll figure it out."

Mags jumped like a popcorn kernel. "Oh! What time is it? I forgot I'm supposed to go pick up Hamish!" She pulled out her cell phone and screeched at the glowing screen. "He's texted me seven times. I better go."

"Wait! Where was Hamish?" I called after her, but the front door slammed.

Sighing and feeling like something forgotten was gnawing at me, I grabbed my bag and checked on the workshop. Upon further inspection, it looked like the source of the crash had been a pestle that tried to break its way through a simmer pot. It was still lazily tapping against the dented bottom of the pot like it was tired from all the effort.

"What a strange hex," I muttered to myself and trudged upstairs. As long as marble pestles and simmer pots didn't start flying at *us*, we were okay.

Albis and Puck were both curled up on my bed like a little orange and gray yin-yang sign. It was so adorable that I didn't disturb them. Instead, I shucked off my cute outfit and donned my oldest—and comfiest—pair of gray sweatpants and a ginormous chunky-knit cardigan over a white crop tank.

Those girls who can go braless are so lucky. I will never be one of them, but I'm also in my at-home braless era. For the sake of *cozy* and Hamish's delicate constitution, the sweater does its job of maintaining propriety.

I tied my hair up in a top knot and washed all the day's makeup and grime off my face before sitting at my desk and digging out the evidence notes. I laid them out, snorting at how silly they looked next to my Witchy oddities, nicknacks, and fashion board. Tapping a finger to my chin, I studied them through their little baggies. There had to be some sort of spell or physical clue that would show me who wrote these notes to two different men sent to kill the same Dead Monster.

It was strange that they seemed to arrive in Gloam Hollow around the same time, too. Did their boss just think two was better than one? Or did they not trust one or the other of them?

Questions, questions.

I was still pondering all this when the doorbell rang.

Hush, Albis hissed from the bed as I got up.

"Oh, stop it, you old grouch."

I bopped down the steps, trying to peer out the thin side windows bordering the door, but they're mullioned glass and it only warbles whoever is out there. They're more for letting natural light in than anything else, I supposed.

Upon opening the door, I found a mascara-tear-stained Maeve standing there, her bottom lip wobbling.

"Blair." She hiccuped my name. "Can I come in?"

CHAPTER 11

Maeve sank onto the couch, her shoulders shaking with her soft sobs. I dropped down beside her and wrapped an arm around her shoulders, rubbing my hand up and down her arm.

Many people think that Vamps cry tears of blood and the truth is that they do—sometimes. It has to be something truly heinous or dreadful *and* they have to have been on a diet of mostly blood.

Maeve was more likely to cry tears of wine than blood.

"Wine," I said. "We need wine."

Maeve nodded emphatically, her face buried in her hands.

I rushed off to the wine cabinet in the kitchen and snagged a deep, aromatic Cabernet Sauvignon and two of our best stem glasses—the fancy kind made of glass so thin you fear a fingernail tap could break it. On my way out of the kitchen, I spied a bag of cheese puffs and snagged those, too. I didn't know yet what had happened, but I had a feeling junk food was in order.

I set the glasses down on the coffee table and poured two generous servings of wine as Maeve wrangled herself out of her coat and burrowed into one of our five hundred cozy blankets. Handing her a glass, I shot a spell to start a fire in the hearth. While it roared to life, Maeve took a large gulp of wine and sighed.

Sitting across from her on the edge of the table, I put a hand on her knee. "Tell me what's going on."

"Tom and I broke up." Her bottom lip wobbled.

"Oh, Maeve, I'm so sorry. What happened?"

She inhaled a shaky breath, cradling her wine glass. "He's just been so weird, you know? He doesn't want me to come over and he hardly comes by my place. After basically avoiding me for weeks, I'd just"—she snapped—"had it."

I sipped my wine as she spoke, trying to keep my face even. I couldn't say this had come as a shock. The two of them had been on the outs for weeks, since the night of Anon's attack when the two roommates began acting strangely. Really, it had begun before all that. Tom's own gran, my Grandmother's friend Tina, had been so angry with Tom for the way he'd been so aloof recently that she tried to set Maeve up with Andrew.

We all thought the strangeness had something to do with Anon's attack and with their mysterious new *friend* who supplied Tom with the glowing tattoo ink, but none of the rest of us had met the guy...or girl. My stomach flipped at the thought and what that might mean for Maeve.

"So," Maeve continued after another sip of wine and a hiccup, "when I found out he'd texted Lacuna about her tattoo appointment but he hadn't responded to any of my calls or texts, I just sort of lost it. I stormed over to his house this afternoon on my break. I couldn't handle it anymore." I nodded along, waiting for the other shoe to drop. "He wasn't home. Anon was there on his lunch break, but he wouldn't talk to me. So I hightailed it over to the tattoo parlor. There he was, doing some girl's tattoo and he acted like he didn't even know me. Like I was some huge inconvenience to him."

Her crying began afresh and I set my wine down to move to the couch. Simultaneously wrapping an arm around her and taking her glass away, I soothed her until she was ready to talk again.

"I can't stand for being treated like that, you know?" she cried.

"Absolutely not, Maeve. *Absolutely* not. So you called it off?"

She nodded, swiping at her nose. "I didn't want to do it over the phone or text, that's just so lame, you know? But he wouldn't talk to me, so I left a note on his motorcycle outside the tattoo parlor. I'm sure he's found it by now."

Maeve reached into her purse on the couch beside her and pulled out her phone. "Oh, no you don't." I snatched it from her and shoved it into the pocket of my huge cardigan. "Not tonight. This is too fresh to talk to him or make any further decisions." I glanced at the cuckoo clock and winced. "Hamish and Mags will be home soon. Do you want to go up to my room? Hibernate?"

Maeve sniffled and I handed her a tissue box from the side table. "I would love a night like the old days, actually." She tried for a watery smile.

I knew exactly what she meant. "Yes!" I hopped up, clapping my palms together once. "Absolutely that! I'll call Mags and have her pick up some ice cream and I'll get every other junk food you can think of delivered."

Maeve started crying again, but this time she was laughing too. "You are the best, B."

I waved her off and ran to the landline. In twenty minutes, my cousins were pulling up in Mags's beat-up yellow car that looked like a bug and bustling in with six flavors of ice cream from *Goodman's* (we unanimously decided to boycott the ice cream and boba parlor owned by Tom's mom for the night) and a roll of cookie dough. I'd called to have pizza, tacos, and Chinese takeout delivered.

Mags and Hamish had Maeve almost giggling over some crazy story that had happened that evening and I'd popped half the cookie dough in the oven and was handing the rest of the raw dough to Maeve in a bowl when the doorbell rang.

"And now we feast!" I shouted as I flung open the door.

My mouth fell open, and my heart plummeted to my toes. "Oh my Goddess," I whispered, staring wide-eyed at the beautiful Dread Monster standing there holding up a ridiculous amount of takeout food and looking almost anxious. I suddenly recalled with stark clarity what I felt like I'd forgotten...

"I– Aramis, I'm so sorry. I can't believe I forgot our date!"

Aramis only smiled, but it didn't reach his green eyes. "No apologies necessary. When you didn't show, I thought I'd come to make sure everything was alright." He held up the mountain of takeout bags and boxes, one of which I did not order. "I figured you were okay once I met three delivery guys on the walk up to the cottage. Want me to bring this in?"

I opened the door wider and gestured him in, my heart in my throat. How could I have been so thoughtless? Goddess, he looked so *sad*.

Shouts of *'hello'* and *'hey'* and *'join the party'* echoed across the living room when Aramis walked in, depositing the takeout on the coffee table. My cousins and Maeve all dug in like a pack of wild animals and Aramis snatched back a *Spectre Café* bag, muttering through a chuckle, "Easy there."

He turned to me with the bag. "I brought a couple of burgers."

A couple. Two. I wanted to slam my head against a wall. "I'm so sorry, Aramis." I pulled him away from the ruckus and into the dark dining room. "Maeve showed up crying. She and Tom broke up and I just—" I hung my head. "I completely forgot. I'm so sorry."

Aramis made my hand take the bag of burgers, then ran a thumb down my cheek. "Stop apologizing, Wardwell."

"Stay," I said softly when his hand dropped away. "Please."

"Your friend needs you and your food is getting cold." He turned away toward the front entry and I wanted to snatch his arm and make him stay, but I didn't. "I'll see you."

And then he was out the door and I was banging my head against it (lightly. I'm not a masochist). But Aramis was right. Maeve needed me and I would just have to find a way to make it up to him.

~

Lacuna

After hours of regulars and new patrons alike ordering my confections and comforting brews, I finally locked the door and switched off the *OPEN* light before padding to the back office to run payroll. I sat, bent over the books, one hand on my ink pen, the other on the moonstone tally. I'm not fond of running payroll or jotting down the days' totals, but I do enjoy the *click, click,* the gemstone tallies make as I manually calculate the moonstone earnings of the day. It's the little things in life that really give it magic, even in a realm where everything glitters with it. In fact, that's why I feel it is even *more* important to find small magic within our mystical realm. It's far too easy to take it all for granted and miss everything.

That was something Blair had taught me over our many years of friendship. It's not always easy being friends with a Witch who has such amazing powers while my only power is blending in as a Shadow Nymph. Blair and Maeve would fight me on that notion, though, claiming I stand out more than anyone for my 'beauty and charm.'

I smiled to myself. That's what I love about my friends. For a long time I would roll my eyes at their compliments, but then I realized they weren't empty words, but how they truly saw me. A girl can move mountains when she knows her friends truly *see* her and have her back. Warts and all.

Quickly, my smile faltered. Anon was one of those friends too until recently. He hadn't quit today, but he hadn't changed his attitude either and I didn't know what to do about it.

Oliver.

The peculiar name assaulted my mind out of nowhere, and I reared back so hard my violet office chair nearly toppled backward with me in it. I touched a finger gingerly to my temple. It felt almost like the name had just seared itself into my mind and I winced.

I sucked in a breath as fog rolled over my vision, thick

and inky, like up in the mountain cave... Somewhere in the distance, I heard the moonstone tally hit the floor of the office, but I was staring at a foggy image of a man.

Oliver, my mind whispered again.

I couldn't make out anything but a tall, lean form. He was walking through...a house? An apartment? It felt like annoyance was radiating off of him. I watched as he approached a figure lying on what had to be a couch and they exchanged words, angry ones, but I couldn't make them out—like my head was underwater. Other shadowy figures appeared around him and there was a muddled blare of music, but I could only feel the bass. *Feel* it. The man kept looking over his shoulder as if searching for someone, but he wove through the crowd without speaking to another person. The music and talking faded as he entered a dark room and shut a door behind him.

There in the quiet, I could sense how familiar he was. Tears sprang to my eyes as I begged the vision to become clearer, crisper—to show me this Oliver. He fell backward onto the faint outline of a bed and I could feel his exasperation. His loneliness and depression. He reached for a book somewhere next to him and its title was crystal clear. *The Catcher in the Rye*. But it looked brand new.

The vision disappeared and I suppressed a sob at how deeply I felt the loss of it. Scrambling, I pulled out my worn copy of the contraband book and hugged it to my chest.

Shaken, I finished up in the office as quickly as I could, knowing I probably made mistakes I would need to correct later after being so distracted.

As I was rushing through the shop, flicking off lights and making sure all the ovens and appliances were off, I caught the scent of fresh coffee grounds wafting from the small employee espresso machine in the back.

I found Anon there, silently making two to-go cups. He placed the lids on and handed me one without a word. I wavered only briefly before deciding I definitely *did* want a cup, peace offering, or not.

My phone buzzed as Anon silently stood there, and I gave him a weak smile before checking the text. It was the new group text we'd started...without Anon and Tom. Someday, we'd have to convince Blair she needed a phone, too.

MAGGIE WARDWELL:

Maeve and Tom broke up. Hang sesh at Wardwell Cottage, NOW!

 be there in ten

Anon had already grabbed his bag and gone out the front by the time I responded to Mags. I considered catching up to him, inviting him, but it wasn't my house and I wasn't sure where any of us stood with him right now.

I locked up and headed to Wardwell Cottage, snippets of my earlier vision dancing around in my head like sugar plums.

Oliver.

I was either going insane or I needed to get into the Mortal Lands.

Blair

The fact that I'd disappointed Aramis hung heavy over my head, but Maeve was no longer crying. She was laughing and had eaten just as much as the rest of us, so the evening had mostly been a success. Halfway into our first old RomCom movie, Lacuna showed up and we sank into more snacks, more wine, and two more movies before everyone passed out.

I'd fallen asleep crookedly in a wingback not meant for dozing and woke with a crick in my neck to find Hamish on the floor, his legs up on the loveseat. Mags was laid out on said loveseat, using Hamish's shins as what had to constitute as the worst pillow in history. Lacuna was curled up on the couch with Maeve, an arm slung over her middle.

Stretching my sore neck, I traversed the chaos that was the evidence of our night and shut off the television. The absence of the blue glare sent the room plunging into darkness, so I wisped magic out to fan the fire's embers and conjured four glowing orbs that offered just enough light to keep anyone from tripping if they got up before morning.

I blew a little kiss to my sleeping friends and padded up the stairs to an actual bed. I barely managed to toss off my sweater and make it into sleep shorts—cute pumpkin ones —before I sank into the blessed comfort of my pillow.

And then the doorbell rang.

My first instinct was fury. Didn't the entire world know I'd just gotten comfortable? That all of us were wine-soaked and asleep?

I flopped over and my arm hit one of the three sleeping cats I didn't even know were there. "Sorry, Puck," I mumbled.

Grabbing my glasses, I carried them out into the hall and made my way back downstairs rubbing at my eyes. They felt like they were made of sandpaper.

I put on my glasses and blinked several times, trying to focus my vision. It appeared Hamish had managed to extricate himself from being Mags's pillow and stumbled his way to the entryway looking quite hungover.

"Who could it be at this hour?" I asked him as I descended the steps, but only received a very disgruntled grumble in reply before he flung open the door.

"'s for you," Hamish slurred sleepily, stepping out of the way.

I froze on the second to last step.

Aramis ducked inside, leaving the door open, the chilly air flowing in after him. He crossed the entryway to stand at the foot of the steps, the height difference putting us at eye level. In his hand rested a bulky, rectangular box, and he held it out to me. "Here."

"What is this?" Four thousand thoughts were racing through my head ranging from '*oh, good, it wasn't an assassin at the door*' to '*woah Goddess, why does he always look so good?*' and '*am I drunk?*' '*Do I have sleep breath?*'

"It's a cellphone."

I'd definitely had too much wine to decipher his tone. Or maybe I'd had too much sugar? Doesn't alcohol turn to sugar in your veins? Probably shouldn't have paired a bottle of wine with an entire sleeve of caramel coconut cookies then... Great, even my brain was rambling.

"How did you get one this late?" Cool response, B.

"It doesn't matter." His other hand went up in surrender when I opened my mouth to protest. "I know you hate cell phones. I don't have the number for it." He sounded almost placating. "But I did put mine in it. Just— " He shoved his empty hand in his pocket, the other one still holding that box out to me, and sighed. "You're investigating murders and searching for assassins *alone*. I know you can take care of yourself, you just—" He shuffled on his feet. "You're shaving years off my life, Wardwell."

My heart did a little tumble and a wide grin stretched slowly across my face as I realized what was happening here —why he'd been so curt tonight. It was more than me forgetting our date. "You're worried about me."

Aramis tucked his lips into his teeth for a second, an adorably nervous gesture, and jostled the box toward me. "Just take the damn phone, please."

I couldn't keep the grin off my face or the teasing out of my voice. "Fine," I sighed breezily, channeling my most dramatically resigned tone. "There are enough assassins after you, I can't be shaving years off your life, too." I took the box from him with a cheeky grin, and he lost some of the tension in his shoulders.

He stepped away, but then his gaze slid down my body once, then back up, as if just noticing what I was wearing. It wasn't until one corner of his mouth tipped up and he lazily said, "Nice pajamas," that *I* realized what I was wearing.

Standing there in only my skimpy pumpkin sleep shorts and a thin white crop top, I blinked at him.

"Goodnight, Wardwell." It was *his* voice that held all the teasing now and I swallowed.

Back in bed and mortified in equal measure to elation, I stared up at my ceiling, twirling the silver phone in my hand, unable to sleep.

Finally, I gave in. The thing said '*slide to unlock*', so I slid my thumb across the screen and searched all the little labeled squares for **Contacts**.

"There, that wasn't so bad," I encouraged myself, already irritated at the bright light of the screen. Surely there was a way to change the brightness. Everything was so *white*.

I found the one and only contact: *Hawthorne,* and clicked his name. There was a cute little message bubble next to it, so I clicked that next.

It took me an embarrassingly long time, but I typed out a short message.

Save the number

Almost immediately, three little dots appeared, bopping up and down in rhythm. "Well that's cute," I said to the screen just before a little ding sounded, accompanied by a vibration and a new message under mine.

Sweet dreams, Wardwell

CHAPTER 12

I did not have time to do my nails.

And yet, here I was ripping open the package of polish I'd ordered and rushing to the workshop to use it. For once, Hamish had set my mail by my bedroom door as requested and I was starting my day off *right*.

"Mags!"

She looked up at me as I ran in, the nail polish nearly flying out of the wrapping when I finally got it open. "Oh my Goddess, is that the new polish?" Mags dropped her crystals and herbs on the tabletop and met me with grabby hands. "Let me seeeeee!"

I held up the polish to the morning light streaming in the window and we both marveled at the olive and silver paint marbled together and shimmering in its little glass bottle.

"It will be perfect for Yule!" Mags squealed. "I get to borrow it, right?"

"Obviously. Samhain is in three days. I should wait,

right?" I looked down at my coffin-shaped matte black nails. "I should wait."

Mags shrugged, wandering back to her tincture work. "Depends how much time you'll have to redo them for Samhain, but I can tell you right now that Aunt Moira was already here demanding we go to the inn tonight and help Grandma with the bonfire prep. Whatever polish you have on now will likely be ruined by the time we accomplish that." She rolled her eyes and I laughed.

"Fair point..." I already had the polish open and the brush gliding over the first nail. It covered the black easily and I could always redo them again to match the Samhain spirit. "Too bad I have plans tonight with Lacuna." Mags met my sinister smile with a frown. "So I will not be helping with this bonfire prep."

"We can easily just wait for you," she teased.

I had all my nails painted in a jiff and cast a little spell to dry them quickly. The color in the bottle had been a pale comparison to how it looked actually on. It would be a struggle not to stare at my nails in different lighting all day. "Would you look at that, it perfectly matches the green of my cardigan, too."

"Ooo, it does!" Maggie agreed.

I slid the bottle across the worktable toward her and she immediately tested the color on her pinky nail. Like everything else, it looked amazing on her, the color taking on more of a jade hue against her warm brown skin.

"Alright, I have to get going. I haven't been to *Copper Cauldron* in days and Grandma insists I need to stop by and have Mom read my tea leaves today."

"I need to head out soon, too." She twisted the lid back on the polish bottle, blowing on her pinky. "I have a client in about an hour and I need to go change." Her attention slid to my sweater and she nodded her head toward me. "You might want to as well."

I looked down at my black tights, black mini dress, and dusky olive cardigan, then back at her. "Uh. Why?"

Mags pulled an amused face and walked over to the back door of the workshop as I followed her.

"Oh, no," I groaned, already feeling it the moment I stepped one booted foot outside. We had been completely flung back into the middle of spring. Pink and yellow blossoms dotted the garden, the trees had little green leaves budding along their branches and birds were singing. Not one single pumpkin or gloriously dead leaf in sight. I immediately sneezed. Then shouted my verbal irritation again, startling a veritable flock of starlings out of a perky green bush.

Maggie winced. "Yeah..."

I should have known by how early the sun had risen. I thought I'd accidentally slept in late.

"Ugh." I turned around and stomped inside to take off my tights and boots, replacing the latter with some black and white canvas shoes. Fine. It was a cute look with the mini dress and sweater.

I managed to stop my grumbling by the time I reached *Moonrise Manor*, but barely. The sneezing, however, had lingered like a bad joke.

Aunt Millie was on the porch swing with a cup of coffee and chatting away with Andrew.

"Hey, Andrew," I said as I climbed the steps. "Morning, Auntie."

"Morning, Pumpkin Squash!" she sang. I could see the telltale signs of her lack of sleep in the daylight, but her mood was downright chipper. My best guess was the sudden shift from late fall to mid-spring was momentarily distracting her from her Samhain woes.

"Pumpkin Squash, hm?" Andrew mused, his mouth curving up in a smile that most would consider quite dashing. "I like that. It's cute." He turned the smile on me and I had to fight the urge to balk at him. I'd seen him flirt with Maeve and Lacuna, quite heavily I might add, but never me.

"Um." I shook my head and looked at Millie. "Is Mom in, by chance?" Usually, she was already at *Toil & Truffle* by this time, but she had been keeping weird hours since I broke Corbin. She'd been taking a *long* time to answer my magical notes, too.

Millie smiled behind her cup in what I can only describe as a coy manner. "She is."

Everything felt off-kilter and strange today. I didn't even want to ask what that look was about. "Alright then," I said awkwardly. "See you guys later."

Grandma had taken all of her Samhain decorations down and I felt the little tingle of my seasonal depression trying to sneak in, accompanied by two consecutive sneezes. See, most people who suffer from seasonal depression experience it in winter. Me? Nope. Spring and summer—it never fails. I really needed to get to the apothecary and brew a remedy or I would slip into a deep sullenness by the end of the day.

Tina came to the front desk as I walked through and said good morning. "How is Maeve?" she asked me with a wince.

I hadn't seen her since I woke up the morning after our junk food and wine night to a scribbled note of thanks. Mags had gotten a text later that day confirming proof of life as well, and Hamish had taken her to dinner last night, but I hadn't seen her.

"She's doing as well as can be expected, I think. How is Tom?"

Tina sighed heavily. "Last I heard, he'd only stopped playing sad guitar ballads long enough to sleep. Rinse and repeat."

"Yikes." I grimaced. "I'm supposed to see him tonight. Want me to give you an overview after?"

"Please." Tom's grandmother pushed her palms together in a show of thanks. "That would be excellent. He won't answer my calls or Linda's texts. She's been so worried."

"It's no problem." I gave her a little wave and went up the stairs toward Mom's private wing of the inn.

Grandma stopped me at the top landing. "Pumpkin!" When I turned to face her, her smile fell. "Sudden spring got you down?"

I sneezed and it was enough of a response.

"Aw, dear." She came over and hugged me. "Sometimes we bloom, and sometimes we gloom, remember? Don't you worry. I'm sure Sister Spring is just in a tiff. Probably angry the seasons skipped Beltane this year. Autumn will be upon us again in time for Samhain."

"You're right." I tried to smile. "Why did you take all your Samhain decor down?"

"Oh, you know how Bill is." Grandma snapped and gorgeous florals wound themselves up the stair bannister. "If it's spring out there, the décor has to match." She kissed my cheek and gestured toward Mom's wing. "Go, go. You need those leaves read."

We set off in opposite directions. I walked through the bubble of magic protecting Mom's privacy from inn guests and made my way toward her kitchen while Grandma bopped down the stairs.

There was a kettle already on Mom's stove and still steaming, so I called out letting her know I was there and began making myself some tea. She had a lovely stoneware cup that perfectly matched my new nail polish, the evergreen slipping down into silver that ended in a crescent moon on the front.

As I was pouring the water over my black tea and bergamot leaves, a chime sounded from my bag. At first, I was confused, still not used to the rectangle Aramis had given me. I do not like technology, but...I do like the little messages Aramis sent me throughout the day.

As I pulled out the phone, I realized I'd apparently gotten more than one before I'd looked at the thing today.

Fair Warning: it's spring today

Darn. Wish I would've seen that one an hour ago.

Let me know when you're in at work, I'll bring you coffee

"Aw! Look how cute that tiny coffee is!"

10-4. Show me how to do the cute pictures

Hey, I was getting slightly faster at this texting thing. I drank my tea and pulled out a book, wondering what was taking Mom so long.

I heard shuffling behind me and I stowed my phone away. I was not prepared for other people to have access to me at any given point in time. "Morning, Mama. Grandma says—"

I stopped mid-sentence when I turned to find it was not my mother walking in at all, but one Sheriff Oliphant in nothing but a bathrobe.

"Blair," he said slowly, his wide eyes mirroring mine and a flush coloring his cheeks above his graying beard. Have I ever mentioned I look quite a lot like my mom from behind? Yikes. At least he hadn't called me Bacon.

"Sheriff," I squeaked out. "I guess Mom, uh, fixed the spell problem?"

Corbin cleared his throat and shifted nervously on his feet. "She did. Last night."

Oh, Goddess. I did *not* like that accidental implication.

"Good. Great." I stuttered, grabbing for my bag and book. "Um. Could you have Mom read my tea leaves and message me?" I pointed to the mug and high-tailed it out of there before Corbin could answer.

CHAPTER 13

Lacuna

I shouldn't have driven my moped up into the woods alone, but it was my day off and the sun was shining.

Spring is the season I adore most of all. What's not to love about mild warmth, a cool breeze, flowers, and creatures galore? I parked my moped next to a tree on a well-traveled path and breathed in, smiling as a little bee buzzed around a flower etched onto my arm in ink. Surprised at the little guy buzzing about the tattoo on my dark skin, I chuckled. "No pollen in my flower, I'm afraid."

He buzzed away and I hopped off the moped. I'd expected more people out on the trails this morning with the warmer weather that would most likely be short-lived. It appeared I was quite alone, though, and I ventured off the beaten path and onto the one I know better than I know all the tattoos covering my body.

As I walked toward the hidden cave, I sent out a silent

search, a quiet plea to Oliver. All I heard was the chirping of birds and the babbling of a brook to my left. From that direction, something caught my eye. Veering off course, I paused to watch a group of Sprites dancing just above the brook's glittering surface. As always, they were a sight to behold, with their sparkling wings beating quick as hummingbirds', their porcelain skin and ethereal dresses...

Out of nowhere, it was there again. The entanglement. And I gasped. This time, it was synesthesia. Music from nowhere and everywhere, yet I could *see* it. A sound that mirrored the vision before me, eerily similar to Pixies reflected on the water. But the vision-sound kept going dark as night.

I snapped back to reality. *Stars.* My Mortal was looking at *stars* reflected on the water. The visions or entanglement or insanity I was seeing were growing stronger. In a rush, I headed back toward the cave, desperate to go inside and see something tangible. To try and see *Oliver* tangibly...

Just as I was about to step out of the trees and into the cave clearing, I heard voices. I jumped behind a tree trunk and watched in mute astonishment as Mildred Wardwell came out of the cave's fog, talking to someone.

I slammed my hand over my mouth to stifle the gasp when I saw who she was with.

Blair

I sneezed the *entire* way to the center of town.

All my spring-allergy-repellent supplies were just on the

other side of the square. All I had to do was make it there, down a potion, and then I could get back to work trying to figure out who killed Steven, and who was after Aramis.

"Hiya!"

"Ah!" I nearly jumped out of my skin at the voice behind me. Whipping around, I was met with Zar, who, humorously enough, had no skin to jump out of, but he did have on a dapper little top hat and a striped vest that kind of made him look like a hotel doorman.

"Zar! Jeepers creepers, it's good to see you, buddy!" Despite how feverish I was beginning to feel, I was delighted to see our friendly neighborhood skeleton—er, Unbodied Person—and we exchanged our secret handshake.

Zar's bones clickety-clacked with the movement. "It's a fantastic day, don't you think?" He spread his skeletal arms wide and tipped his eye sockets toward the sun that I was very much angry at for making me sticky along with the allergies. I'd already had to discard my sweater by the time I made it to Maple Lane.

Achoo!

Zar frowned in the way that only a skeleton can, which is more a clack of the mandible and a sag of the clavicle. "Shucks, hun. I forgot about your allergies." That toothy grin was quick to return and Zar hopped toward his mint green candy cart with a matching striped awning. "Gelato?" he asked brightly. "Salt water taffy?"

I can get on board with spring and summer if only because of Mr. Brightside, Zar. Never mind that it was hardly eight in the morning and I hadn't eaten any breakfast yet.

"I would be delighted to have some gelato, my friend."

This earned me a happy click-clack. "Since when do you sell more than candy?" I asked as Zar lifted the lids of three chilled compartments of gelato on his cart. By the looks of them, it was chocolate, strawberry, and something so deeply purple it was almost black.

"Which flavor, hun?"

I pointed to the purple one.

"Blackberry," he confirmed. "Shoulda guessed." Nimbly, Zar jostled a narrow waffle cone free from a towering stack. "The gelato came about because I was up there bored as snot in my apartment, tired of playing video games." He waggled his phalanges at me before grabbing a spatola and scooping out some gelato into the cone. "And I just had this brilliant idea that Linda and Art should combine frozen treats and candy to maximize the fun, you see?"

He handed me the cone and I took a *Gelato by Zar* napkin from the cart. "It really is a brilliant idea," I chimed before taking a lick. "And this is phenomenal, oh my Goddess."

Zar beamed. "I've been up there for weeks with a fire roaring while I wrote out letter after letter of instructions. We finally settled on a good deal a couple weeks ago that Ginny signed off on."

Ginny is one of two Gloam Hollow attorneys. As far as attorneys go, she's a peach, also a Banshee like her grandmother, Ms. Cooper, but with none of the scary fuss unless she's in court.

I stifled another sneeze. There's a little non-Witchy trick to that—all you have to do is press the area right under your nose and above your upper lip with the side of your finger, like you're making a little mustache. Really. Give it a shot.

"That's great, Zar."

He gestured to his cart. "Even had that construction fella build me a new cart and everything."

I wondered if my lips were turning purple from the gelato. "Construction fella? You mean Dean?" Dean Wigglesworth, a distant relative of our Bartholomew the Ghost, ran the only construction crew in town.

"No." Zar closed his gelato containers. "Dean and his crew have been working on other projects like a new facility for the Interweb company coming to town." He leaned in and put a bony hand to his cheekbone like he was about to tell me a secret. "Heard they knocked out the schools' Interweb for hours the other day when they bulldozed into a tower." Zar laughed and I mentally checked off another low-level mystery solved: why there were so many kids at the library the other day.

"Nah," Zar went on. "This fella was here to help with opening *Spectre Café*. He left there for a bit to pack up and then he moved to The Hollow, he loved it here so much." Zar gestured down the square toward the café. "Heard Dean didn't want to hire him, though, so he went back to working for Aramis. I just met the kid." He jostled me with his shoulder. "I like him."

I assumed he meant Aramis, but went ahead and played coy. "Who, your cart builder?"

"Hardy-har," Zar joked. "Your boyfriend!"

Cue the blush. "He's not my boyfriend. We haven't even been on a date yet." Thanks to me. *Le sigh.* "I'm glad he has more help at the café, though." He sorely needed it, and I couldn't help but hope it meant I'd get to see him more.

"Maybe you'll finally get that date then." If a skeleton was physically capable of winking, Zar did. But more people were flocking onto the square and he saw his opportunity. "Ope! Gotta go, hun!"

He tipped his hat and bustled off to convince more patrons to eat gelato for breakfast. I wondered how long it would be before Mom was after him for stealing her morning customers. Granted, she would have to leave her unclothed *sheriff* to do that.

Thankfully, I was distracted from that line of thinking by a very interesting kerfuffle beginning on the sidewalk in front of *Spectre Café*. I wasn't yet close enough to hear what they were saying, but Bill Winslow was waving his arms wildly at Aramis, who had *his* arms folded across his chest and a very distinct gleam in his eye that signaled his temper was hanging from a very thin string.

I debated just eating my gelato and watching from a distance. It would undoubtedly be an amusing show. But, I wouldn't get to hear what the commotion was about.

Hmm. The more I looked around, though, it seemed all the shop owners had a disgruntled look about them. Why were they all outside, arms full of decorations...

I inhaled a sharp, offended breath when it dawned on me, and I threw my gelato in the garbage, headed for Bill.

"Samhain is in three days!" I interrupted his spat with Aramis. "Tell me you aren't making everyone take down their decorations just because it's spring *today!*"

"That's exactly what he's doing," Aramis snarked. One look in his direction and I could tell his temper had taken on a bemused air when I walked up and started shouting at Bill. I pushed the warm fuzzies away and scowled at the mayor.

"Now, you listen here, the both of you." Bill pointed a

finger at Aramis and then me, but Aramis dropped his arms, hands going into fists.

"Get that finger out of her face, Winslow."

Jerkily, the mayor lowered his hand. "I will not have backtalk from either one of you. Tourists come here expecting an immersive experience and we will abide by that. If it is spring today, the decor is *springy*." Spittle flew from his mouth on the last word and I tried not to make a face. "If winter shows up tomorrow, it will be *wintery*. Do I make myself clear?"

"I'm not putting out flowers, Winslow. The best you're getting is the Witch hats down." Aramis's forearms flexed as he folded them across his chest again.

"I'm a Witch who owns a business with *Cauldron* in the name." I shrugged nonchalantly. "My spring is still Witchy."

Aramis smirked at me and Bill growled. His next words were incoherent as he stomped away, but I had a feeling they weren't very demure.

A full, wolfish grin slid across Aramis's face. "Your lips are purple."

I touched my fingertips to my mouth. "Gelato."

"This early?" He *tisked*. "What a rebel."

"No one can say no to Zar," I offered.

Aramis laughed. "I'd say you're right about that. I had two scoops of strawberry at dawn about three seconds after meeting the dapper Unbodied guy. Coffee?"

"You know the way to a girl's heart." I folded my hands over my heart and blinked dreamily.

"This girl's, anyway," he uttered as he held open the door for me.

The café was all hustle and bustle per the norm since opening day. "So you got to meet Zar even before Samhain, hm?" I asked Aramis as we made our way between the tables toward the back.

"I did. How ever will you get me to Samhain now?" He raised an eyebrow at me over his shoulder.

"Oh, I have my ways." I looked around. We were passing the clatter and chaos of the kitchen. "Where are we going?"

"Good work, Oscar." Aramis nodded to who I could only guess was the new employee Zar had told me about.

"Who knew these hands could fry up eggs as well as they hang drywall," he shot back, flipping a skillet with expert precision. He nodded to me with a genteel smile and I thought maybe he looked vaguely familiar from my time in the café before construction was all the way complete.

"I'm Blair," I said cheerily, holding out my hand.

Oscar offered me a pleasant smile but held up his frying pan. "Germs!" He knocked his elbow against mine instead of shaking my hand and I worried he'd drop the skillet, but he didn't. "Pleasure to meet you, Blair."

"BLAIR!" I jumped, startled by yet another genteel creature, only this time it was a ghost only Aramis and I could see right now. "Aramis let me watch a movie with him a couple of nights ago!" Henry beamed.

I looked sidelong at Aramis who was grumbling something about being off his rocker that night. I wondered sadly if it was the night I'd stood him up.

"That's great, Henry!"

"*Bye*, Henry," Aramis said and kept moving.

He could pretend all he wanted to loathe our ghost buddy, but I knew better. I followed him into his office where he shut the door and the noisy kitchen out with it.

"Whew," I said as I sat in the only *guest* chair in the small space. "I don't know how you deal with all that noise all day."

Aramis shrugged a burly shoulder and sat on the edge of the desk in front of me. "You get used to it. It's not that different from being in the bullpen of busy a police precinct."

I looked around his messy office. "Didn't you promise me coffee?"

"I did." He inclined his head and his bright green eyes went squinty. "But you haven't exactly updated me on your investigation and, seeing as I'm the next in line to be murdered and the sheriff is comically under the weather, I'd like to hear what you've got."

Frowning at him, I squared my shoulders. "You really expect me to believe you've just been serving up delicious waffles and burgers and not investigating your own assassin?" I squinted my eyes right back at him.

"Fair enough." He wove his fingers together and rested them in his lap. I dutifully kept my eyes on his face. "A trade, then."

Stone cold and without so much as blinking, I said, "Coffee first. Then a trade."

He tried to hide it, but I saw those lips twitch. "Deal."

When Aramis returned a few moments later with two steaming to-go cups of coffee, I already had the scraps of notes in their little baggies laid out on his desk. He handed me a cup. "What am I looking at here?" He leaned in closer as I took a tentative sip of the coffee.

"Ohhhh. It's gingerbread." My shoulders inched up toward my ears. "It's delicious but I hate you for reminding me it's spring outside and not winter."

"Patience, Wardwell. That's key in an investigation."

I looked up at him. "You better watch it or someone might think you've classified me as a real investigator."

"If the shoe fits."

I halfway hated him for all the warm fuzzies I had to shuck off in his presence. Mama Wardwell always taught me to chase dreams, not men. Now that I'd spent a very long time following that advice, I wasn't exactly used to letting a man chase me.

Aramis must have mistaken my silence for a different sort of self-consciousness, because he shifted on his feet and said, "I only mean to say that you have a keen eye and seem to have a knack for this investigation stuff. Not everyone does. It's hard, thankless work."

"But somebody's gotta do it," I finished for him. "There are people in danger. *You* are in danger, and I know you're all big and macho and whatever, but no one expects to have their family called and told to get a casket. Thankless or not, Steven's family deserves closure and you deserve people in your corner."

Aramis looked at me for a long moment and I watched his throat bob as he swallowed. Eventually, he cleared his throat and rounded the desk to sit opposite me. "What have we got here?"

I looked down at the two nearly identical scraps of paper. "A lot of something and a lot of nothing." I explained to Aramis that one scrap was the one he'd known about—handed over to Sheriff Oliphant by the Mimic, Boris Leek, when he was arrested for the murder of the Golem John Doe—and the other I'd found rolled up in the pocket of John Doe's jeans.

Aramis ran a hand idly down his short beard. "This handwriting is definitely a match, so we can assume that they were most likely sent by the same person. I can't see how we could infer much more than that, though. Unless you have something magical."

He looked across at me and I shook my head. "I do think they're written by a left-handed person, but that doesn't mean it was the killer. I didn't find anything that indicated an obvious Lefty as Steven's killer."

Aramis nodded and took a sip of his coffee. "Stab wound trajectories can sometimes give that away, but that wasn't evident in this case. Not for sure, anyway. I did hear the coroner toss the idea around, but nothing was definitive."

Well, it wasn't confirmation, but it still left the idea as a possible lead. "Have you fared any better?" I had to fight off the disappointment flooding my chest.

"Kenny has been doing some digging for us, too. He's confirmed that none of the people on the list of those less than pleased with me are Golems or Mimics, but we already expected as much." He leaned back in his chair. "I started looking into the names being linked to anything represented with a sparrow considering both men had sparrow tattoos. I haven't gotten very far on that front, but I thought it would be a good place for you to pick up if you're willing to use the Interweb for more than your fashion boards."

He gave me that winning smile of his and I mocked exaggerated frustration, rolling my eyes. "I guess I can take one for the team."

"Good. Now,"—he leaned forward and slid his forearms along the desk—"can I take you to dinner tonight?"

I deflated. "I have plans with Lacuna tonight. I'm going with her to get her tattoo with the new glowing ink Tom has."

Undeterred, Aramis nodded. "Following the ink trail. Clever Witch."

Achoo! "Argh! " I grumbled. "I'm *indoors!*"

Aramis rose and went to the door. "Come on. I'll send you off with some breakfast. Oscar really does make a mean omelet." I walked past him back out into the bustling kitchen. "Oh, and you should be on the lookout for a package delivery at the apothecary today."

CHAPTER 14

The allergy potion wasn't immediately or totally effective, but almost, thank Goddess. Sitting around doing nothing at the apothecary didn't sound good at all when I was itching to find a computer and violate my anti-technology moral standards to do research. Alas, I was equally curious as to what sort of package Aramis claimed would be delivered, and I'd have to stick around to see what that was.

A plan conjured itself in my mind, one born of my impatience. I pulled out my personal grimoire containing all the spells, elixirs, and potions I've designed and perfected over the years. On several occasions, I've not had the patience to sit and wait for a package that needed to be waited for. (Yes, I'm aware the proper remedy is not magical but *mindful*, but what's the point of being a Witch if I can't use magic for minor inconveniences? Haven't *you* stalked the mailman waiting for a package? Ha! I knew it.) Thus, I long ago concocted a spell that would re-route whatever package was headed for me to my current location a wee bit faster.

Once, Bernie the mailman asked if I could cast the spell for him. He'd seen me re-route a *Toil & Truffle* delivery and wanted me to do the same for a package he'd forgotten to deliver. That was the history of how I got my first job outside of Mom's bakery or the inn, working at the Gloam Hollow Post Office alleviating mail mix-ups and late package deliveries.

A good spell is a good spell, plain and simple.

But I couldn't find any of my ingredients. Standing in front of one of my shelves, I spun in a small circle. What in the world had happened here? Did a thief come in and not take anything but decided to rearrange my entire apothecary?

Meow.

This was followed by an entire chorus of mews. I looked up to see all three Wardwell cats that aren't ghosts lounging high on a shelf near the ceiling. "Did you three do this somehow?"

Do what, darling? Beetle examined her claws.

And then I remembered. Mom had been the last one in here, days ago when she needed the sample of my potion that broke Corbin. "I specifically told her *not* to clean up," I mumbled, stomping around trying to find the proper ingredients.

It was all for naught anyway, because Corbin himself walked through the door then, carrying a large parcel. "Bernie was dropping this off outside," he said by way of greeting and handed me the box.

Curious as all get out, I reined in my desire to rip into it right then and there and slid it off to the side of the counter. "Where's your fancy robe?" I teased poor Corbin.

Color rose high on his cheeks above his graying beard, and he looked at his hands. "About that. I'm sorry— Well—" He stuttered and stopped a few more times.

Listen, Mama Wardwell and Sheriff Oliphant are adults. They can do whatever they please. But watching him squirm was a *little* fun. Until it became just plain painful.

"Corbin." I cut him off. "You don't owe me an apology. If anyone should apologize it's—"

It was his turn to cut me off. "Nope. I was the buffoon who decided to try and pick my breakfast order when I knew full well I was under a spell to memorize whatever it was I was looking at. The buffoonery rests solely on my shoulders."

When my dad left Mom and me high and dry many years ago, Corbin stepped in. At the time, it was mostly human decency and just a man trying to be there for someone he'd briefly dated ages before she'd married my dad. Eventually, I began to suspect he'd held a torch for my mom for many years, and I'd absolutely let him assume a fatherly role in my life without ever having a verbal conversation about it. It just sort of...*was.*

Even so, he's never been much for outward shows of affection or communication of feelings, and this might be the deepest conversation we'd ever had about feelings—if it even constituted as such. Usually, it's gentle mutterings of *'take care of yourself', 'here, I brought you a sandwich', 'put on a coat before you freeze.'* If we were headed toward deeper territory, whether due to his budding relationship with Mom or our investigating together, I was definitely here for it.

But right now, I had to put this man out of his misery.

"That's enough of the mushy stuff, Sheriff, *gah*." I smiled at him and he visibly relaxed. Until I continued with, "Erm. I also might have some evidence I stole and some I found."

All of Corbin's touchy-feely aversion fell into a mood I was very familiar with: exasperation. "*Blair*." It was frankly hard not to giggle at the censure in his tone.

I spent the next several moments filling him in on everything Aramis and I had found while he was incapacitated. Or, rather, the dead ends we'd hit. "Has Deputy Pete happened to stumble across anything?" I asked, not bothering to hide the skepticism from my voice as I handed over the evidence baggies I'd been carrying around.

"Pete did call and have another chat with Steven's family that lives up in Dornwich, but they still don't know anything. Unfortunately, I think Steven was just in the wrong place at the wrong time."

And that happened to be Aramis's café when it was set up as a haunted house for the Harvest Festival, at which point an assassin either made an attempt on Aramis's life or wanted to frame Aramis for murder.

"Why do you think this person who was hiring hitmen to assassinate Aramis also wanted to frame him for murder?" I mused.

Sheriff pointed with the evidence baggies toward the cozy reading corner of my apothecary. "Let's sit."

I followed him over, kicking my sandals off and curling one leg under me. The fire in the hearth was lit as always, but I'd left it mere embers for ambiance since we didn't exactly need heat today.

Sheriff crossed his ankle over one knee. "We don't have *proof* that whoever killed Steven meant to frame Aramis, or that they are also involved with the two sent to assassinate him. The first rule of investigation is to not get ahead of yourself," he cautioned.

I frowned. "Aramis says the first rule is not to make assumptions."

Corbin chuckled. "He's not wrong. Find a lead and follow it. That's what we do. Anything else is shoddy investigating."

"But we have no lead on who killed Steven." I was starting to get frustrated. "There were no prints on the knife and Aramis's kitchen is always full of people. He had a building crew in there, a haunted house going... Anyone could have taken a knife or seized an opportunity."

"It's a tough case. But we do have evidence that links the other two men, both the papers found on them and the sparrow tattoos. Those are leads we can follow while we keep an eye out for one that could lead us to Steven's killer."

I nodded, mind already whirring and a buzz beginning under my skin reminding me to look into the sparrow tattoos. "I was just about to head to the library and see what I can find about the list of names Aramis gave us—see if I can find a sparrow link."

Sheriff stood. "Good. That's a great place to start. I'm going to the office to catch up on paperwork I missed and check in with Mrs. Cobblepot." He patted his pockets. "Oh, wait. I almost forgot. She gave me something a few days ago." He pulled out a folded paper from the pocket on his shirt. "She found this under her desk, it must have fallen and gotten stuck down there. I meant to give it to you at the café before things went haywire." He passed the paper to me. "Maybe you can look into it."

"What is it?" I asked, unfolding the paper.

"Someone called the department the night we arrested Aramis, claiming to have information about Anon's attack. I still agree with Aramis and don't think the boy really was attacked, but it's worth looking into."

Scrawled in Mrs. Cobblepot's looping cursive on pretty blue stationery bordered with baby ducks was a phone number and the words: *possible tip concerning Anon Bishop.*

The buzz under my skin was ratcheted up to an entire hive of bees, making my mind amp up into overdrive until that tell-tale Witch sense dropped over me like a veil. "This doesn't mention the attack. Did the caller specifically say it was about the attack?"

Sheriff's bushy brows met in the middle and he cocked his head. "I didn't hear the message and chances are Mrs. Cobblepot can't remember. It was left on the answering machine, she did remember that. She didn't speak directly to anyone."

I gnawed at my lip and shoved the phone number into the pocket of my dress. "I'll check into it. I'm meeting Lacuna for dinner tonight and going with her to get her new tattoo with the glowing ink. I plan to subtly question Tom about his and Anon's new friend and what happened that night."

Sheriff nodded and strode toward the door. "Excellent plan, darlin'. I'll see you."

I was so excited about a lead on one branch of the case that I almost forgot about the box that was delivered. It was plain old boring brown on the outside, but inside there was a gift receipt complete with a typed note.

So you can research wherever you want

-Hawthorne

A little thrill skittered up my neck. Setting the note aside, I pulled out the plethora of brown paper shielding whatever was inside to reveal a white box with a picture of a laptop on it. "He did not," I whispered in disbelief.

Meow came just before Albis jumped up onto the counter. *Who didn't do what?*

"Aramis!" I pulled the box out of its wrapping and tossed the larger shipping box to the floor. "I think he bought me a *laptop*." Gently, I set the white box on the counter and slid the lid off. Inside was, indeed, a shiny new laptop in the most gorgeous midnight purple color with an enchanting scene of forest flora and the night sky on the front.

You don't know how to use one of those, Beetle mewed after she and Puck both jumped up onto the counter to see what the commotion was about.

Beauty doth hide a beast, Puck put in.

I glared at them both.

Successfully wrangled out of its snug box, I put the beautiful laptop on the counter and opened it, quite proud of myself for knowing how to turn it on—thanks to commandeering Hamish's laptop on multiple occasions. The glowing screen had just come on, displaying the classic pear logo and a prompt to '*set up device*' when the bell above the door jingled.

"B!" It was Lacuna, rushing in and looking rattled. "Can we hang out a little early, because I have some *tea*, babe."

I looked at my new laptop and back at my friend. There went my few hours of sleuthing...

"Sure, Lac. What's going on?"

Her lavender eyes were as bright as her lilac hair, whether from excitement or trepidation, I couldn't tell.

Maybe both. "You will never guess who I saw in the woods with your aunt."

My stomach dropped to my toes.

CHAPTER 15

Lacuna

"*A*ndrew?" Blair looked at me quizzically, and I could tell she was trying to hide minor frustration. "That's not that strange, Lac. Aunt Millie has been showing Andrew all around the woods for his documentary." She gestured mildly toward the direction of the woods we couldn't see from her shop. "I just saw them together this morning at the inn like they were about to head out on a hike."

I wrung my hands. I'd kept this a secret for so long, just between Anon and I. Maybe I shouldn't tell her. Go straight to Millie. Or never tell a soul...

But I felt like this entanglement was about to drive me mad. There was this *something* in the back of my skull since seeing those Sprites over the water this morning. If Millie knew about the portal—or whatever it was—into the Mortal Lands... I don't know. I didn't know what it could mean.

"There's something I've never told you," I blurted,

watching Blair's face blanch before she covered it with concern.

"Lac, you can tell me anything, but you're also allowed to have secrets you keep to yourself." Her words were gentle, kind, but they also had that Blair sass that I so wish I could embody.

"This—" I shifted on my feet, feeling that *otherness* in my head again. "I think I need to show you."

Blair nodded, petting Puck as he purred on the counter. "Absolutely. Sure. I'll close up here and we can grab some coffee on our way."

My head was still foggy, but I was feeling lighter already. Blair would understand. I think.

"Perfect. It's my day off so I'd rather have Aramis's coffee, if that's okay with you." I gave her a little wink and she blushed. "Meet you there in a few, babe."

Blair

The apothecary door closed behind Lacuna and I turned to the cats. "What in the realm was *that* about?"

Puck rolled over for me to scratch his ginger belly, but I wasn't falling for that trick. As soon as I did, he'd attack my hand with his murder mittens and needle teeth.

Albis was asleep on my new laptop, his silvery fur splayed out over the keyboard.

Beetle purred, *Probably something to do with that book she always has with her.*

I looked at my cousin's black cat sidelong. "What do you know about a book Lac always has with her?"

Of course, Beetle didn't answer but began daintily licking her paw. Typical.

I glanced out at the town square through my shop's windows and debated if I had enough time to call the number Sheriff had given me. Whatever Lacuna had to show me could wait a few more minutes, surely. It might even give her time to collect her thoughts. She'd seemed abnormally shaken. Lac was always only half present, like her mind was living somewhere else, but my Witch sense was giving off more of a clanging bell tower vibe than a gentle jingle.

Still, I needed to make this call. Quickly, I fished out the cell phone from my bag, pausing to grin stupidly at a text from Aramis, and pulled the paper out of my pocket with the number.

I'd not used the phone for actual phone calls and didn't enjoy the idea of using it to contact anyone aside from Aramis. Alas, it's what a phone was for. I dialed and put the phone to my ear, waiting for it to ring. But it never did. Instead, the call went straight to voicemail, a chipper voice coming over the line as my veins filled with ice.

"Hey there, hi there! You've reached Steven Littlebottom's phone. I'm not available but—"

I didn't hear the rest due to a dull roaring beginning in my ears. Dumbfounded, I pulled the phone away from my ear and watched the screen light up with the number. Mouth gaping open, I compared the number on the screen with the one on the paper from Corbin. I'd definitely dialed correctly.

Adrenaline was coursing through me and setting my fingers into a slight tremor, but I managed to end the call and grab my bag. Snatching the paper off the counter, I shoved it into my pocket and ran out of the apothecary, mind spinning.

Spectre Café was abuzz with the lunch rush, but I found Lacuna at the bartop chatting with Aramis while he helped nearby customers.

"Hey," I greeted them both, a bit breathless as I took a seat on the stool next to Lac.

"Hey babe." My friend already seemed less shaken, but there was still a note of distraction in her tone.

Aramis was already pouring me a huge black mug of coffee. "Wardwell," he greeted, but he was watching me closely, his brow furrowed. Lacuna looked down at her cup, and Aramis mouthed, '*What is it?*' at me.

Barely moving, I shook my head severely. Aramis frowned, but Lacuna interrupted our silent showdown.

"Oh, can we get these coffees to go?" she asked. "I didn't even think to tell you that, Aramis, I'm sorry." Lacuna's smile glittered, but Aramis seemed to be picking up on her strangeness as well as my own because he murmured '*sure,*' though he was looking between both of us with great suspicion before he withdrew our mugs and headed for the coffee station.

Not much gets past the Dread Monster detective, I guess. Ex-detective. Hm. Had I somewhat pulled him out of retirement?

"Eggs benedict!" a voice called from the kitchen door. Lacuna and I both looked in that direction. Oscar held a plate aloft, scanning the dining area.

"Who is that?" Lac asked me quietly of the blonde-haired, blue-eyed man. "I think he came into *Stonewood* a couple of days ago, but someone else took his order."

"That's Aramis's newest employee, Oscar. A rehire, I

suppose. He was on the construction crew here but left once the café was done. He loved Gloam Hollow so much that he came back and Aramis hired him to cook."

"Well, that worked out, now didn't it?" Lacuna perked up on her stool. "Oh! There's Kat! I haven't seen her in days. I'll be right back." She hopped down and hustled over to where Kat was sitting with a couple of her friends, while her sister Kendall took their order.

I watched Lac slide into a chair opposite Kat and Aramis slid my to-go coffee cup in front of me, taking Lacuna's vacated stool. "Spill it, Wardwell."

Leaning in close, I tried not to look suspicious or too wired, but judging by Aramis's smirk, I didn't think I was successful. "Sheriff gave me a number to call. Someone who phoned in with a tip about Anon's attack and he hadn't returned the call yet."

"Alleged attack."

I frowned. "Why would someone call in with a tip about an attack that didn't happen?"

"Maybe that *was* the tip. It wasn't real."

Narrowing my eyes at him, I pressed my mouth into a hard line. He had a valid argument. "Fine. But the point is, I called the number back and it was Steven's phone."

Aramis balked, almost indiscernibly, but the action from him was jarring. "So this was an old message?"

I nodded. "From the night you were arrested."

"The night Steven was killed." His voice pitched low, distant. "He must have made that call just before..."

"This changes everything."

"Maybe. Let's not get ahead of ourselves," he cautioned.

"Aramis, someone who possibly wanted to frame you also wanted Steven dead and he had information about

Anon's mysterious 'attack.'" I made air quotes with my fingers.

"Or," he countered, "someone wanted Steven dead and Steven worked at my café near my knives."

I pursed my lips. "I don't believe in coincidences."

Aramis ran a hand down his beard. "Yeah. They're not usually real." He blew out a breath and checked over his shoulder to make sure Lacuna was still with her friends. "Alright, then we—" His words dropped off mid-sentence and his expression took on a spaced-out look.

"Uh... Come in, come in, Space Cadet." I waved a hand in front of his face.

Aramis's attention snapped back to me, his back going ramrod straight. "This was a phone message Mrs. Cobblepot took or an answering machine message?"

I mocked a deep-thinky frown. "Corbin didn't specify. Wait! Yes, he did. It was a message. He said she didn't speak to anyone directly. Why?"

The crease between Aramis's brows was etching deeper. "I think I heard it. The morning after I was arrested, I heard Mrs. Cobblepot checking messages on the answering machine." He squeezed his eyes shut like it might help him remember the details. "There were a few about petty things I tuned out, but there was one..." He opened his eyes, still looking strained. "It was hard to hear from the granny cell, but it was about Anon. I think they were claiming they had evidence about the attack."

"And this detail never caused you to consider that maybe you were wrong and Anon *was* attacked?" I knew full well I'd focused on the wrong part of his statement, but I couldn't take the words back.

"See, that's the thing..." He trailed off again, undeterred

by my snarky comment. "I remember that what I heard of that message was what solidified my suspicion that he *wasn't* attacked. But I can't recall now what it was."

Then he turned to me, those green eyes sharp. "And you should challenge people more often, Wardwell." He gave me a wry smile and stood as Lacuna returned. "Let me know when you two are done with your shenanigans tonight."

I handed Lacuna her coffee. "Lead the way."

When we were out on the square, I was thrilled to find the breeze had cooled considerably since this morning. With any luck, this bout of spring would be gone before morning.

"Um." Lacuna scrunched her nose, looking at my outfit. "We might need to stop by the cottage so you can change."

I looked down at my mini dress and canvas sneakers. On principle, I never went on a hike that my current outfit couldn't handle. "Do you mean because of chiggers?" My legs were bare...

Lac offered me an apologetic smile. "That might be a factor, yes, but it's um...pretty deep in the woods."

I groaned. "Am I going to sweat?"

"It's likely."

Tucking my lips between my teeth so as not to sigh, I led the way to Wardwell Cottage. No one was home and I could only assume all three living cats were still at *Copper Cauldron*. There was, however, a basket of melt-in-your-mouth pumpkin cheesecake cookies neatly tucked into a kitchen towel covered in little ghosties. I was thrilled, immediately snagging one and offering the basket to Lac, but then I saw the card and my stomach dropped.

We need to discuss your tea leaf reading xo

"Ominous," I mumbled darkly around a gooey bite.

"Everything okay?" Lacuna's words were equally as muffled by her bite of cookie and she took a sip of her coffee. "Oh, my Goddess, these pair so well."

"Yeah, everything's fine." ...I hoped. Curious, I took another bite and a sip of my own coffee, immediately nodding my agreement. "Do we need to take this entire basket with us?"

Lacuna laughed. "Steep hike, remember? The less we carry the better."

"Steep hike?" I nearly shouted. "You said '*deep into the woods,*' not *steep.*" Listen, I know whining is unbecoming but ya' girl does not do cardio, okay?

Lacuna's face fell and I instantly felt terrible. She needed to show me something. Reveal a secret she'd kept for who knows how long. And judging by her shock at my Aunt Millie's presence at this secret location, she might very well be involved in the whole thing. Suddenly, I felt sick and put the rest of my cookie and coffee down.

"Hey, I'm sorry. I'm just teasing you." I did my best to smile and Lac returned it, but hers was dim. "Water and hiking clothes. I'm on it."

I trotted upstairs to change while Lac grabbed us some cold water bottles. On the door to my bedroom, there was a neon pink sticky note—Mags.

`Family breakfast at the inn tomorrow about the hex.`

*Grandma said it was urgent, but told them
you were busy tonight.*
—M

Fire and ice were warring in my veins today. Something wicked was stirring, but I couldn't get the threads to untangle.

Quickly, I changed into some yoga pants that flared at the bottom and had never seen yoga in their life and a cropped tank with a sports bra sewn in. Trainers or runners or whatever they are called do not exist in my world, so my black-and-white canvas sneakers went back on, and I tied a brown and black plaid shirt around my waist just in case that cooler wind dipped back into autumn while we were in the mountains.

"Let's do it," I told Lacuna with a grin as I took a chilled water bottle from her.

CHAPTER 16

I am not built for exertion.

"Lacuna," I gasped, hands on my hips and basically doubled over but still moving—at a snail's pace. "Didn't you say you rode your bike up here?"

My friend laughed. "I rode my moped. Big difference."

"I was about to say, whatever your legs are made of, they should be studied."

Lacuna stopped and I made no qualms about it. "It's just past this copse of trees but we have to leave the path."

Nodding, I chugged my water. "Can I just ask why we didn't ride the moped? Can mopeds hold two people?"

Lacuna laughed as if I wasn't completely serious. "Come on."

"*Little petite Sprite of a woman*," I muttered (not kindly) under my breath.

There were a few narrow misses of branches to my face, but we cleared the trees and I followed Lacuna to what looked like your typical rock face.

She turned to me, wringing her hands. "Promise me you

won't want to end our friendship for not telling you about this."

To be honest, I didn't know if I should bark a laugh at the absurdity of her statement or be scared. "Lac, need I remind you that we have a lot of years of friendship under our belts?"

"Okay. But I also need you to promise not to tell anyone."

That one gave me pause. How could it be something that serious? And if it was that serious, what were Millie and Andrew doing out here? Was it why Aunt Millie was acting so strange and not sleeping? She'd seemed just fine to me this morning and so had Andrew…

"Lac, I've got your back. If you've unalived some people and buried them out here, we might have to have a chat, but barring that level of sinister behavior, we're good."

She let out a long, slow breath and I watched her shoulders lose some of their tension. "It's not sinister. At least, I don't think it is. But—" Lacuna looked toward the rocks then back to me. "I'm not completely sure anymore."

Well, that didn't sound good.

"Lead on, my friend."

As we approached the rock face, it became clear that it was actually a cave mouth essentially camouflaged by the rocks. That made sense why Millie would say she'd found something she'd never seen before. Until we walked right up to it, the cave was completely invisible.

"You may not be able to see me in here," Lacuna explained. "My Shadow Nymph powers blend with the air in the cave."

Now that piqued my interest. Lacuna had velvety night skin but it was only a few shades darker than Aramis's unless her Shadow Nymph powers were, for lack of a better term, activated. When that happened—and it was rare—Lac *was* shadow.

"Oh my Goddess, I'm so ready for this," I whispered, excited. This took a fraction more of the tension out of my friend and she stepped into the cave.

Dear Reader, I was not, in fact, ready.

The moment we stepped inside, Lacuna all but disappeared. There was a preternatural fog in the cave, so thick that I wouldn't have been able to see her even if her powers hadn't ensconced her in shadow. My magic crackled, begging to be let loose. The hairs on my arms were standing on end. There was even a faint hum in the air.

Lacuna

I pushed through the ghostly fog, its heaviness heating me to the point that I removed my overshirt and slung it over my shoulder. Blair was spinning in a slow circle next to me. I doubted she could see what I could, hear what I could, but I knew she could sense it.

The voices of the Mortals tickled my ears like they were whispering secrets, and I saw flashes of them as they passed by. Having them near brought tears to my eyes as it always did, but I couldn't make them out clearly. Not every trip had revealed a Mortal enough to remember their essence and capture it via a tattoo, and this was shaping up to be one of those unsuccessful outings. I'd stay all day—all the time—if I could, but Blair was restless next to me. Surely she was confused and possibly a bit scared.

With the dense fog swirling around us, I concentrated

on the tether between me and my Mortal, Oliver. *There*. The air cleared to a gentle mist and I spotted a gas lamp. Next to it sat a man on a bench. A Mortal man staring out at a river, starlight dancing on the ripples.

It was him. I desperately wanted to see his face. This Mortal I somehow knew.

Quietly, so as not to frighten Blair, I edged around the misty scene, my hands in front of me, worried I'd fall right out of this Inbetween place into the Mortal Lands.

Just as I caught sight of the man's jawline, he started. "Who's there?"

I froze.

Blair

"Lac," I squeaked, "what is this place?"

Lacuna's voice came from beside me and I jumped. "This is a portal into the Mortal Lands."

Immediately, I summoned the most powerful orb of light I could. I needed to see my friend's face. Even with it, I could only make out a shimmery outline of a person. "I think you need to start explaining, friend."

I felt Lacuna's hand clasp around my wrist and she pulled me out of the cave, back out into the glaring sunlight, her form materializing again. "Maybe sit down."

She didn't have to tell me twice. I sat hard on a boulder to the side of the cave. I knew I was watching her with wide, wild eyes, but I couldn't help it. "How does no one know about this? Oh my Goddess, does *Millie* know about this?"

"I don't know." Lacuna sat down on a shorter rock across

from me, but not before pulling a tattered book out of her back pocket. She rested it on her bent knees. "Do you remember the day when we were kids when Mags sliced her hand while cutting lemons? We were all at the inn playing out back and you ran in to help."

I nodded mutely. My magic was the only one of the Wardwell Witchlings strong enough to help. "I do. Everyone else left."

Lacuna inhaled. "Anon was squeamish of the blood. Maeve was worried she'd do something she'd regret. When she went home, Anon and I took a trek into the woods to calm him down—he didn't want to shift into his Wendigo form."

He almost shifted over a little blood, and yet he hadn't shifted the night he claimed he was attacked? I shoved the thought to the back of my brain and refocused on Lacuna, nodding for her to continue.

"We stumbled upon this cave. I went in because I could hear voices."

"Voices?" I leaned in. "What voices?"

"People," she clarified. "Mortals. I–" She began fiddling with the tattered and frayed edge of a hole in her jeans. "I can see them through the mist."

I blinked at her, sitting still as a statue on my rock.

"This is the part where you say something." She almost sounded scared. "Please, Blair."

About a thousand responses raced through my mind. She'd known about a portal into the Mortal Lands since we were children and had told no one? It was dangerous. Foolish. So unlike Lacuna... And hearing voices? Seeing Mortals? A sharp pain was developing above my left eye.

"It's a lot to digest, Lac." I was proud of myself for how calm and collected I sounded when I felt anything but.

"I know." She looked at her hands and my anger with her fled.

"Why didn't you tell anyone? I know there has to be a good reason." At least I hoped so.

"There isn't." Lacuna shrugged. "Not one that justifies it."

"I'd still like to know." I held out my hand, palm up, and gestured toward the book she was cradling. "May I?" Lacuna hesitated for only a second before handing me the tattered tome. "*The Catcher in the Rye*," I read off the front cover. "Does this have something to do with your reason for keeping this massive secret?"

Lacuna nodded, her mouth twisted in a mournful smile. "Ever since the day Anon and I found this portal, I've come to watch the Mortals. It's not exactly people I see, but vague impressions of them—who they are." She held out her arms, twisting this way and that to display the ink on them. "When I see a clear enough impression, I have Anon draw the tattoo by my description, and Tom inks them on."

I suddenly felt quite a lot like crying. "Like a memorium." She nodded. "You've made your body a temple of art, of Mortals."

Lacuna sniffled. "Yes. But, there is one essence, one Mortal that I can feel all of the time, and it's getting stronger. A couple of days ago, I heard enough to gather his name." She smiled and my stomach dropped. I knew that smile. The one that holds a person's heart in its gentle curve. "Oliver."

I didn't want to gape like a fish, so I repeated the name. "Oliver."

"And just then"—she pointed toward the cave—"I saw his face for the first time."

I wanted to be happy for my friend. Happy someone had caused that smile on her face, but he didn't even belong in our realm—if he was real at all. "But you've never *been* to the Mortal Lands?" I held up the book. "How did you get this? It's from there, right? Or am I missing something?"

Lacuna checked her phone which couldn't possibly have a signal way up on the mountain. "Come on. Let's get some food before it's time for my tattoo appointment. I'll explain on the way down the trail."

As we made our trek down the mountain, Lacuna explained, "I don't know how the book got here. Anon surprised me with it a couple of moons ago. He said it was a very rare book and I wouldn't have even known it was from the Mortal Lands except that I'd seen glimpses of the cover with its vivid red and yellow amongst the essence of the Mortal I can always sense."

I twisted the lid off my water bottle, brows furrowing together. "Oliver?"

Lacuna nodded, looking down, but I saw the tilt of her lips. "I searched every database I could get my hands on for *The Catcher in the Rye,* but it never existed here. Then, when Anon brought me the books from the library about the Mortal Lands, I saw a mention of it."

Blinking a few times, I shook my head to clear the thoughts rattling around in there. "Didn't his and Tom's mysterious new *friend* help him sneak those out of the library?"

Lacuna nodded again. "From what I can gather."

The trek down the mountain was only mildly easier than going up it and I guzzled the last of my water.

"Anon doesn't strike me as the type to wander into the Mortal Lands at all, let alone do it without mentioning it to you. If that's even how it works. I would venture to say someone very powerful would be needed to make it through."

"Yeah," she agreed. "Anon's freaked out enough by going near the cave, and he's not exactly a powerful type of creature."

"So how could Anon end up with a copy of a book from the Mortal Lands? Someone else must know about this cave and it seems like it has to be this elusive friend."

Unless he was an entirely different person than I've known for almost my entire life and a terrifyingly good liar, Anon had found himself mixed up with some seedy people.

We broke through the treeline and I could smell *Tito's Taco Stand.* I looked at Lacuna, who was practically drooling. "Are you thinking what I'm thinking?"

She grinned. "*Tacos.*"

Three bags of greasy tacos and two sodas in hand, Lacuna and I made our way to the gazebo at the center of the square. The sun had begun to set, painting the sky in persimmon and aubergine, but a storm was rolling in over the mountains. The sunset would soon be drowned out, but for now, it was stunning. It had also grown quite chilly. I'd already put on my plaid overshirt, but I considered summoning a sweater, too.

"Yesss," Lac crooned as we climbed the few gazebo steps. "It's empty!"

I held one of the taco bags up to point out Bill Winslow outside the bank. "I think he might be the reason the square is deserted."

Bill had one finger up, wagging it in Norm the bank manager's face. Norm had a plastic skeleton in one hand and a trailing vine of faux flowers in the other, gesticulating wildly.

We sat on one of the three benches in the gazebo and dug into the *divine* tacos. "Hiking makes me hungry," I said around a delicious bite of seasoned beef, crunchy shell, lettuce, and cheese.

"Mm," Lacuna agreed, smothering hot sauce on her next bite of taco. "Same."

We ate in silence for a few minutes, watching Bill walk from shop to shop as the air grew colder and the storm inched closer. I had about a million questions for Lacuna about her alleged connection to a Mortal, but I didn't want to word them carelessly and make it sound like I didn't believe her. And, I supposed, I didn't fully—not yet. But Lacuna would never make something like that up. She did, however, have a great imagination, and maybe all her daydreaming had begun to feel real. Or it was all real and she wasn't daydreaming at all, but truly seeing a man named Oliver from the Mortal Lands.

As far as evidence went, she did have a book that wasn't known to exist in our realm. Just to be sure, I'd have to see if Hamish could look into it for me. Maybe he knew how Anon could get something like that without entering the Mortal Lands.

That was the other issue: I couldn't let this remain a secret. Lacuna might think of the portal as hers and she might believe that only she and Anon know about it, but it stands to reason that she's wrong. Anon clearly has someone helping him do some shady things. Not to mention Millie and Andrew were seen coming from the cave as well.

Andrew. I almost choked on my taco.

"Are you okay?" Lacuna slapped me hard on the back.

"Yeah," I croaked. "I'm fine. Hey, what were Millie and Andrew doing at the cave when you saw them?"

Lacuna dabbed at her mouth with a *Tito's Tacos* napkin.

"I don't know. I saw them come out and I panicked. Ran straight back to my moped and pushed it halfway down the mountain before I hopped on and rode the rest of the way down. It wasn't long after that when I went to find you at *Copper Cauldron.*

That reminded me that I probably needed to open up the apothecary and stay in it long enough to refill my moonstone coffers because they were looking pretty grim. (By *'coffers'*, I mean bank account. We're not archaic.) If Lacuna hadn't bought the tacos, there was a good chance my card would have declined, and I was sure there were only about a coffee's worth of moonstones rolling around the bottom of my bag. I fought the urge to groan and pushed that anxiety away.

"Did Andrew have his camera with him?" I asked my friend.

She thought hard for a moment while I sipped at my soda until I slurped at the bottom—empty.

"Hmm. I turned away so quickly that I couldn't be positive, but I think he did. He definitely had something in his hand."

Swiftly, I ticked through all my encounters with Andrew between book club and seeing him around Grandma's inn. Which hand did he hold his book in? His coffee or wine?

Aha! A memory surfaced of seeing him in the *Moonrise Manor* restaurant eating lunch one day. Yes, he was definitely holding his fork in his *left* hand.

"Which hand did he have something in?" I prodded Lacuna.

She quirked her lips to one side and shifted on the bench like she was trying to position herself as Andrew from her vantage point in the woods. "Left," she said confidently. "Millie was on his right."

"And it wasn't small, like a cellphone?"

She shook her head. "Definitely not. It wasn't huge, but it was electronic and black."

Most likely his camera, then.

It was downright cold out now and I whispered a spell to summon my favorite Fairycore hoodie. I'd prefer to have had on something better for this evening, but cozy comfort gets points, too. "Do you need me to summon a sweater for you?"

Lacuna shook her head. "I'm good. I always run hot when I'm getting a tattoo. Still get nervous, I guess. Plus I have a leather jacket in my moped compartment. It's parked just over by the coffee shop."

I started combining all of our trash, wadding it up into the bags, and Lac went to toss them in the bin outside the gazebo.

"Red alert," she said through all the flower vines wrapped around the gazebo. "Bill incoming! Bill incoming!"

She ran back up the steps into the gazebo and we hopped over the back railing, landing with a *thud* on the other side. Laughing hysterically, we made a beeline for the tiny alley next to *Curl Up and Dye Salon*, Bill shouting at us something about a citation for endangerment to public property.

We didn't stop running or giggling until we were safely behind the salon. "He's the worst," Lacuna laughed.

I stopped next to her, leaning against the wall. "A complete menace," I agreed breathlessly. "If I hang out with you anymore I'm going to be a proper athlete." The woman had made me hike *and* run all in one day. "I know they say working out is healthy, but Goddess, is it worth it?"

Lacuna laughed again. "Come on, babe. I have a needle and some glowing ink calling my name."

We meandered past the salon and I didn't see Maggie's bicycle out back, so I assumed she didn't have any clients this evening. After a couple of turns and a stop to talk with Ms. Lilly about the latest gossip (Katarina won't leave *Spectre Café* because she thinks the new chef, Oscar, is 'cute'), we finally made it to Tom's *Tattoo Parlor*.

"Hey, guys!" Tom called from the back where he was bent over a burly man's arm. "Be right with you!"

Lacuna started perusing all the art and tattoo ideas on the walls, and I pulled out my phone to text Aramis.

> Heard you have a permanent Faerie fixture in Kat

I sat on one of the very stylish but very uncomfortable waiting area couches and watched the little bouncing dots on my phone.

> I'm about to sic Henry on her 👻

> Ha! Tell her there's a news scoop at the gazebo. Bill is making everyone trade their decor back to Samhain

Hey, I was getting pretty good at this texting thing. Little dots again...

> You're a genius, Wardwell

Lacuna plopped down next to me on the hard leather

couch and began twiddling her thumbs. "Whatcha gonna get?" I asked her.

She shrugged. "Maybe not something new..." She turned to me with a bit of a grimace and a wild look in her eyes.

"Uh oh..." I sat up straighter. "What are you thinking, friend?"

"Don't be mad."

Popsicle toes, I inwardly Grandma-Wardwell-Cursed. "It's *your* body, Lac."

"I want Tom to use the ink to trace over all my tattoos."

My heart rate immediately calmed. "Oh! That sounds really cool. I like this idea."

"The thing is..." She squirmed in her seat, brightening. "All day I've been able to see Oliver better."

Sinking feeling back.

"And," she continued chipperly while I tried not to make a face, "I think it's partly because stars were glowing on his side. I could see the stars and then it all became clearer."

"This translates to the tattoos by..." I prompted, increasingly nervous because I already suspected the answer.

"If *I* glow in the Inbetween, maybe he can see me, too."

"Oh, Lac, I—"

"Ready?" Tom beamed at us from behind the counter. "Let's get to it, guys!"

Lacuna hopped up, effectively ending our conversation. I followed her and Tom back to his booth and perused his collection of faux hands encased in display jars like specimens, their tattoos stark against light skin and contrasting with the dark green walls of the parlor. My favorite was the one on the middle shelf next to an austere figurine of a fox in a tiny waistcoat. (Technically, the dapper fox is my favorite thing on the shelf.) On that particular hand was a vintage mirror, ornate with filigree and a skull cameo. In the reflection of the mirror was the faint outline of a Faerie with gossamer wings, but her hand was outstretched, obscuring her face in the reflection.

As much as I love tattoos and have several of my own, part of me has always thought our Gloam Hollow tattooist Tom Huang should put his art on paper and canvas as well. I'd mentioned it to him once, and he'd merely thought for about half a second and said, "*Nahhh. People are my canvas.*"

I watched Tom as he talked with Lacuna, his long, lean form making the stool he sat on seem tiny. Just about every inch of Tom's skin was inked in every color imaginable, all the way up his neck. His dark, wispy hair curled up at the tips of his ears, and I noticed his brown eyes were brighter than I'd seen them in weeks.

While I considered how much I did not want to ruin his good mood, I knew I needed to ask questions regarding the investigation. Tom set out all his supplies and chatted amicably with Lacuna as an inward debate raged within me. The man sure was handling his breakup pretty well. No sign of those guitar ballads his grandmother mentioned to me...

"Oh, my Goddess," Lacuna and I breathed in unison when Tom pulled out the vial of glowing ink.

"I know, right?" It lit up his face. "This stuff is *sick*. It glows in the vial, goes on the skin black, then glows in the dark."

What kind of sorcery...? My gut clenched. As insanely cool as the ink was, its origin wasn't sitting well with my Witch sense. I didn't gather that it was dangerous by any means, or that Lac shouldn't have it inked into her skin, but

I was definitely gathering that it was obtained in a less-than-typical way.

"Where did you find something this amazing?" I asked Tom nonchalantly.

He set it down next to his other supplies and stood to wash his hands with Lyme soap at a nearby sink, calling over his shoulder. "Anon found it, actually."

Lacuna and I looked at each other with wide eyes, then back at Tom when he strode over, wiping his hands dry.

"It was the craziest thing. He surprised me with the idea of it a couple of moons ago—said he knew a supplier—and it finally came in a few days ago." Tom pulled out his box of black latex gloves, but it was empty. "Oops. Let me go grab another box. Be right back."

As soon as he was out of earshot, I stood right next to Lacuna where she was sitting on his adjustable tattoo chair. "Another peculiar surprise from Anon?" I hissed in her ear. "What is he up to?"

"I don't know!" she whispered back, even though we were the only two in the shop.

"You two sure do have a lot of secrets."

"Hey," Lac sounded wounded. "Unfair, babe."

Was it, though? I'd had about enough of their dangerous secrets for one day.

Tom returned and sat back on his rolling stool, tugging on a pair of gloves. "So what are we doing today, Lac?"

She glanced at me before facing Tom. "I wanted to see if we could trace all my tattoos in the glowing ink."

Tom furrowed his brow, taking Lacuna's arm in his hand and looking at a few of her tattoos. "That would take hours, Lac. And I don't know if I have enough ink. I've only got the one bottle. Supposedly it's made from firefly bioluminescence. I don't know how that works, but Anon made it sound rare. I don't know if he can get me another bottle."

Did anyone else want to storm Anon's house and demand answers? I swear I was about ready to do just that.

"If he got one bottle, he can get another, right?" I said, and Lacuna glanced at me again.

"I mean, maybe... But it's going to be expensive."

"I'll pay," Lacuna chimed in. "I don't care the cost."

Oh, *turtle shoes*, my friend had it bad for a possibly fictional person...

Tom considered the proposal for a minute before sputtering a breath through his lips. "If you say so. Where do you want to start?"

Lacuna grinned, her face lighting up. "My arms."

Tom got to work and I discreetly sent a thread of magic out toward the ink's glowing vial. Again, I didn't sense anything sinister about it, but I couldn't shake the feeling it was deeply mixed up in all this Anon and Mortal Lands business.

One thing at a time.

"Hey, how is Anon, anyway?" I asked Tom casually. "Neither of us have seen much of him lately."

I watched Tom's shoulders stiffen ever so slightly and he pulled the needle away from Lacuna's skin. "Doesn't he go to work?" he asked Lacuna.

"Yes," she replied, "but he's so sullen and quiet. When he's not quiet, he's downright rude to me."

Tom and I both looked at her, shocked. She hadn't mentioned that to me.

Gingerly, Tom went back to work tracing the outline of a

butterfly on Lacuna's forearm. "He's been out of sorts since the whole...*thing* before the Harvest Festival."

"You mean his attack?" (Listen, I know tact isn't my strong suit sometimes.)

Tom kept his attention on his work. "Yeah, that." His tone was borderline cross.

"Were you with him that night?"

"Ouch!" Lacuna cried out.

"Oh my, Goddess." Tom scrambled with a paper towel, swiping at her arm. "Lac, I'm so sorry. I slipped."

But Lacuna was glaring at *me*. I mouthed, '*Sorry,*' and winced. "It's okay," she told Tom. "No biggie."

Tom moved to pick up his needle again, but he sagged, his hands falling limp to his lap. "Can–" His gaze shifted toward the door. "If I confess something to you two, will you promise not to go to Sheriff Oliphant about it?"

A little tingle shot up my spine.

"I know you're buddy-buddy with Oliphant now, Blair, and I just—" He looked over at the door again. "I don't want to get Anon in trouble, but I'm dying trying to keep his damned secrets, you know?"

I needed to choose my words very carefully. "I can't promise that, Tom." I rose from my chair and put a hand on his shoulder. "But I can say that unless *you* did something illegal, you'll be okay. Anon will understand. Anyone who is a true friend wouldn't ask you to hold onto potentially dangerous secrets that make you uncomfortable."

I just caught sight of Lacuna's attention as it fell to her twiddling thumbs out of the corner of my eye.

Tom shook his head vehemently. "I've done a lot of petty stuff Oliphant loves to bust me for... Tagging buildings, pranks, double-parking my bike... But I know lying to the police can be an obstruction of justice and I've purposefully avoided answering any questions."

"Because..." I prompted.

"Because... Yes, I was there that night. And Anon wasn't attacked."

Bingpot.

CHAPTER 18

"Then what happened in the park?" I dropped back into my chair and awaited Tom's explanation with bated breath as I watched lightning illuminate the parlor's front windows.

Lacuna was anxious too, judging by the fact she was leaning so far forward I thought she'd tip out of her seat.

Tom scrubbed at the back of his neck. "Anon texted me and said to meet him in the park that night. I was supposed to get the firefly ink and I thought I would finally get to meet this elusive supplier of his. But when I got there, Anon was all worked up. He said the guy bailed on him and he was kind of busted up." Tom's face twisted. "I don't know this guy he's been dealing with and I assumed he was the reason Anon was bleeding, so I called Oliphant." He shook his head. "Anon was livid with me. He said I was going to mess everything up."

"Okay," I said slowly, confused. "If he wasn't attacked, what happened?"

Tom rubbed his palms together furiously, like he was

about to start a fire. "I don't know. I kept pestering him and he finally told me it wasn't an attack, but I don't know what happened. By then, Oliphant was already on his way and I don't know, it was all happening so fast... We decided to make it look like an attack, but I still don't know *why*."

"That explains why he didn't shift," I said quietly, thinking. "He wasn't scared."

"He was plenty scared alright, but not of some attacker. He didn't shift because I kept telling him no one would believe an attack on a Wendigo. He had to keep it together."

"But you forgot to actually make it look like an attack by taking his wallet or at least busting up his glasses," I added.

"Uh. Yeah..." Tom shook his shoulders, a gesture remarkably like a dog shaking off water. A Werewolf to his core. "I feel a lot better telling you guys. Thanks." He gestured toward Lacuna's arm. "Want me to keep going?"

"Please." She gave him a small smile.

As Tom got back to work inking her arms, I peppered him with questions, hoping he wouldn't maim Lac again. "Anon has never mentioned why he would want to fake an attack? Maybe it has something to do with his friend."

The thunder rolled outside.

"Nope," Tom answered. "For a while, I worried it was all a distraction for the bakery murder. You know, the body you found outside *Toil & Truffle*?"

How could I forget? "I thought so, too, for a while. But we caught that guy and Sheriff Oliphant believes he's telling the truth that the Mimic responsible wasn't involved." Although, that didn't rule out the *victim* of that murder... "You've truly never met Anon's friend?"

Tom huffed a humorless laugh. "Nope. And that jerk is what made Maeve and I break up."

"I didn't want to bring her up," I said cautiously, "but I did hear it was related. You stopped talking to her when this *friend* showed up."

He was still bent over Lacuna's arm—he'd moved on to the third tattoo, a lightning bolt—but I could see his jaw clench. "I couldn't involve her. I don't know how dangerous this guy is. He always meets with Anon in the woods, like it's some huge secret."

Ice filled my veins again. "The woods? Where? Do you know?"

He shrugged a shoulder. "Behind *Moonrise Manor* is all I know."

Oh, I was feeling sick. "Have you met Andrew? The filmmaker staying there?" I tried to sound casual, but Tom's head jerked up, his eyes flashing.

"I hate that guy."

I felt Lacuna's eyes on me. "Oh? Um... Why is that?"

"He's always flirting with Maeve. Always." Tom sneered. "Pretty intellectual boy pretending he's not a wolf in sheep's clothing?" He huffed through his nose. "Mark my words"— he pointed his tattoo gun at us—"watch out for guys like that."

The conversation ascended into lighter topics as my questioning fell silent, and Lacuna asked Tom simple things. Eventually, I relocated to the uncomfy reception area couch and pulled out a book. I tried to read, but my mind was a swirl of information. It didn't seem wise to message Aramis any details, but I went ahead and shot him a quick text letting him know I needed to give him some big information. Several moments later, my phone buzzed.

Same. We need to talk ASAP.

Ha. Gettin' the hang of emojis, I see.

I could almost see his smirk through the phone.

Unable to read and unwilling to sit and daydream about a Dread Monster, I wandered back over to check Tom's progress.

He worked at remarkable speed. He'd outlined all of Lacuna's arm tattoos and most of the ones on her legs when a shiver jolted her. "I need a break, I think."

"Of course." Tom rolled his stool back. "There's water and soda in the back and a couch if you need to lie down." He snorted a laugh. "What am I saying? You knew that."

Lacuna gave him her million-watt smile and went to the back. Tom looked up at me from his stool. "Want anything tonight?"

"Tom Huang, when have I ever turned down the opportunity for fresh ink?"

"This would be a first, should you choose not to accept the challenge."

I laughed, sliding onto the raised tattoo chair. "Challenge accepted. Lac and I shouldn't be here too late, though, so let's just add..." My lips quirked to one side as I thought. "Some more delicate finger tattoos." I pointed to my pinky, just under my cuticle. "Maybe a crescent moon here and some constellations on the other fingers."

"Sick," Tom said, holding onto my hand to inspect my fingers. "Tiny stars like the ones we did climbing up your wrist?"

I nodded my confirmation.

"Perfect." He dropped my hand and slid over to his

worktable, picking up the glass vial of firefly ink. "Think Lac will mind if we use this? It would look dope to have the moon and stars glow…"

"I wouldn't mind at all," Lacuna said with a smile as she returned from the back carrying a cold bottle of water.

My tattoos took no time at all, and I relished the sting of the needle. I'll never be able to explain it, but the steady buzz almost lulls me to sleep. As soon as Tom was done, I grabbed Lacuna by the arm and pulled her toward the bathroom.

"Where are we going?" she giggled.

"I need to see these glow," I answered, Tom on our heels.

"Hey, wait," he held the bathroom door open for us. "I'm coming too."

"Oh, my Goddess," Lacuna breathed as soon as Tom flicked the fluorescent light off.

"This is unreal." I felt Tom next to us, and I could vaguely see his outline, but Lacuna had become one with the shadows. "I *have* to get more of this ink," he whispered.

It was truly remarkable. Lacuna looked like the night sky lit up with stars or a velvety horizon aglow with fireflies.

"People will come from all over to get this ink, Tom," Lacuna said, breathless with awe. A second later, her sparks were barrelling toward the bathroom door. "I have to go."

She opened the door and Tom flicked the lights on. "Wait, what?" I asked, catching up with her.

"Can you calculate the total and I'll come by with moonstones tomorrow?" she threw over her shoulder at a dumbfounded Tom.

"Uh. Yeah, that's fine, but I thought you—"

"We need to go." This was directed at me and said quite

seriously. I shared a befuddled look with Tom and shrugged helplessly.

"I need to make sure all those have ointment and wrap them," Tom argued. "You can't just leave."

But Lacuna was already handing me my bag and picking up her own, headed for the door. Panicked, I snatched a bottle from Tom's stash and held it up. "This stuff, right?" I looked up to see Lacuna already out on the dark, damp street.

Tom nodded and tossed me a box of cling wrap. "Yeah. Make sure she takes care of those!" he was shouting at me when I stepped out into the night after my suddenly deranged friend. Thank the Goddess the rain had stopped, at least.

"Lacuna!" I whisper-shouted at her, but she was a Shadow Nymph on a mission. "*Purple penguin prancers*," I cursed through gritted teeth.

Lacuna

I knew Blair was behind me, calling my name, but I didn't stop. Not until we reached Hollow Hill.

"What– in– all– the– realms?" Blair huffed, catching up to me.

I looked at my friend, her red hair glowing under the lamp post, and I wondered if I should do this on my own. But that would be reckless. By nature, I'm not a reckless person. But I've also been hearing voices in my head and— I just need to know I'm really hearing Oliver. That I really saw him today.

"Lacuna?" Blair shook my shoulders gently. "Lac, you're scaring me."

Her voice was drowned out by...a number?

4592681

4592681

Over and over again. I blinked rapidly, a series of lights flashing behind my eyes. No, not just lights, but gas lamps. Lamp posts just like the one Blair and I were standing under. I gripped my friend's forearms for balance and her fingers dug into my shoulders.

4592681

It's in Oliver's voice. But what is that number?

"4592681," I said quietly without realizing it. "Gas lamps."

I felt Blair pull away, saying something, but her voice sounded far away. Farther than Oliver's.

"He's looking for something," I uttered, sounding every bit like a zombie to my own ears. "4592681. A lamp post with that number."

A little *whoosh* of air hit me as Blair spun around. "Like this one?"

Her voice made it through the haze and I shook my head, clearing the fog that was Oliver. Blair was pointing at the bottom of the very lamp post we stood under, its warm light spilling on us and turning the cold, wet night air buttery. There, at the tip of her shimmery nail was a golden plaque.

4592681

"I think it's a serial number?" Blair guessed.

"Blair, we have to go." Tears were crowding the back of my throat, making it burn as they crawled up toward my eyes.

"Go where?" she called after me as I shot up Hollow Hill.

I didn't bother answering. My shoes pounded the asphalt and then the damp dirt and leaves as we skirted *Moonrise Manor,* disappearing into the woods.

"This is a bad idea!" Blair hissed at my back every few feet, but I didn't listen.

Just before the clearing for the cave—for the portal to the Mortal Lands, to Oliver—Blair pulled me roughly to a halt.

"Get down," she hissed through her teeth.

A second later, I heard it. Voices. Low and gruff.

Blair

A starling landed on the bush next to my head, where Lacuna and I were crouched in the dark, freezing woods. What was with all these starlings? I definitely needed to scry like Mags suggested. I looked up through the tree branches, barely catching sight of the moon.

Yup, a *full* moon.

"What are those voices?" Lacuna whispered in my ear.

That's exactly what I was about to find out. Though potions were my specialty, I'd learned a fair amount of spying spells from my nosy, meddlesome Wardwell coven and perfected them on my cousins. Carefully, I wove the magic together in my mind and sent it slithering through the trees toward the source of the voices.

As soon as the image slipped back up the magic and into my mind, I stifled a gasp.

"*What*?" Lacuna pushed me hard on the shoulder and I almost toppled over. "What is it?"

"Guards." My voice was all but inaudible and Lacuna gasped. "They're guarding the cave. Trolls and Gargoyles mostly. They're in their true forms and armed."

"Did you tell someone?" she accused me and I balked.

"Absolutely not!" Not yet, anyway...

Lacuna was silent, so I risked the magic of the barest of dull lights to illuminate her face. Immediately, I wished I hadn't. Her features were set like stone. I watched as she ripped off her jacket, all the firefly ink on her arms sparking to life. Without another word, she stood up and tore through the trees, headed for the cave.

"No. No, no, no, no." I rocked on my heels, mind whirring. If she'd left the jacket on, she could have at least been discreet.

Oh, Goddess. If she gets worked up, her hair is going to glow like a lilac beacon.

"*Ghosts in a sandwich!*" I whisper-cursed, standing and darting in the opposite direction of the cave—of Lacuna.

"Who's there?" I heard one of the guards shout near the cave.

Panicked, I lifted my arm toward the sky and shot magic up into the night, setting off a ridiculous spray of fireworks. They popped and sizzled and popped again, shouts of alarm going up near the cave.

Goddess, I hoped it was enough of a distraction.

CHAPTER 19

Lacuna

Magic fireworks lit the sky above the treetops and I sent out a silent thanks toward my Witch friend.

As I ran for the cave, I let my Shadow Nymph power bleed me into the night. I knew my tattoos were glowing, and my hair would be so bright it was almost white with this much adrenaline coursing through me. With any luck, my eyes would be as well.

I dodged the last Gargoyle who'd stayed behind in the excitement, skirting behind him and into my cave.

Finally, I was alone in the Inbetween, pulling on that entangled tether through the dark fog. It was aglow around me with the light of my tattoos, my tresses.

"Please," I whispered into the swirling. Into the thin place separating me from what I felt was missing from me.

I searched for Oliver, my heart racing. There was no way to know how much time Blair's fireworks had bought me.

There.

A lump formed in my throat. Oliver was there, walking along a busy sidewalk. I could see him, clear as day.

I inched closer, holding my breath, terrified he'd disappear.

The Mortal man's step faltered, and he looked over his shoulder. I watched as his gaze landed on what looked like a coffee shop window. Then, I watched as he caught sight of a thousand stars in its reflection. As he caught sight of my tattoos in the reflection.

He whirled around.

It was *me*. He was seeing *me*. My tattoos. My hair. My eyes.

A sob bubbled up out of me.

The recognition in his eyes. On his face. It hurt to look at.

Without warning, he turned and snuck into a vacant alleyway, looking over his shoulder as if he wanted me to follow.

My pulse fluttered.

The fog grew denser and darker, but I followed this man —Oliver.

His gaze was searching every shadow. "Are you here?" he whispered into the emptiness—into the void—and I inhaled a breath.

"I'm here."

He turned sharply toward the sound of my voice.

"Where are you? I've waited so long to meet you. *Please*...tell me where you are. I'll come get you."

"I'm here." My words were choked, my eyes blurring with tears. He was so beautiful. Big brown eyes and carob curls. "I, I don't know where I am," I whispered. "I call it the Inbetween."

Oliver turned in small circles, searching for me. *For me*. I watched as his eyes lit up with a realization. "A window!"

He raced to a shop door at the end of his Mortal alley and I followed, going deeper into the cave on my side. He looked in the dark reflection of the door at my shimmering markings.

"I can see your outline like this," he whispered, his voice cracking, just a little.

He turned around and held up his hand, placing it against the glass.

I did the same, inching closer and pushing against the fog. My fingers brushed his and we both drew in a sharp breath. How had it worked?

He was fading. Floating off into the fog. "What's your name?" His voice was hardly audible, a distant whisper on wind.

"Lacuna."

"*Lacuna*," he repeated it almost reverently, and then he was gone.

Blair

"I don't see anyone. Do you?" Two Gargoyle guards walked right past me where I was pressed up against a tree trunk wrapped in a cloaking spell.

"Nah. Probably some punk kids playing a Samhain prank."

The acrid scent of smoke from the fireworks filled my nose and curled around the tops of the naked trees.

"We should still report it." They lumbered through the

woods, their bulk more than a little intimidating. The taller of the two flexed his back, his massive, leathery wings fanning out. "We better tell the boss before that old fogey of a sheriff finds out we're up here.

"Yeah, okay. Lester can hold it down here, I'd wager. Where's the boss at tonight?" the shorter one asked as they began to walk away, back toward the cave. I hoped with all my might Lacuna had come back out and was safely away from there by now.

"At the inn, last I heard." The tall one said, and my heart stopped. "But we can just use a phone, you idiot."

They disappeared from view and I sank to the damp bramble on the ground.

This cave—a portal into the Mortal Lands—was being guarded, and those men weren't sent by Sheriff Oliphant. There were only two other men I knew about who were aware of this portal: Anon and Andrew.

My instinct was to break off a branch and see if I could fly it like a broom down the mountain, find Grandma and Mom and my aunts, and get this family meeting going down a much more serious path much sooner.

But Lacuna.

And I needed more information. The best option was to slow down. Maybe consult Aramis. We all know Wardwell Witches would take things into their own hands and who knows how that could go. Not well would be my guess.

First things first, I needed to get Lacuna home.

Once I finally found her in the woods, dazed and distant, I convinced her to head down the mountain toward her apartment.

Like many of the Gloam Hollow Square shop owners,

Lac's place was above *Stonewood*. However, chaos ensued on the square as the rain picked back up again.

I summoned a pair of umbrellas for Lacuna and me, and we watched in dismay and delight in equal measure as Bill Winslow ran around with a megaphone, demanding everyone finish setting up for Samhain despite the misting rain and soggy decor.

"It's two days to Samhain and we've returned to fall!" he was shouting. "Get that decor up before sunrise!"

At least one *Goodman's Grocery* employee was near tears and Bill's hyper-chihuahua of an assistant, Marcus, was repeating everything the mayor said while waving around a fall-themed flag. What that was for, I didn't even want to hazard a guess.

"It's almost midnight, Winslow!" Aramis was standing on the sidewalk in front of *Spectre Café* which had long since closed. He did not need a megaphone to be heard.

In truth, neither did Bill. In fact…

"I'll meet you upstairs," I told Lacuna, dropping her and my umbrella off at the front of *Stonewood*.

I marched over and snatched the megaphone right out of Bill's hands mid-tirade, nearly dropping the slippery thing. It squealed in protest of being cut off, much the way Bill did, and I winced.

"How dare you!" Bill whirled on me.

"'atta girl, Wardwell!" Cheers echoed Aramis's praise across the square. "Get out of the rain, everyone," he called. "We'll decorate tomorrow!" He directed the last loud declaration toward Bill with enough venom that I was certain his vipers were trying to slither loose. We could do with a stone Bill Winslow statue in the square—I'd be okay with that.

"You are not the mayor, Aramis Hawthorne!" Bill shouted as he waddled in that direction. "They don't listen to you!"

"They listen to *reason*, Winslow. Run along before the rain washes you back out to sea."

So I wasn't the only one who thought he looked like a disgruntled walrus. I stifled a giggle and Bill turned to glare at me.

"HEEEEELP!" someone screamed out of nowhere.

I locked eyes with Aramis across the square. Shoving the megaphone against Bill's chest, I took off at a run across the green toward the cry for help. Aramis, much closer and much faster, was already there by the time I made it.

He was standing over a wet pile of screeching bones, his hands on his hips. "Never a dull moment, hm?" he mumbled as I approached.

"Aw, Zar." I knelt beside my Unbodied friend. "What happened, buddy?"

I was just—" His skull rolled in the opposite direction from me. "*Fooey!*"

I duck-walked around to face him, ignoring Aramis's great attempt to conceal his entertainment at poor Zar's expense, and probably mine for the duck-walk. "Does this happen often?" he asked.

"More than I'd like," Zar grumbled. "I finally got my gelato cart stowed away behind the party barn and was trying to make it home, but my bones all locked up with the cold. When the rain started again, I just—" His phalanges wiggled separately on the sidewalk with little *tip-taps*. "Fell apart."

Aramis sputtered a laugh at the animated, detached

finger bones, but covered it with a cough when I glared at him.

"I'll put you right as rain," I told Zar, but his bones all clattered against the wet concrete.

"Please, not rain."

"Right. Right. I'll put you right as a clear, warm summer day."

Instantly, the rattling ceased and Zar gave a lung-less sigh. "Ah. That sounds nice."

I'd put Zar back together again on more than one occasion, so the spell came to me quite easily. In no time, the bones were fusing back together by whatever means kept Zar erect without muscle and tendon, and our resident Unbodied was swaying on his feet.

"Oh, thank you, Blair."

I caught him around the pelvis and Aramis jumped to help, hooking one arm behind his knees and scooping him up.

"Help me get him upstairs to his place?"

Together, we gingerly carried him through *Art's Candy Shop* and up the stairs to Zar's little apartment. I'd been up here a couple of times, but Aramis had not and his shock at the place was written all over his amused face. When I say Zar prefers summer, it's not an exaggeration. His entire place is one sun away from a beach bungalow, with the palm tree and beach wallpaper a nice backdrop for his bamboo furniture and hibiscus motif. Not to mention the full tiki bar and his thermostat set to a balmy 95°.

"Zar, your place is a vacation waiting to happen," Aramis complimented him as we laid him on the palm branch-patterned couch.

"Aw, thanks, big guy. It's my oasis." He pointed a skeletal

finger toward the huge flat screen on the wall. "Do me a favor and flick that on and grab my controller, would you?"

"Sure thing." Aramis did as he was instructed and also grabbed Zar's headset. "What are you playing?"

Zar placed the headset over his skull. "Elder Crossing. Wanna see my garden?"

Aramis chuckled. "Next time, bud."

"Are you going to be alright?" I asked, already anxious to get out of the sweltering heat of his apartment.

"Sure thing, Blair, now that I'm up here."

"Okay, we'll see you at Samhain Night still, yeah?"

"Scout's honor!"

We hustled downstairs and the rush of cool air was glorious when we made it back out onto the square. Aramis was pulling at his shirt to fan himself, but I was thankfully distracted by the fact I'd dropped my umbrella at *Stonewood* when I stormed after Bill and it was still drizzling.

"I have to go check on Lacuna," I told Aramis. "Then we *need* to talk."

"Yes, we do. I'll walk you home after?"

Aramis headed for the café and I high-tailed it up to Lacuna's place.

Upstairs in her purple and stormy gray apartment decorated in a vibe I lovingly call, 'Goth Boho Chic,' Lacuna was already fast asleep on her velvet couch. I smiled down at her, so serene and beautiful. My friend had caused a great stir tonight and I was beginning to fear the whole of Gloam Hollow soon. I desperately wanted to ask her about what happened in that cave—what she saw; if what she hoped would happen had taken place. But it would all have to wait until tomorrow.

Pulling out the tattoo ointment and cling wrap from my

soaked bag, I bent down next to the couch and gently spread a little bit on each tattoo I could reach without waking her. The cellophane, however...it wasn't going to happen.

I set it on the coffee table and found a purple notepad in the kitchen where I jotted down a reminder to wrap her tattoos the second she woke up. After leaving the note and a glass of water on the table next to her ointment, I pulled the gold chain of her lamp and left her to slumber, tattoos aglow in the dark.

CHAPTER 20

Aramis was on the square waiting for me when I came down from Lacuna's apartment and locked *Stonewood* up for the night. It took me a moment to find him because he was next door helping Tom's mother, Linda, hang her Samhain decorations since the rain had stopped.

"May I?" I asked Linda with a smile, pointing up to the front of her ice cream and boba shop with a finger crackling with magic.

"Please!" Linda dropped what she was holding and backed up, Aramis doing the same.

In a jiff, I had her decor hanging back up, the spring florals packed in a crate, and I'd even added some moody lighting and a design to her sign.

"Ah!" she squealed. "You made the ice cream black! And the cherry is a Jack-o'-Lantern! It's lovely, sweetie." Linda gave me a hug and bid us both goodnight. Or was it *'good morning'* by now?

Aramis held out his elbow and I took it as we started the

trek to Wardwell Cottage. "I'm sorry you have to walk me all the way home all the time just to come back to the square."

"There are two things fundamentally wrong with that statement," Aramis said seriously. "One: there you go apologizing for no good reason, and two: I *get* to walk you home. We aren't teenagers without responsibilities, who can see one another at the drop of a hat. I will gladly take any second I can get with you."

I looked up at him sidelong, a teasing grin sliding across my face. "You're *nice*."

Aramis barked a laugh. "Mm, I'm not sure many would say that."

"On the contrary. You might think you're a scary Dread Monster, but there's a fair amount of cinnamon roll hidden under all that protectiveness."

He grunted, looking displeased, and I hid a smile. "About this chat we need to have," he said. "Who's going first?"

"You'd better." A fraction of my joy slipped away. "My news might take some time to digest..."

"Ominous."

I grimaced. "Kind of, yeah."

Interest had his eyebrows hitched up, but he finally just nodded. "Well, my news isn't a doozy, but it's a possible step forward."

"Do tell," I prompted, watching the moonlight glisten in the puddles we passed as we walked.

"On my dinner break today, I went to the Sheriff's Department and spoke with Mrs. Cobblepot about the message I heard the morning after I was arrested—the one you said the callback number belonged to Steven. I didn't recall what was said or that what I heard sounded like

Steven, so I asked her if she happened to still have the tape."

I turned my head toward him slowly. "Did she?"

Aramis nodded. "Lucky for us, they don't get many calls and she still had it."

"Anddddd?"

Aramis chuckled at my intrigue. "I listened to it several times. The first couple listens it didn't sound that much like Steven, but by the third time, taking into consideration the differences voices can have over the phone versus in person, it did sound like him but...stressed. A little scared. I didn't register that when I heard it from the granny cell that morning. I was too far away.

"What I couldn't recall earlier was *why* that message had solidified my suspicion that Anon wasn't attacked in the park, despite the message specifically saying the person *'had evidence regarding the attack.'*"

"Well," I asked impatiently, anxious to get to the meat of the story, "did you remember?"

"I did."

"Hawthorne! Spit it out!"

He laughed, a deep sound I felt land in my chest. "Steven said he had evidence about *'that night in the park with Anon.'*"

"You realize that means...nothing, right?"

His grin widened, wolfish, and he pulled me to a stop just before the tree tunnel road and we sat on a bench. Aramis took out his phone and pulled up an app with little audio recording lines on it. He hit a button and a voice came over the speakers.

"I'd like to report an ex-employee of mine accosting me in the park tonight on my nightly walk, arguing with me about a reference I gave to his new employer."

I looked at Aramis and he hit pause. "That sounds like Bill."

"Yup. This was two messages before Steven's. I asked Mrs. Cobblepot how often she checks the messages and she said every day, but she doesn't know how to skip over ones already listened to. So, I heard this one the same morning I heard Steven's, but it was actually a few days old."

"What's the connection?"

"Bill Winslow was Steven's employer before I was and I'd just received a scathing employee reference from him. That was mostly why I hired the kid, just to piss off Winslow."

"So, you think Steven saw Anon there that night? But wouldn't Bill have seen what happened too, then? He was already there when I arrived, but so were Corbin and the EMT."

"I don't think Bill was still there to witness what happened, but I do think Steven was there."

"That is the perfect segway into me telling you I now know for a fact that Anon was not attacked."

Aramis frowned at me. "That would have been handy information."

I shrugged. "You're the one who said not to discuss case things over the phone."

"Touché." He flourished a hand. "I'm all ears."

I explained what Tom had told Lacuna and me about that night. Anon claimed he was meeting his friend who never showed, and when Tom showed up, Anon was already busted up and wouldn't explain.

"Tom panicked and called the police, thinking Anon had been attacked by this friend that, by the way, Tom has never actually met."

Aramis mocked an exaggerated frown. "Color me surprised."

"Yep. It turns out that Anon just went with the lie of an attack and Tom still doesn't know why."

Aramis scrubbed at his beard for a moment, then stood, holding out a hand. I took it, letting him pull me up.

"The timeline does add up," I explained as we walked down the tree tunnel road to the cottage. "When I used my tracking potion, I saw older trails through the park, which would have been Steven and Bill. The other three I saw would have been Anon, Tom, and..." I halted. "Do we even know who? I assumed it was Anon's attacker since it wasn't Boris Leek. Could it have been Steven?"

Aramis's mouth quirked to one side. "Do you mean the trail that led all the way to the back of the café and then behind Art's?" I nodded and he blew a breath out. "Could have been. Maybe he saw something that night that he wasn't supposed to see."

"Are you thinking what I'm thinking?" I asked cautiously, worried he was *not* thinking what I was thinking.

"If you mean that we need to search a dead man's house, then yes."

I gave him a wicked grin because that was *exactly* what I was thinking.

"Now, what's this jarring news you have for me, hm?"

My grin faded and I explained in great detail what Lacuna had told me about her Mortal. About the portal in the cave and the guards and fireworks...

When I was done, Aramis whistled. "That is a doozy. We'll go up and check it out in the daylight."

I nodded too many times, worry taking hold, and he reached out to gently lift my chin. "We'll figure all this out, okay? We have ourselves a full day tomorrow. Get some rest, Wardwell."

He dropped me off at my front door, but I walked around to the back, wondering if maybe I could catch any clues about the hex on our cottage.

Nothing seemed out of the ordinary, so I entered through the back porch door, and I was met with a cacophony of clanging and rustling. The hex at work again?

But it wasn't coming from the direction of the workshop. I rounded the corner into the kitchen to find Hamish.

My cousin sometimes has some pretty gnarly nightmares. Grandma insists it's all to do with his particular brand of magic, how he weaves spells out of nothing because he's so in tune with magic's essence. It makes for vivid, wild streams of consciousness in his brain.

When Hamish has these nightmares, he spends the rest of the night cleaning. Judging by the 'it gets worse before it gets better' style of mess in the kitchen well past one in the morning, it was safe to assume tonight's nightmares had been a doozy.

"Whatcha doin' there, Cousin?" I dropped my bag to the floor and my booty into a chair at the table.

He didn't bother with more than a quick glance over his shoulder at me. "You have your glasses on, genius. What does it look like I'm doing?"

He ripped the lid off a plastic container and the offending smell hit me way across the kitchen. "Gross," Hamish muttered, dumping the mystery goop into the trashcan he'd hauled over to the open fridge.

Ignoring his vile temper and stifling a yawn, I put my feet in another chair, crossing my ankles. *Man*, my arches were sore. "Wanna talk about it?"

"About how you're dripping all over the kitchen floor and you and Mags need to throw away your old takeout?" He sniffed a box of obviously stale pizza and tossed it in the trash. Next was a take-out container from *Santiago's Seafood*. The styrofoam protested as he opened it and he made a face.

"Hey!" I jumped up from my chair, a wisp of magic darting out to catch the container before it landed in the trash soup. "That's only two days old." My magic set it back in the fridge and Hamish rolled his eyes.

"Mags said starlings have been following you again," he mentioned off-handedly, dumping a pot of moldy spaghetti into the trash. "Goddess, we need to clean this out more often."

"Or stop saving leftovers." I leaned my hip against the counter. "What do you mean starlings following me *again*?"

"Ew, I got spaghetti guts on my waistcoat!"

He began swiping at the red and very-un-spaghetti-like green. Only Hamish wore a waistcoat over his pajama set. Well, technically sometimes his mother did, too.

"Don't you remember right after university," he explained as he swiped, "when you dated that absolute tool from out of town?"

"Uh. No..."

Hamish's eye roll was on par with Sheriff Oliphant's famous sigh. "Come on. The Incubus who always had his nose in a book and hated everyone but you, except he didn't know how to treat you and I threatened to boil him like a toad?"

"Oh yeahhh," I hummed. "And then he pushed you into the pool at Maeve's parents' place. Ha. I remember that."

"Wrong part to focus on." Hamish pinned me with his

signature withering stare. "Starlings followed you around for days, warning you that *Sam* was bad news before he just left town without a word."

I frowned. "I mean, he wasn't the best, but I wasn't exactly heartbroken or anything..."

Hamish scoffed. "Tell that to the mascara stains on the shoulder of my favorite New Haven University hoodie." He waved a bottle of lumpy milk at me.

"Hey, aren't we supposed to be walking about *your* issues?"

Hamish lifted one eyebrow and snorted. "The point is: Don't ignore the starlings, B."

He was right. And so was Mags. I needed to scry and figure out what in the realm the starlings were trying to tell me. "Thanks, Hamish," I said on a sigh. "Make me a cup of coffee, pretty please?"

He pursed his lips. "Finnnne."

I trotted into the workshop to grab my cobwebbed scrying mirror and found Mags asleep at the table. I considered waking her, but she had crystals and herbs spread out everywhere like she'd been working at something for hours. Careful not to disturb her, I peeked at her notes and the open grimoires in front of her.

The hex.

It didn't appear she'd made any definitive conclusion, but to be sure, I'd just have to wait until our family meeting when the sun came up.

Which was way too close to now.

I snatched my mirror off a dusty shelf and quietly snuck out the door into the garden.

Kneeling down in the damp grass, I set my mirror in front of me and looked up at the foggy moon. I'd never had trouble with the art of scrying under a full moon, but it had been ages, and the art of deciphering what I'd seen...I was less apt at.

Scrying is not a process to be rushed. I spent several moments with my eyes closed, face bared to the moon as I centered my mind. It's important to keep the questions at the forefront of your mind's eye without directing an answer—the magic, the Goddess, the ether must reveal it. Otherwise, you end up with nothing more than a dream or nightmare of your own imagination. Much like Hamish when he isn't in control while sleeping.

Speaking of Hamish, I heard him tiptoe through the grass and leave a cup of coffee on a saucer next to my hip before he disappeared back inside.

When I was ready to call forth the image meant for me, I opened my eyes and looked down at the mirror, eyes never straying, never distracted.

The mirror's black depths were swirling, coalescing into a violent vortex that had my heart hammering against my ribs. I heard the trill of a starling somewhere in a tree and another on the greenhouse. Finally, the swirling began to dot with sparkles darting around until I realized they, too, were starlings in flight within the image, just before it all slowed and went gray—misty. I watched with my lips parted as I saw myself running through the woods, breathing hard...

It didn't make sense. That had happened tonight with Lacuna... I'd never seen an image from the past before.

But that's when I noticed I wasn't wearing a hoodie and canvas sneakers. I was in a black cloak.

I watched as I took one look behind me, my face set in fear, and then it all went dark.

I gasped, scrabbling away from the mirror as my skin turned ice cold.

"*Rotted oak trees*," I cursed. "What does *that* mean?"

I was so distracted that I almost missed the distinct hoof print in the mud next to the greenhouse as I gathered my belongings. It was most definitely not a deer print, and way too big to be any small, hoofed creature...

Twisting around to survey the grounds, I tried to remain calm as I rushed inside.

CHAPTER 21

"We don't need three kinds of muffins and two kinds of quiches, Minerva!"

"You're just angry because you can't resist my cooking and you don't want your butt getting any bigger!" Mom shot back.

"Who wants their butt bigger?" Aunt Moira flailed her arms.

"Some women purposefully make their butts bigger," Aunt Millie added to the argument not-so-helpfully as she poured herself a glass of orange juice from the carafe. Both her sisters glared in her direction.

I stifled a laugh from my position at Grandma's dining table, and Hamish elbowed me, sipping his tea. The poor guy had massive bags under his eyes. Best I could tell, he never did make it to sleep after his nightmares. Not that I'd gotten much sleep of my own after my scrying.

"The longer they argue, the longer we're here," Hamish sniped in a whisper.

Maggie was attempting to massage the crick out of her

neck due to her night asleep on the workshop table. "Remind me why you didn't wake me up and send me to bed?" she griped at me.

Cheese and newts, I did not have time for this. "Pipe down, everyone," I called over the ruckus. "Where is Grandma? We need to get started."

"Who died and made you the Matron Witch?" Hamish scrunched his nose at me.

"Is everyone in this family five years old?" Grandma's voice boomed from everywhere and nowhere, effectively silencing us all. A moment later, she stepped into the dining room, her deep plum Witching robes billowing out behind her. "I am tired from a night of divination and we all have much to do before Samhain tomorrow." She spun and regarded each of us with narrowed eyes. "And I *know* one of you set off those fireworks in the mountains last night!"

Thankfully, no one said a single word and we all looked guilty when Grandma was in this mode.

"Mildred and Margeret, you called this meeting, so you speak now." When Maggie rose slowly, Grandma clapped her hands together. "Quickly, child!"

Hamish and I grimaced at one another. When Grandma was in Witching robes and reverted to a more vintage mode of speech, we were a blink away from being turned into frogs if one toe went out of line.

(Once, I'd spent a week as a frog for criticizing Mom's lemon meringue pie while Grandma was present and in this sort of mood. And don't go thinking you should call protective services. This is common Witch practice, so calm down. It was actually a very relaxing week by the pond, but I've never told Grandma that.)

Maggie cleared her throat and pulled at the hem of her

moody, flowing boho blouse. "I've been looking into the hex placed on Wardwell Cottage and its source. I haven't exactly figured out where it came from yet, but I have been able to deduce it came from something in nature but not of it."

"What?" Hamish asked, deadpan.

Mags let out a sigh that sounded like her last breath. "I mean the hex was tangled up in something natural." She tumbled one hand over the other as she explained. "As in, it was probably dragged in on someone's clothing or shoes—maybe a bag or something—from somewhere they'd been."

"Outside," Mom clarified.

"Yes." Mags nodded.

"Didn't we already establish that?" Hamish was on a roll of bitterness this morning and I smacked him in the back of the head. "Ow!"

"You two stop it," Moira snapped at us.

"Do go on, Margaret." Grandma waved a hand at her, still in Ancient Crone Mode.

I watched Maggie's gaze slide to her mother. "Well, Mom was the only one in the workshop between the time of No Curse and the time of Now Cursed—"

"*Hex,*" my Mom pointed out. "Not a curse. Quite different, dear."

I mean, that was sort of debatable, but I didn't go there.

"*Hex,*" Mags amended saltily. "Anyway, we think it was something Mom brought in from the woods."

We all turned in unison to my Aunt Millie, and I tried to keep my face even, my pulse steady. This did not sound good.

"Mildred?" Grandma pressed with a quirk of a gray eyebrow.

Millie put her hands up. "If I brought it in, it was

without my knowledge. This means we don't know if the hex was intended for Wardwells or not. It might have had little effect on the cottage and its inhabitants for that very reason: the intent and ritual behind the hex creation were meant for someone else."

"So basically we're still at square one?" Hamish stood and pushed in his chair. "I'm going to go to work. If you lot figure anything else out, let me know."

"Hamish Jasper Wardwell!" Grandma stomped after him out into the hall and we all looked at each other with various expressions of ill ease as we heard muffled berating.

"I have a client first thing," Mags broke the tense silence. "I'd better be going."

"Me too," I added.

Mom frowned. "No one even blasted ate anything." She gestured to the island full of food and threw a fist on her hip.

"I'll take some to go," I offered, though it wasn't an inconvenience in the slightest. 'Cause food—duh. Huffing and muttering, Mom's magic made quick work of compiling several quaint to-go containers, each with a little note inside and a name on top.

"Aw," I said when I saw *Aramis* scrawled across the container under mine. "You made one for Aramis, too?"

Mom rolled her eyes. "I assumed you'd be seeing him soon, and he enjoys my cooking."

I wanted to snort at this because he'd only had a few tastes of her baking that she'd thrust upon him, but the simple fact remained that most couldn't resist Mom's cooking, so she was probably right. "Well, thanks, Mama."

"Of course. Now"—she looked between Maggie and me, her sisters, and then toward the hallway where heated whispers were still coming from—"who wants to sneak down the back service stairs with me and avoid Grandma?"

All in favor said, '*aye*.'

Everyone bustled toward the back stairs, but Mom caught my arm. "We need to talk about your tea reading, Pumpkin Pie," she whispered as we descended and I balanced my to-go boxes. "Your leaves very clearly warned to be wary of a fake friend."

My stomach flipped.

"But," Mom continued, "they also spoke of success in following your intuition." She squeezed my arm as we landed on the ground floor. "Listen to your Witch sense and everything will be fine."

That did not feel overly helpful.

GLOAM HOLLOW WAS THOROUGHLY THRUST BACK into fall, the trees bare again, muted autumn leaves underfoot, and that crisp chill in the air that just makes life feel *better*. Not to mention the fact that, despite Mom's tea reading, I felt steadier during the full moon and in proper fall attire.

I had great trouble sleeping last night and awoke well before dawn. It was the perfect opportunity to change my nail polish back to something Samhain-appropriate (I went with matte black) and curate an outfit for my sleuthing morning with Aramis. After careful consideration, I'd chosen brown corduroy trousers, rolled up two turns at the ankle to show off worn, brown kiltie boots, and a navy and brown plaid blazer open over a dark blue velvet halter top. In my world, it's all about styling versus wearing, so I'd added a belt, a dainty three-tiered necklace, and batwing earrings. I went for a more natural lip stain this morning, a dusting of taupe eyeshadow with brown mascara, and your Witch was ready to face the Wardwell Witches and the Dread Monster's breaking and entering plans.

Step one had gone...not to plan.

I considered the short and possibly useless meeting I'd just had with my family as I walked toward the square to meet Aramis. Maggie had obviously narrowed down the hex culprit to her mother—as far as who'd tracked it into Wardwell Cottage, anyway—but the inception of the hex was another matter altogether. My concern was that Aunt Millie had brought in something from the portal cave. Even worse...from the Mortal Lands. The idea that my aunt had been waltzing in and out of the realm of Mortals was unsettling. To think she'd been doing so with Andrew—a veritable stranger—was worse. Not to mention the hoof print I'd seen behind the cottage.

A shiver raked down my spine and three starlings flitted by at the same moment.

To be honest, I hadn't let myself consider what my scrying vision had meant, either. For all I knew, it was a vision of me running through the woods last night shooting fireworks in the air, and I was in a cloak because...cloaks look cool? I screwed up my face at the terrible logic but pushed it all away. This wasn't difficult to do, considering good ol' Bill was on another tirade.

This time, he was waddling about passing out neon green flyers. He thrust one in my face.

"Town meeting tonight," he groused. "Samhain is tomorrow and someone is running amok shooting off unsanctioned fireworks in the woods!"

Before I could do more than clutch the flyer that I guess

I'm now the proud owner of, Bill bustled off to hand out more from his huge stack. "Too bad he didn't put this much care and effort into, I don't know, the murders of Gloam Hollow," I mumbled to myself.

"That's what we're here for."

I turned to find Aramis standing there with a smile and two cups of coffee. "*Cheese and rice*, you scared me! Lurk much?"

He laughed and leaned closer, looking oh, so good in black jeans and a jean jacket over his usual plaid flannel and t-shirt combo. "You do appear to be juggling two fancy to-go boxes and that one on top looks to have—" He bent in further to have a closer look. "Yup. My name on it."

I narrowed my eyes on him. "One box for one cup."

"Deal." Aramis took my flyer between his fingers so I could take the cup from him, and then he crumpled it up and tossed it in the nearest trash bin. He took the food box from me with his name on it and sniffed. "I'm starving. Let's eat before we head to Steven's."

"Aramis Hawthorne!" Bill shouted, waddling at hyper-speed toward us. "Did you just throw away a flyer?"

"Uhhh let's eat somewhere else." Aramis all but took off at a run and I tried to keep up, but I couldn't stop laughing. "Wardwell!" he censured as I kept falling behind. "If you get me caught by our walrus mayor, I'm going to make you ghost-sit Henry after his day terrors!"

"Stop it," I laughed, bending over to clutch my stomach and nearly dropping my food. "I can't," I sputtered.

"Give me that." He laughed and took my food and coffee, creating a very precarious tower.

"How can a ghost have terrors?" I spit out between laughs. "He doesn't sleep!"

"That's why I said *day* terrors," Aramis clarified. "Sit before you pull a muscle." He jutted his chin toward a nearby bench and we sat.

"So your ghost has anxiety, then?" I took my food and coffee back from him, balancing the food on my knees and setting the coffee on the sidewalk next to me. It was really a picturesque spot, nestled under an oak tree with a view of the same street as the record shop.

"Huh." Aramis hummed. "I hadn't thought of it like that." He inspected the food Mom sent.

I didn't need to inspect it and already had a huge bite of quiche in my mouth. "Yep," I said around the mouthful of fluffy egg, flaky pastry, and savory spinach and cheese. "If he's awake during these terrors, they're just anxious thoughts. Maybe even PTSD. We might need to figure out how your buddy passed."

"I forgot no one knows how he died. I thought for sure he just needed to figure out his unfinished business or something." Aramis took a bite. "Oh my Goddess," he groaned, "is this zucchini and parmesan quiche?" He chewed a couple more times. "With thyme?"

I shrugged. "Sure?"

"If I move into the inn, would this be breakfast every morning?"

I laughed. "Mom doesn't do the cooking there normally, but you do know you have your own restaurant where you can serve whatever you want, right?"

He waved a hand. "It's different when someone else cooks for you."

I watched his profile as he took another bite of quiche and then gobbled down the triple chocolate espresso muffin. It hadn't occurred to me that Aramis cooked for everyone else and never had anyone cook for him. Even on our first evening together taste-testing the foods on his menu, he'd done almost all of the actual cooking. I helped, but it was minorly.

I filed that notion away for later.

"Eat up, Wardwell," he said, sipping his coffee. "We have a house to search."

"You mean to *break into*."

"Semantics." He nudged my shoulder with his. "We'll tell Oliphant afterward. You know the saying: ask for forgiveness, not permission."

"This is why you were a better PI than a cop, huh?" I teased.

"Hey now, I was good enough to make enemies doing both jobs, you know."

Ah, yes. The list of enemies Aramis had made was quite literally burned into my brain. "Here's hoping our breaking and entering can lead to a conclusion about your assassin."

Aramis grinned that wolfish smile of his and tapped his coffee to mine. "Cheers to that."

CHAPTER 22

Lacuna

Never in all my years had I taken two days off work in a row. Not even when I was working as a maid at *Moonrise Manor Inn*, let alone now that I owned my own business.

But the fog inside my head was beginning to drive me batty.

I'd seen him. Heard him. *Touched* him. I know that I had.

I wanted to talk to Blair about it and should have. But I fell asleep before she came up to my apartment last night and nothing could have stirred me from dreams of Oliver.

Maeve would call me a sap at this point, and Anon... Well, I don't know what Anon would say. He'd agreed to open *Stonewood* this morning which was all I could ask for at this point.

And that was why I was marching through the cold woods toward a cave guarded by some very scary dudes. There was no way for me to know how long Blair could keep my secret. Especially with the knowledge that her aunt was mixed up in whatever this was.

It wasn't my secret to keep, not really. It never should have been. I was being selfish and more than a little erratic, but these things don't just happen, right?

It all felt...kismet.

Kneeling behind a boulder to watch the guards milling around outside the cave, I saw Millie Wardwell off to one side talking with them. They didn't seem at odds or surprised by one another's presence at a cave housing a portal into another world.

I didn't have time to consider Millie though, or her intentions. Blair could handle that. All I wanted to do was sneak past everyone, go into the cave, and hope against all hope that Oliver would meet me there.

I watched for far too long for an opportunity that never came. I couldn't stay any longer and there was no guarantee Oliver would be here, anyway. It was possible he was asleep. It had been daytime for him when I came last night...

Frustrated and dismayed, I made my way back down the mountain to *Stonewood* and Anon.

Blair

If you had asked me even five minutes before our arrival at Steven's house what I thought it would look like, I never in a million years would have guessed correctly.

"Well, this is—" Aramis broke off, shoving his hands in his pockets and looking over the white picket fence.

"Quaint," I finished for him. The house was small, but

painted a robin's egg blue, with two picturesque windows and a rather lavish garden that had to have been tended by magic. I sent out a tiny tendril of my own power to see who had warded the house and lent such lushness to the garden.

"Aw," I cooed.

"What is it?"

"My Great-Grandma Wardwell is the one who protected this little house and put a prosper spell on the garden."

That also meant it would be easy-peasy to get in. If I'd been born at the time she warded the house, anyway. Apparently, I had been, or at least in the womb, because my Wardwell birthright opened the door right up.

"*Is it* breaking and entering if your family did the warding?" Aramis asked, his tone sly.

The inside of the house had cute bones, but it definitely lacked a proper interior design touch. Over the floral wallpaper that probably went up ages before Steven arrived, he had hung massive framed photographs. They were stunning pictures of mountain scenes and even a lovely one of the Gloam Hollow gazebo with my apothecary just visible behind it.

"What are we looking for?" I asked, walking slowly through the space.

Aramis had a flashlight that he was shining on everything he looked at. "Anything that looks suspicious or out of place. Oliphant stated in his report that he and Deputy Pete had been through here"—he stopped to shine his light on a pair of sneakers—"and he didn't see anything. My thought is it's been a few weeks now and whoever killed him might have come in here looking for something and left a clue."

"If Steven had anything incriminating, that is."

"Exactly. He might just have been the closest available victim when someone wanted to frame me, but I'm thinking less and less that was the motive. If that other trail you clocked in the park was Steven, he very well could have seen something the night of the first murder and someone came to take out a witness."

I paused in front of a particularly beautiful black-and-white photograph of foggy woods. It was almost as tall as me, in a classic black frame. Speaking of *frames...* "I'm starting to think the perp's desire to frame you is incorrect, too, or it was just a bonus for him. I think it's much more likely we're dealing with someone who wanted Steven out of the way."

Aramis paused his rifling through a desk drawer, his brow pulled low. "Hunch or Witch sense?"

Allowing myself the briefest of moments to consider his question, I quirked my lips to the side...and ignored his attention dropping there—neither of us needed *that* distraction. "Just a hunch. If someone wanted you dead, why would they frame you for murder? You'd be infinitely more difficult to kill in prison."

"You'd be surprised. Someone with connections inside, whether a guard or an inmate that an ex-con has ties to, it can happen. Still, I think you're right. I was there in a dark, haunted house, distracted by my—" Embarrassment flashed across his green eyes and he cleared his throat. "By you." One shoulder lifted. "I was easy pickings if he was already there."

I harrumphed. "And really anyone could have been in there. The square was crawling with tourists and the haunted café was a huge hit." I shuffled through the magazines and takeout menus on the coffee table. "You're sure Henry didn't see anything?"

"Nope. He was banging pots together near the bathroom." Aramis opened the fridge and made a ghastly sound, quickly shutting it again. "Goddess, no one has cleaned that out I guess. Poor guy's been dead for weeks and no one's come to pack up his place."

We both looked around. "Death is harder for the living than for the dead."

Aramis quirked a sad smile. "You're amazing, you know that, Wardwell?"

"Oh, stop." I flapped a hand at him and moved down the hall. "Let's check the bedrooms."

"Good idea. I'll cover the master since, you know...guys are disgusting."

I laughed, happy to dispel the melancholic energy shrouding Steven's place. "I've lived with Hamish for a very long time, but he's so immaculate I can't say I know quite what it's like to experience boy mess."

Aramis stopped in the doorway of a larger bedroom, his hand on the doorframe. "Count yourself lucky, then."

He ducked into the bedroom and I continued past a bathroom to the end of the hall. The door was closed but not locked and I went in, surprised to find it wasn't a second bedroom at all.

The windows were blacked out and when I flicked on the switch, a dull red light bled into the room. The walls were covered with photos, not a single bit of empty wall space visible. The ceiling was strung with cords that had even more photos dangling like clothes on a line. In the center of the room where a bed or rug would normally be, was a long table with empty plastic trays set up over old newspapers. The only other thing in the room was a shelf containing bottles of liquid and several canisters of film.

Steven has taken all those photos? Who knew he had such a raw talent for photography and even developed them himself? Sadness coursed through me as I considered his loss and what his life might have been like if he'd pursued his hobby as a line of work, rather than take odd job after off job.

But it does not do to dwell on the past.

I shook the sad sallies loose and wandered around the room. The photographs were beautiful and would have fetched Steven a pretty moonstone, but nothing really stood out. Until...

"Aramis!" I called over my shoulder, not realizing the alarm in my tone until he came rushing in looking ready to rip someone apart.

"What? What is it?" he asked quickly, his chest heaving.

I smiled sheepishly at him. "Um. I found something."

Aramis visibly relaxed and let out a long breath. "Let's lead with that next time, Wardwell." He came to stand next to me. "What did you find?"

I pointed silently to a photo hanging from one of the many rope lines strewn around the room.

"Well, would ya' look at that." Aramis snorted. "Now we know why Steven was sure Anon had not been attacked."

"And what evidence he had proving it."

It was a lovely photograph of Dew Park at night, eerily empty save for one lone person. This person was, however, not strolling or sitting on a bench or even feeding the Goose-Toad hybrids we were supposed to stay away from.

No, this person was captured mid-fall, flailing as he tipped over, his head and shoulder headed straight for a gnarly fallen tree trunk just waiting to inflict damage on poor Anon.

"Hm," Aramis made a sound deep in his chest. "It's a wonder he didn't break those glasses after all," he mused.

"Seriously. That's quite a tumble. Makes sense why he would say he was attacked. I guess he thought it was better than admitting to a nasty fall."

Aramis nodded. "He just wanted to save face, I bet. Didn't consider there would be any harm in it."

I started wandering around the array of hanging photos again. "Bill saw Steven at the park and they argued, but Bill isn't usually out too late. He likes to have dinner with his mother, go for his walk, and head home for the news by nine. Anon's fictional attack must have taken place after that, and Steven was just enjoying himself taking photos that night."

"The question is if his camera is what got him into trouble." Aramis rubbed a hand along his beard thoughtfully and pointed at the photo in front of him. "I didn't know he was this into photography, but he did bring his camera to work one day."

I came around to look. Sure enough, there was a row of prints of *Spectre Café* in various stages of construction. It had been mostly up and ready to go by the time Steven was hired on, but not completely, and he'd done a bang-up job of documenting. "He took all these in one day?"

Aramis nodded. "Yep. I told him he couldn't bring the camera back after that. He was in everyone's face all day." He flicked one of the photos with his thumb and forefinger. "It was right after this gem here."

The photo in question was a pretty chaotic shot of Aramis hovering over someone, holding their hand in his.

The two of them were in the small alleyway behind *Spectre* and *Copper Cauldron* with a few other guys, and there was a massive oven—that would later be named *Beast*—on the sidewalk.

"Oh!" I realized what was happening. "This was when one of the guys cut their finger unloading the oven! It's the blood I found when I traced the path from the park."

"Good memory, Wardwell." He shook his head, laughing. "Steven had only been working for me a couple of days and he had that camera in everyone's face."

I was still studying the photo, squinting at it. "Hey, isn't that Oscar?"

"Sure is. Good eye noticing that from the back of his head." Aramis chuckled. "Oscar was livid, too. Hurt his thumb and couldn't do much of anything for a bit."

Aramis thought for a moment then grabbed my hand. "C'mon. Let's get out of here. I don't think we'll find anything. If what got Steven killed was in here, it's long gone by now. They might have snuck in while Oliphant had the house open."

My brain had already moved on, anyway. "You're right. There were some empty hooks. Maybe Steven took more photos in the alley that night and caught our assassin on film."

Aramis looked at me and frowned. "*My* assassin. Don't think for one second I'm going to let you be caught in danger."

"That's all very valiant of you, but that cuts both ways, sir."

His frown only deepened. "How about you show me this cave portal, hm? Maybe we can figure out who hired all the guards and why they chose to do so all of a sudden. Then we need to, unfortunately, debrief with our good ol' sheriff. I have to be back by the dinner rush."

MAKING it past the armed guards and into the cave was impossible in the daylight.

Aramis did offer to turn them all to stone with his viper dreads, but we mutually decided we didn't need to be the ones sent to jail.

"You really can't un-stone-freeze people?" I whispered to him where we were crouched behind a huge boulder. To be fair, I was asking more to distract myself from his very close proximity than sheer curiosity.

"I really can't."

Oof. His voice was so low it made my toes curl. Mmk. It was time to go. "We'd better head back."

I sort of duck-walked toward thicker trees and Aramis followed. Once we stood upright and hit the hiking path, I regretted not looking back to see if he had duck-walked, too.

"This was a bit of a bust, but it was a nice hike."

"Says you," I grumbled and Aramis laughed. "At least I wore boots this time, I guess." I looked down at them. "But now they're all dirty."

"There, there, Wardwell. We'll get you some coffee and you'll feel much better." He looked me up and down in what can only be described as a medical diagnosis sort of way. "Maybe a taco or two as well."

I perked up. "You know the way to a Witch's heart."

Aramis laughed. "So this isn't a total bust, tell me more about this Andrew guy and his documentary. You haven't expressly said it, but I get the impression you think he has something to do with the hex on Wardwell Cottage, maybe even more than your Aunt Millie."

I chewed on my lip in thought before answering. "Maybe. I did find a hoof print behind our place that had a distinctly *Centaur* feel. And I find it strange he's with Millie so much. I know she's more or less his tour guide, but Lacuna specifically said she saw Andrew and Millie leave the cave together." I shook my head. "Why would Millie let Andrew in on something so bananas and not tell the family?"

"She doesn't know you're aware of the cave and her knowledge of it?"

"No. I've only told you, and then Lac knows, of course."

Aramis let out a long breath. "It's certainly strange. I wonder if they've encountered the armed guards up there, or if they're the reason the guards are there in the first place."

I turned sharply toward the Dread Monster. "As in they hired them?"

Aramis shrugged. "Possibly. Or whoever did hire them caught wind of a Witch and a Centaur poking around where they don't belong and hired them."

There was that shiver again. And the trill of a starling.

"I have a couple of hours before I need to be back at the diner," Aramis said. "Maybe I should go meet this Andrew fellow and pay a visit to the Marvelous Matron Wardwell while I'm at it." He grinned a charming smile.

"Ha. Schmoozing my mother and now my grandma?" I *tisked*. "You're somethin' else, Hawthorne."

By the time we made it down the mountain and procured coffee and tacos, I was sweaty and exhausted. Aramis ran a knuckle down my cheek tenderly, bid me farewell (yes, he said *'farewell'* in the dramatic accent of a lovesick lord), and left me at the doorstep of *Copper Cauldron.*

It was then that I recalled I had a lovely new tool I'd received as a gift from him and never even said thank you for.

"*Ghost puffs,*" I whisper-cursed to myself, then shouted, "Aramis!" at his back.

He turned with one hand in his pocket—the one that had grazed my cheek where it still tingled—his eyebrow raised.

"Thank you for my laptop. And my phone. I don't think I properly thanked you for either and—"

He pulled that hand from his pocket and held it up. "No thanks needed, Wardwell." With a handsome smile, he turned and walked down the sidewalk.

I went into the *Cauldron* and pulled out my new laptop. I packed it up, along with a few elixirs and potions meant to sprinkle in a bath, then made my way home where I had every intention of completing the following:

- Research Aramis's enemies on the Interweb
- Make a margarita to go with the last taco
- Take a long bubble bath

When I passed *Stonewood*, I decided to pop in and check on Lacuna. I hadn't heard from her since last night when I'd left her up in her apartment after visiting the cave, but I found only Anon and Luke working this afternoon.

Anon saw me and faked an emergency in the back. I rolled my eyes and walked out. It wasn't like Lacuna to take two days off in a row, but I didn't have the mental capacity to worry about it. She was a grown woman and there were guards to keep her from the portal. That had to be enough.

"*Newts knees, that's good,*" I whispered reverently and took another pull from my deliciously tart margarita.

Maggie giggled as she made herself another. "I agree, but I think I need some food with number two. You already ate?"

"A while ago. I could eat again." I winked at my cousin.

"There's no time!" Hamish shouted from the hallway. He rushed in, grabbed my margarita, and downed it in two gulps, then slammed the glass on the table so hard I thought it would shatter. "Let's go, let's go, Witches!" He waved a hand in the air like he was herding cats and headed for the front door.

Mags and I exchanged a look. "What is he on about now?" she asked me in a hushed tone.

But we were already following him. This time, he didn't bother turning around but thrust a bright green flyer in the air. "It was your firework extravaganza that caused a town meeting so step to it."

"Oh, great," Mags muttered.

"Hey, at least we have a buzz." We looked at each other seriously, then burst out laughing.

"*Please* do not be menaces at this meeting," Hamish harped. "I'm begging you."

"Oh, get your cravat out of your butt, Hamish."

The thoroughly appalled look that crossed his face at Maggie's joke only made us laugh harder.

"Walk it off, you two!"

The meeting was pointless. Almost no one was there because they were preparing dishes and crafts and goodies for Grandma's town-wide Samhain bonfire night. There was, however, an opportunity to throw popcorn at Winslow when he wasn't looking.

"Fourteen!" Maggie crowed, counting the number of pieces we'd managed to stick to his tacky sweater.

We were kicked out soon afterward, and—despite the meeting being my fault entirely—I was rather irritated that I'd never thought to get myself kicked out of the boring ones until now.

Headed for the *Bunny's Burger Joint* on the corner, someone behind me latched onto my forearm with a death grip and swung me around.

"Blair." It was Andrew, looking very perturbed. "I need to speak with you."

I felt Hamish's magic crackle at my back at the same moment Mags said, "All good, B?"

"I'm good, guys," I replied over my shoulder, not taking my eyes off Andrew who had at least let go of my arm. "I'll meet you at *Bunny's* in a second."

I didn't exactly have training in how to avoid abduction, but I did know you *never go to a second location,* and several people were milling about on the square. *Bunny's* was just a walk-up window, so Hamish and Maggie would be able to see me the entire time. I was also a bit proud of myself for purposefully saying I'd meet up with them in a second, clueing everyone into how long this conversation was allowed to last before someone intervened.

When Mags and Hamish were out of earshot, I glared at Andrew, my jaw clenched so hard it hurt. I did not enjoy being *grabbed* and his aura was far too dark for my liking. "Spit it out, Andrew."

His perturbed demeanor descended into menacing in a blink. "You wanna explain to me why your PI boyfriend came knocking at my door at the inn this afternoon acting all buddy-buddy and asking questions about my film?"

Oh, this mother trucker was *really* getting on my nerves. Every civil bone the Wardwell Matrons instilled in me went flying out the window.

"Wow, Andrew. Sounds like you're not accustomed to people wanting to be your friend. Or is it just Aramis that bothers you?" I crossed my arms over my chest, my pulse racing. Between his audacity and my snappish dig at his motives, my adrenaline was through the roof.

Andrew all but snarled at me, his lips pulled back from his teeth. A warbled wave passed over him and I fought the urge to step back. I knew the tell-tale sign of an unintentional creature shift when I saw one. And I did not want to confront a Centaur.

The warbling slowed and he leaned in far too close. "You and your little PI need to watch yourselves, *Pumpkin Squash.*"

My hand connected with his cheek before I even realized I'd moved. He looked at me like a startled deer in headlights. I heard Hamish calling my name and feet pounding on the pavement behind me.

"Don't you *dare* call me that again," I bit out through gritted teeth. "And if anyone needs to watch themselves, it's you, unless you'd like to talk to Sheriff Oliphant about your treks into a certain mysterious cave and what you're doing lurking outside Wardwell Cottage at night." Fear flashed in his eyes and I couldn't help the smug smile that crawled across my mouth.

Andrew darted away just as Hamish and Maggie reached me. "Oh, my Goddess!" Mags cried, wheeling me around by the shoulders to face her. "Did he touch you?"

"That son of a—" Hamish was stomping after Andrew with his hands in fists, but I flung a rope of magic around him and he yipped. "Stop roping me like a heifer, Blair!"

"Thanks for your willingness to fight for my honor and all that, but I'm fine. He didn't touch me. He's just—" What? Possibly the one who wants Aramis dead? The one getting Maggie's mom entangled in something bonkers? "He's just a jerk. Can we go home?"

Maggie held up three hefty bags of food. "Sure. Let's go."

Back at home, Mags and Hamish traded off looking at me with furrowed brows and various other shows of concern when they thought I wasn't paying attention, but they said nothing as we each recapped our day.

There hadn't been much progress in the assassin/murder case or in the hex culprit case. Though now I was very worried Andrew had something to do with at least one of those, if not both.

I did not mention the cave and was just beginning to feel guilty about that when Mags announced she was going up to bed.

Samhain preparation would begin very early in the morning for us all. Hamish claimed he needed sleep, too, after her since he hadn't slept well the night before, and I gave them both an elixir from my stash I'd brought home from the apothecary—a peaceful sleep shower steamer for Hamish, a relaxing bubble bath for Mags.

Actually, a bubble bath sounded like exactly what I needed after two hikes in the last twenty-four hours, multiple strange encounters, and a minor assault on someone I thought had become a friend.

With a sigh, I trudged upstairs and drew myself a milk bath. As I sank into the steaming water and fluffy bubbles, I couldn't help the knot of worry and guilt tying itself up in my belly. I needed to tell Maggie what I suspected was going on with her mom. But tomorrow would already be such a hard day for her... Was it better to wait? Or would that only make it worse?

I still hadn't decided by the time the water turned tepid.

Clean, in comfies, and tucked up in my room for the night, I scratched Puck behind the ears on my bed and opened my laptop to finally take an opportunity to research some of the names burned into my memory. Before I began, though, I shot Aramis a quick text.

> We need to talk

While I waited for his response, I found the search thingy, which was thankfully pretty close to the same setup as the library's computers and Hamish's, and entered the first name on the list. It pulled up a few articles and an arrest record, which I read. Apparently, Aramis had tackled the guy (an Orc) to the ground at a horse race and arrested him for money laundering.

I would have paid great money for video footage of this tackle. All the moonstones to my name. Which wasn't many, considering I never kept the apothecary open long enough for customers. Whoops.

I'd looked into three more names on the list with nothing to show for it when Aramis finally texted me back.

> Come in for coffee in the AM

> Aye, aye, Captain

Hardy-har. Sweet dreams, Wardwell

Alone and therefore free to wear the goofy grin Aramis often caused me, it stayed plastered on my face as I typed in the next name plus the word: *birds.* It was worth a shot, right?

Trust the process. Await the serendipity.

All I found was a fairly lame arrest record and a strange bird cartoon drawn by a guy with the same first name. A bust. But I continued on in this way, adding '*bird*' to each name searched, and '*bird tattoo*' when that pulled up nothing.

Just as my eyes were beginning to feel heavy, something interesting came up within the search for: *Arnold Comfrey bird*

ATTORNEY ARNOLD COMFREY
CHARGED WITH EMBEZZLEMENT

A local legend of an attorney and well-known philanthropist of charities such as The Starling Bird Sanctuary and Hearts for the Helpless was arrested late Thursday night at his Upper West Side residence in New Haven by the 99th precinct's star detective, Aramis Hawthorne, and charged with embezzlement. According to the arrest report, Comfrey had forced his assistant, Janet Bonham, to transfer portions of employees' pension funds to his own personal bank account.

Hawthorne was tipped off by a
complaint by an unknown paralegal at
the firm claiming they suspected the
misappropriation of employee pensions.
According to an anonymous source in
the 99th precinct, Hawthorne went
undercover as a janitor in the law
firm to obtain evidence that led to a
warrant for Comfrey's arrest and could
see the 8th-generation New Haven
attorney facing years behind bars.

Did I think Aramis was somehow even more attractive
than when I'd sat down with this laptop he bought me? Yes.
Yes, I did.

But did my Witch sense zone in on a certain portion?
You bet your Witch's broom it did.

A local legend of an attorney and well-
known philanthropist of charities such as
The Starling Bird Sanctuary

"*Bingpot.*"

CHAPTER 24

Lacuna

I couldn't sleep.

I'd swear I heard Oliver calling my name. Like a chant, or a search. A one-man search party.

Arms folded across my stomach, drumming my fingers, I finally gave in.

Throwing off my blanket, I rushed to dress in whatever was on the floor of my room. After grabbing a black jacket to cover my glowing tattoos, I slipped on a dark knit cap over my glimmering hair and a pair of shades to hide my bright eyes. Between the get-up and my Shadow Nymph powers, it was going to have to do. I shoved *The Catcher in the Rye* into my back pocket and locked up my apartment. The square was quiet and empty as I walked my moped toward where I could start it without being heard.

Up the mountain as far as I was willing to take my moped, I hopped off and stowed it in the bushes, taking the rest of the way on foot. It was freezing out again, but I didn't care. Oliver's voice was growing louder in my head.

At the cave clearing, Millie was nowhere to be seen and most of the guards were gone. The three still patrolling were half-asleep and all it took was bleeding into the shadows to make it past them.

Deep into the fog of the cave, I removed my sunglasses, hat, and jacket, revealing every glowing part of me to the portal—to Oliver.

My hands were shaking. I didn't know how long I could wait. How long before one of the guards would sense that something was off and come in to check? The longer I waited, the more foolish I felt. Until—

Lacuna.

It started as a thought in my head, not mine.

"Lacuna." And then it became corporeal.

"Oliver?" My voice shook.

"I'm here," he said, a smudged outline of him appearing in the haze. "Reach out your hand."

I did as he requested, the fog sending tingles up my skin. Oliver, this Mortal man, laced his fingers with mine —invisible, but I could feel his skin. I wanted to keep him with me long enough to truly see him. I tugged him toward me with all my might, a heady desperation possessing me.

As if the veil swayed, I watched with clarity as he fell and fell. Out of the sunny morning on his side. Out of the alleyway I'd seen him in before. Into the dark fog of the cave. Into the Inbetween. Into my starstudded nightfall.

With me.

Breathing heavily, Oliver gathered himself and found my lavender eyes. "It's really you."

He didn't shrink away from me. He didn't run. He knew me. And I knew him.

I couldn't speak. My eyes filled with tears. If this was crazy, I didn't want to be sane.

A tear tumbled down my cheek and Oliver reached out to brush it away. He was so handsome with that brown, disheveled mess of curls, and his warm brown eyes. "Hi," I squeaked.

A wide smile broke across his face and I'd never seen anything that made me so happy. "Hi," he repeated. "Did you get my gifts? I've left them here since I first realized where you might be." He laughed in a self-deprecating way and shook his head. "That sounds crazy. Maybe it was..." He pushed his fingers through his hair nervously and I pulled my hand from his to reach into my pocket.

He watched as I showed him the torn and battered book I'd kept with me for moons, his smile returning. "This was from you?"

Oliver took the book and ran a thumb over the cover. "It was mine. My favorite. And I wanted you to have it." He handed the book back to me, then tenderly took my arm in his hands, as if he'd done so a million times. I swallowed hard as he marveled at the glowing tattoos. "The ink worked."

"The ink was from you, too?" I didn't understand.

"I made it. It took me months..."

"You did this?" I couldn't believe this. I didn't understand.

Oliver simply nodded.

"But, Anon— How do you know him?"

Oliver's face contorted. "Anon?"

A rock skidded behind me and I gasped, turning back to

Oliver, my eyes wide. "Go!" I whispered urgently. "You have to go back!"

"Meet me tomorrow. *Please*." He squeezed my hand and dropped it, melting back into the fog as I rushed to put my disguise on and bleed back into the shadows.

Blair

In the dark of my bedroom lit only by the glow of a laptop screen, I listened to the ring of the phone at my ear. I'd never called Aramis before and it was incredibly late, but when his raspy voice came over the line, I worried I'd want to do exactly that more often.

"Wardwell," he said without preamble. "Are you okay?"

"I'm good. I know it's late, but I think I found something. Can you come over?"

"On my way."

The phone went silent and I looked down to see my home screen—a cute little wallpaper of ghosties in witch hats.

Aramis was knocking quietly on the front door of the cottage in record time. I let him in and peered outside, wondering how he'd managed such a speedy arrival when I saw a motorcycle Maeve would have *drooled* over.

I closed the door and raised an eyebrow a him. "I didn't know you had a bike."

"There's a lot still to learn about me, Wardwell," he smirked.

And I grinned mischievously. "Like how you were

written about in the *New Haven Times* for tackling an Orc to the ground at a horse race?"

Aramis laughed and rubbed at the back of his neck. "Uh, yeah. Like that."

"Why didn't I hear that bike coming up the drive?"

"You don't miss a thing, do you?" The warmth in his eyes had me fighting the urge to preen beneath his attention like a sap. "Part of investigating is keeping a low profile," he explained. "A Warlock buddy of mine spelled the bike to run almost silently."

"Impressive." I led him to the dining room because I didn't quite trust my judgment so late at night when he'd shown up all ruffled and handsome. I had, however, had the forethought to change out of my pajamas and into leggings and an oversized sweater after the last time he showed up at night and I was in skimpy sleep clothes.

We sat across from each other at the table and Aramis drummed his fingers on the wood. "Lay it on me. What did you find?"

I scooted the laptop to where we could both see the screen and showed him what I'd found and highlighted: **A local legend of an attorney and well-known philanthropist of charities such as The Starling Bird Sanctuary**

"I completely forgot that windbag was a principal donor to the bird sanctuary. He loved that place."

I watched Aramis closely, his face taking on a blueish tint in the laptop's glow. "Enough to have a bird tattoo, or weirdly make his hired assassins have one?"

He chewed on his bottom lip. A very distracting habit. Eventually, he shook his head. "I don't think that's his MO. This guy is almost out now. He knew all the great attorneys and he ended up with only a few years' jail time. He wasn't my biggest fan for obvious reasons, but all-in-all, he was reasonable during the trial. Even plead guilty."

My shoulders sagged. I was tired and irritated, and now my bubble had just been popped.

"Did any of the other names pull up anything about birds?" Aramis asked, moving his hand deftly across the mouse pad to scroll through my open tabs.

"No. No connection that I could find."

"Hmm," he hummed to himself. "I could have Kenny pay another visit to our Mimic friend in jail. From what he's gathered, it seems like the hired hands of this guy were all expected to be tattooed, not just Boris Leek. They weren't told why, but maybe he knows something more he's not saying."

"Like maybe he did see who did the tattooing?" I offered.

Aramis quirked his mouth. "Nah. He told Kenny he was blindfolded for it, just like in his interview with Oliphant."

He sighed and I leaned back hard in my seat.

"Hey"—his hand landed on my thigh for a second, so hot I could feel it through my leggings—"you did good work. I still think we should look into the bird sanctuary lead." He looked down and froze, like he'd just realized where his hand was, and pulled it back.

"It's officially a lead, you think?" I asked, brightening at the thought.

"I do. But for now, you should get some sleep. Samhain waits for no Witch."

I laughed and we both stood. "Especially not when my grandmother is in charge."

～

"IF YOU DON'T REMOVE yourself from my presence I am going to cut your hand off with this ax."

"Woahhhh, Blair." Mags stepped between me and our cousin and carefully took the sharp tool from me. "Hamish, maybe go see if Grandma needs anything inside, yeah?"

I glared at her. "It is way too early for this," I snapped.

Hamish groused something similar but stomped away.

"Too early for you to hold an ax around other people?" Mags replied. "Yep. But no one made you stay up until after midnight whispering with a Dread Monster at the dining table." She leered at me and my scowl deepened.

"Didn't someone promise there would be—"

"Coffeeeeeee," Mom sang chipperly, balancing a silver tray and bustling across the back lawn of the inn. She set it down on one of the many tables littered across the grounds and handed me a cup.

"Thank you," I mumbled and took it. I frowned so deeply I feared my face might stick that way and made a show of tipping over the cup. "It's *empty*."

"Aren't you a ray of sunshine?" Mom pointed sarcastically to the carafe on the tray that I'd missed. "*Helloooo*. Coffee."

I stomped over and poured some into my cup, the aroma lifting my mood a fraction. "Grandma has me doing manual labor barely past sunrise. Cutting wood wasn't really on my bingo card for today."

Mags set my ax down and poured a cup for herself.

Mom sat at the table and crossed one leg over the other, bouncing her foot. "Your grandmother doesn't believe in doing magic before noon on Samhain, so tough luck, kiddo. We all know Hamish isn't strong enough and Corbin isn't here yet. I did consider asking Andrew."

I scoffed.

Mom looked at Mags, who awkwardly made some excuse that she heard Aunt Moira calling her inside.

"Did I miss something, Pumpkin?" Mom watched me carefully.

I plopped down in a chair across from her, brushing dirt off my old band t-shirt. "A lot."

"Mmm. Care to share then?"

In the way of mothers and daughters and the safety therein...I told her everything. About Andrew being a jerk and my suspicions of him. About Millie and Lacuna and the weird portal cave. Even breaking into Steven's place and finding all those photos. I spared no detail and she sat listening carefully, only raising her eyebrows when things got interesting. By the time I was done, I felt like a million-ton elephant had fallen off my chest.

Mom licked her lips and leaned over the table, cradling a cup of coffee she'd poured somewhere in the middle of my story. "Let me get this straight. Anon was not attacked, but fell and wanted to save face?"

"Correct."

She nodded once. "Okay, and Aramis's attempted assassin might be the one who killed poor Steven Littlebottom, but you aren't certain?"

"Correct."

"And our dear Lacuna Pindle has a friend in her head from the Mortal Lands?"

"Yes?" I wasn't too sure about that part yet.

"But there is definitely a portal in a cave and my sister has found it without telling any of us."

I cringed. "Correct."

"And Andrew is a monkey's butt."

A laugh popped out of me. "He was last night. I don't trust that guy." I had to admit that the evidence was stacked against him, but it was circumstantial at best. If I wanted to prove he was involved in some way, I was going to have to play nice and get him to talk to me. Maybe that needed to be my first step today...

Mom slapped her palm against the table. "That settles it, then. Your tea leaves were quite clear, Pumpkin. Beware of a friend who is a traitor, but fear not. It will all work out. Samhain will bring you answers and this"—she lifted her hands up in a carnival master-esque display—"is Samhain. Mum's the word from me until tomorrow morning."

She rose and I gaped at her. "Wha— I just handed you a bus worth of information and you're not the least bit concerned?"

"No. I'm not. I have full confidence in you and my Witch sense is..." She looked up to the sky in thought or for an answer, I wasn't sure which. "Tentatively optimistic."

Gee. That's reassuring. "You're just going to let Millie wander around the woods tonight? You know she spends Samhain out there. I—"

"Millie is a grown Witch, Pumpkin. And my sister. I trust her, and so should you."

Mom left me alone with my coffee and ax, flabbergasted at her cavalier attitude. Maybe I was overly worried, but that seemed like a stretch with a *murderer* on the loose.

With caffeine buzzing through my veins as sharply as the magic dangling in the air from my mother's words, I felt my head screw on straight.

First things first, I wanted to cross Andrew off my suspect list or draw a bright red circle around his name. Oh, and abandon wood-cutting to magic—screw Grandma's Samhain rules.

I drained my coffee and left a spell to finish the labor of chopping bonfire wood before I strode jauntily toward the inn. An idea sprung up in my mind as I reached the back door and it soon took root.

If Andrew was Tom's mysterious friend who had procured a contraband book from the Mortal Lands and firefly tattoo ink presumably also from there, that didn't mean he'd done anything heinous—yet. But it did mean Millie and Lacuna could be in danger, even potentially the entirety of Gloam Hollow. For all we knew, the voice in Lacuna's head could be a trap. Some creature in the Mortal Lands trying to find their way back and using Lacuna.

A shiver snaked up my spine. Someone had to have opened that portal, and it was not a Mortal. Which led me to believe it was opened on our side. I didn't think Andrew had been the one to open it considering Centaurs don't have that kind of magic, but I did wonder if he was the one who had supplied Anon and, by proximity, Lacuna with the contraband. If I could check the inn records and see when Andrew checked in and cross-reference it with the time Anon's *'friend'* showed up on the scene, maybe it would give us some answers.

Dodging the hustle and bustle of inn guests coming down for breakfast and the employees/my family running around decorating for tonight, I ended up at the reception desk in time to help someone check in.

"I know check-in isn't until this afternoon," the sweet elderly Elf said, one arm wrapped around his wife's shoulders. "We read that in the little brochure we have, but we're early risers, see, and wanted to get a good nap in before the Samhain festivities." He smiled brightly and his wife chimed in.

"Oh, yes. We've heard Penelope Wardwell throws the most amazing Samhain Night."

"She does indeed," I confirmed, searching the dregs of my memory for how the check-in process worked. Aha, the guestbook—my quarry to begin with. "What was your name?"

"Parks. Richard and Ophelia Parks."

I flipped through the crisp pages until I found their reservation, set for tonight. The key to Room 13 was on its little golden hook, so it was unoccupied. If it was already clean was another question. Knowing Tina and Grandma, they'd probably had someone up there to do so, but with the Samhain preparations, they might have put it off. "Your room seems to be ready, but I'd like to go up with you and ensure it's already been properly prepared. Is that alright?"

"Oh, certainly, dear," Ophelia Parks said, looking every inch a jolly Yuletide Elf with her tuft of snowy hair and rosy cheeks.

After jotting down their time of check-in and initialing it, I lifted the little key to Room 13 from its hook and tucked the guestbook under my arm. The Parks Elves followed me —slowly—down the hall to the last room on the right. I gave a quick knock and unlocked the room. We were all three rather pleased to find it immaculate with logs by the hearth and chocolate Witch hats on the pillows.

Once they were tucked up nicely in their room, I snuck up the back stairs to the library. There, I closed myself in the closet not many knew was hidden behind a bookshelf that is actually a door. It was one of my favorite places as a child, and a secret that crowned me the winner of many hide-and-seek or sardines matches. Of course, the first time I sardine'd there with Maeve she told Lacuna about it, who told Anon, and the whole thing was ruined.

To this day, I'm not sure anyone but the Wardwells and our friend circle knows about the secret hideaway.

Huddled in the dark of my secret hiding place, I broke Grandma's rule again and summoned a glowing orb. The little guy floated above the pages of the guestbook and I perused the pages, looking for Andrew's arrival date. According to the records, he hadn't made a reservation, but simply showed up and asked for a long-term room about four days before the first murder.

Lacuna said she'd had the old book from the Mortal Lands for a couple of moons, and the first mention of the glowing ink was prior to Andrew's arrival, too. But what about the hex and the Centaur print in the backyard of Wardwell Cottage?

Frustrated, I growled and slammed the guestbook shut at the same time the door to my hidey hole flew open.

CHAPTER 25

"Maeve!" I jumped up, hiding the guestbook behind me.

"B?" she squinted at me.

"What are you doing here?" I didn't mean to sound accusatory, but it definitely came out that way.

Maeve looked almost bashful. She shifted on her feet, one hip jutted out. "Listen, I love your grandmother. You know I do. But around Samhain she—"

"Is insufferable?"

Maeve sagged with relief that I wasn't judging her. "Yes!"

I nodded empathetically. "Oh, for sure. Until moonrise on Samhain, she possesses Bill Winslow energy."

Maeve snapped and pointed at me. "Exactly that! I finally couldn't take it anymore. Andrew took over my duties so I could sneak away."

I tried not to sneer at the mention of Andrew and vacated the hidey hole. "The hideout is all yours."

"Thank you, thank you!" She pulled a dangling chain to a light I forgot existed and made to shut the bookshelf door.

"Oh, hey," I stopped her. "What did Grandma have you doing, anyway?"

"Setting out about nine thousand pumpkins, gords, and carving supplies at the carving station."

"Ah, yes." I waved goodbye and hightailed it to the carving station. It was time to confront Andrew.

I found him unloading a wheelbarrow full of pumpkins onto a few tables littered with carving knives, little miniature pumpkin saws, scoops, and a ton of newspaper to soak up the pumpkin slop.

"We need to talk," I demanded.

I squared my shoulders as Andrew spun around to face me, a pumpkin saw in hand. His face immediately soured. "I don't want to talk to you, Blair."

"I don't care." My attention darted from his angry face to the tiny saw meant for cutting triangular Jack-o'-Lantern eyes, then back up. "I need to know what's going on with you and that cave."

"Shh!" Andrew threw a panicked look over his shoulder and tossed the tool onto the table. "Would you keep it down?"

That was not the reaction I'd expected. "Why is it such a secret, hm? Are you the one who hexed Wardwell Cottage by putting something on Millie?"

He balked, looking at me like I'd grown two additional heads. "What? What hex?" He shook his head like he was dislodging the idea. "I'm a Centaur, Blair, not a Warlock."

I sighed and rolled my eyes. "A Warlock could have given you a hexed item to give Millie or place on her person."

"Why would I do that?" He did look genuinely confused. But then his face blanched. "A hex... Is that why weird stuff keeps flying around my house?"

"Flying around your house?" I asked cautiously. "Like what?"

Andrew nodded. "Like a jar of mayonnaise flying at my fridge door until I opened it. The mayo went soaring across the kitchen and landed on a window sill."

"Where is it now?"

"Still there. I was afraid to touch it."

Son of a biscuit. Andrew and Millie had carried a hex back to, presumably, the next place they went after the portal cave. "I think you both need to stay away from that cave, Andrew. We need to tell Sheriff Oliphant abo—"

Grabbing my arm, he yanked me toward one of the low garden walls and we sat. In a hushed tone, he said, "Look, I don't know why Millie wants the cave a secret, okay? But she does and I'm respecting that."

Millie wanted to keep the cave a secret? "Why would you keep a secret like that for her?"

Andrew ran a hand nervously over his knees. "My—" After a long pause, he continued. "My mom passed away a couple of years ago. And Millie has been so kind to me, showing me around up there and—" He set to rubbing his hands together, knees bouncing. "She reminds me of her." A wistful smile curved his mouth and my heart ached for him. "Millie has the same zest for life and unstoppable energy that my mom did."

I suddenly felt like the biggest jerk who'd ever lived. "I'm sorry, Andrew. I didn't know."

He shrugged. "How could you know?"

"If you don't mind me asking, how did you and Millie find the cave?"

"We just sort of stumbled upon it a couple of weeks ago. We were up there exploring and filming and Millie said she wanted to show me a path that was hardly ever traveled. Then we found it."

"I had my camera and..." His face lit up and it was the first glimpse I'd seen of the passionate documentary filmmaker—it looked good on him, the excitement. Passion has a way of lighting up a person. "There it was, this cave filled with glittering fog." He pushed the hair back from his face, eyes wide in wonder, like he could see the inside of the cave right now. "Talk about a wonder. A natural phenomenon."

My pulse spiked. A natural phenomenon—not a portal. Andrew had no idea what the cave was... But there was no way Millie didn't.

"Do you know why it's been guarded? The cave?"

Andrew's elation fell into confusion. "Guarded? I haven't been up in a couple of days, but I've never seen it guarded."

I needed to get to Millie. Pronto.

"Thanks for talking with me, Andrew." I stood from the low stone wall. "It was nice to clear the air. I'm sorry I slapped you."

Andrew barked a laugh and stood, too. "I deserved it. I'm sorry for being a jerk. Millie's just been so good to me and I didn't want this one thing she asked of me to get messed up."

"As far as I'm concerned, you and I never spoke of a cave."

Andrew smiled wide. "Thank you."

When I got to the doorway, he called, "Oh, hey. Can you call off your scary boyfriend now?"

I didn't bother denying the allegation that Aramis Hawthorne was my boyfriend. I think I liked the sound of it too much. "Sure thing."

I took the stairs up the back porch two at a time until I almost tumbled back down them. Thankfully, no one was at the check-in desk, and I'd just tossed the guestbook back under the counter somewhat close to where I'd found it when the front door flew open.

"Morning, Wardwell," Aramis announced cheerfully, stomping across the entryway in heavy boots. "I brought reinforcements."

"Kenny!" I ran around the desk and gave my newest (and Aramis's oldest) friend a hug.

"Hey, kid," he chuckled, giving me a squeeze. "Where do ya' need us?"

Kenny stepped aside and I finally registered the others Aramis had brought with him huddled in the doorway. "Oh Goddess, guys! I'm sorry, how rude of me. Come in, come in."

Oscar, Aramis's construction-worker-turned-egg-flipper-friend, and Cole, the record shop owner, crowded the small entry. "I didn't realize you two knew each other." I looked from Cole to Aramis, narrowing my eyes at the latter.

The Dread Monster smirked at me. "Don't worry, Wardwell. I haven't been to the record shop without you."

"You better not," I grumbled, and Kenny snorted. Oscar turned what was probably a laugh into a cough.

Cole laughed. "He refuses, in fact." He clapped Aramis on the back. "Been trying for weeks to get him to come by."

Aramis stepped to my side and slid an arm casually around my waist. "If Wardwell wants to be the first to take me there, she gets to be the first."

I didn't know what to inwardly freak out about first: Aramis's hand hot on my waist, the fluttering moths as a result of hearing him talk about me, or that he had been saving the record shop for so long so he could go with me.

"*Cheeseball*," Kenny coughed into his fist and Armais's arm slid from me so he could punch Kenny in the shoulder.

"Look at all these handsome men!" Grandma crowed as she trotted in. "Aramis you told me yesterday you'd bring help, but you never said three lookers. How marvelous." She clapped her hands together. "Come along, then. I have jobs enough for all of you."

Kenny, Oscar, and Cole followed my grandma to what was probably their doom, but I squinted at Aramis. "Thought you came here last night to talk to *Andrew*."

His lips quirked up to one side. "What kind of guy would I be if I didn't say hello to your grandmother when I saw her and offer help when she mentioned how much she needed to get done, hm?" He bent down and brushed a kiss against my cheek. "You had that sleuthing look in your eye when I walked in. You'd better run away while you have the chance, Wardwell. I'll cover for you."

Aramis followed the direction Grandma had walked away in, and I could hear her doling out jobs as I tip-toed around looking for Millie and trying not to get a job of my own.

Maggie was sending little wisps of magic to dangle hundreds of candles from the ceiling of all the common rooms when I stumbled upon her in the dining area.

"Hey, Mags."

She jumped half out of her skin. "You scared me!" she whisper-shouted at me. "Don't you dare tell Grandma I'm using magic this morning!"

I sputtered an irreverent breath past my lips. "You know I don't give a flying fart."

Mags laughed and sent more candles to dangling. "Did you need something?"

"Have you seen your mom?"

She looked at me with a mixture of sadness and annoyance. "It's Samhian, B. We both know she's already disappeared."

Beavers in a bungalow. "You're right. I'm sorry, that was insensitive of me. Are you doing okay?"

Mags crumpled into a chair. The candle her magic had been lifting tumbled to the floor and I jumped to stomp out the flame before kneeling next to her. "Talk to me, Mags."

"I know Samhain is a hard time for her, B. I really do. But Mom has been acting *weird*." She lifted her chin just enough for her watery eyes to meet mine, her fingers tangled in a knot in her lap. "I'm really worried about her. She's been avoiding me since I figured out the hex was brought into the cottage by her."

Welp. If this wasn't an ethical pickle for me, I didn't know what was. "Mags, there's something I need to tell yo—"

We both froze as a starling materialized out of nowhere and landed on the sideboard.

"Uh..." Maggie looked from the ethereally sparkly bird to me. "Did you figure out what these are about yet?"

I stood and walked over to the sideboard, hunched over to look at the little bird watching me. "No..." I turned to Maggie. "Your owl translation— Can owls interpret other birds for you?"

I was a rare Witch who could understand owls, bats, and cats while most could only translate one of the three. The trade-off was that I couldn't branch out. Many Witches who spend time cultivating their translation gift can often pick up related dialects. I cannot, unfortunately. Maggie, however, isn't exactly fond of the outdoors, so she doesn't often do much owl-talk at all.

"I could try?" she answered me with a grimace. "But it's the middle of the morning."

She had a point. I stood straight and chewed on my lip. "There has to be a spell for this."

"For talking to birds? Probably. This isn't a real one, though." Maggie wiggled her fingers sending the starling's magic whorling about. "Is someone sending you these birds?"

I sighed. "Like my Spirit Guide?"

Mags shrugged. It was an area of magic that Wardwells knew of but didn't pay a great deal of attention to. In theory, we each had a Spirit Guide who sent us warnings and even our familiar as a Witchling. Maybe it was something to look into, but now was not the time.

"Let's finish setting up and get ready for tonight. Closer to sunset, maybe we can try?"

"Try to get an owl to translate what the starlings want?" Mags confirmed with no small amount of sarcasm.

I grimaced. "Yeah..."

CHAPTER 26

The tables were longer this year.

Something about that had tears springing to my eyes as I stopped to take in the stunning display of the grounds behind *Moonrise Manor*. Two long tables were dressed in black cloth, adorned with golden plates and dark, gothic blossoms, dotted with candles, and laden with an absolute feast. They were flanked by a bonfire that would soon be aflame, and an altar that would soon hold mementos of the dead.

Zar was already there, laying out his wife's wedding band, along with that of Bartholomew's wife and Henry's favorite cufflinks. Zar might hate the cold, but he had a special kinship with the ghosts of Gloam Hollow, and always came to honor them, their dead, and his long-dead wife.

"Blessed Samhain, Blair," he greeted me somberly, a much-bedimmed version of his usual perky self.

"Blessed Samhain, Zar. May the road rise up to meet you."

Sweet Zar sniffled. (Who knows where the snot and air came from.) "Thanks, hun."

A giant cauldron bubbled and gurgled with Grandma's special Samhain cider which was mulled with spells, spices, and whiskey in equal measure. "Let's get you some cider, hm?"

I ladled Zar a generous cup. He sipped it through his teeth, the liquid floating between his ribs before dissipating into mist. What a marvel, our Zar.

"Delicious as always." He lifted his cup in salute and strode away as guests began to arrive on the grounds.

The trees were glowing with orbs of Wardwell magic, and spiders had come to decorate the branches with their shimmering webs. Already, bats were tittering overhead, their excitement for the bonfire amongst their chatter. Beetle, who took Samhain as her personal night of self-celebration, had summoned every black cat she knew from across the realm. I could just make out their glittering eyes sprinkled along the treeline.

"B!" Mags called me and I turned to find her rushing over, already in her guise. Soon, the majority of the town would be here in their own guises, preparing to spook away evil spirits. "Cosette came to my window just now."

I blinked at my cousin. Surely she was mistaken. Cosette is the majestic owl we're convinced doesn't actually live in our realm, because she only shows up when something major is going to happen in Maggie's life. It's a bit like when the starlings show up to warn me, except Mags has the advantage of knowing what Cosette has to say.

"I guess we don't have to seek out an owl after all! What did she tell you?" I asked, enthralled.

Mags shook her head, the mask balanced on top of her

hair bobbing. "She said to find you and meet her in the aerie."

Together, we rushed past guests that were beginning to arrive, and up the winding stairs to Grandma's aerie. There, perched at the window was Cosette in all her splendor. She hooted softly to us and Mags bowed her head, almost reverently.

Some unspoken thing passed between them and I tried not to fidget. My Witch sense was on overdrive. I couldn't shake the feeling that this night would change everything for us. For Gloam Hollow. It felt like one part light and one part very, very dark. My grandmother's divination and my mother's words danced around in my head, leaving me off-kilter.

"She says you need to be careful, B." Maggie's voice broke through the haze. I looked at Cosette, her large eyes boring into my soul. "The veil is thinnest tonight."

My Witch sense sent chills up my arms. "What do the starlings mean, Cosette? Why are they here?" I asked her.

A series of hoots to Maggie and then she faced me, her throat bobbing as she swallowed. "She doesn't know. Only that there is danger ahead. Tonight."

I'd gotten that from my own translation of Cosette's hoots, but Maggie's lip wobbled and it didn't make sense to me.

"Mags, what aren't you telling me?" Or did she know what I wasn't telling *her*?

"Something is shifting. Something isn't right." Her words were quiet. "I can feel it."

"So can I." I came forward and put my hands on her shoulders. "But I'm going to take care of this, okay?"

Cosette gave one final hoot and flew off into the falling

night, her great wings pumping. I didn't need to translate that one. It was a warning and encouragement in one.

"She said '*take heart*,'" Mags squeaked out, translating for me anyway.

I took her hand and tugged. "Come on. The bonfire will be lit soon." And mayhem would no doubt ensue.

We rushed back down to the Samhain Night festivities just as they were beginning, Maggie and I both doing our best to remain calm.

"Mags," I eventually said, pulling at her arm. "Try to have fun tonight, okay? Katarina just got here. Maybe go have some cider and chat with her. Try not to think about any of this nonsense."

Maggie nodded too many times and trotted after Kat. I felt guilty for keeping things from her, for lying to her when I knew it was anything but nonsense, but I felt strongly that I needed to keep the case and the things I was feeling to myself—completely to myself—for just a bit longer.

"You look amazing." I felt Aramis's words on the shell of my ear as he came up behind me and bent low, that arm slinging around my hips again as if it belonged there. And it felt to me like it did. His presence sent a dose of calm flooding me like the greatest elixir.

I *did* also look pretty amazing.

Traditionally, Samhain guises are meant to ward off evil spirits, but as I've mentioned before, we mostly don them for fun, and spend the whole of the night honoring the dead and banishing the past. Tomorrow, we will usher in the new, setting ourselves on a fresh path. For Witches, it's the start of a new year. For everyone else, it's a couple of days of remembrance, free therapy, and fun.

Since the costumes worn for the Harvest Festival are

reserved for sillier, jovial styles, we opt for spookier looks for Samhain. I'd elected a white mask with only a thin black line for the mouth and two crescent slits for the eyes. The idea behind such masks was to elicit fear in the evil spirits through the lack of discernible features. For my outfit, I'd chosen solid black leggings and a long-sleeve top to match, all form-fitting. Essentially, I was a floating, spooky, faceless redhead.

Buuuuut, I hadn't put on the mask just yet. I'd wanted Aramis to see me first, and my makeup did look incredible, even if it would soon be covered up.

He lifted one finger and traced it over my sparkling, iridescent eyeshadow. "This is pretty. It makes your eyes stand out even more."

Aramis was dressed in a thick black cloak any Witch would be envious of. Tucked under his arm was a simple skull mask.

"And you're going to make one dashing reaper, Hawthorne."

He wove his fingers through mine. "So what happens at this Samhain Night?"

"Well," I said coyly as I pulled him along on a tour. "First, the bonfire will be lit, then we will hold Silent Supper where we eat in silence to honor the dead. During that, many will go and leave trinkets of their loved ones on the altar, or they'll light a candle for them there. Once the dinner is over, we'll all carve Jack-o'-Lanterns to keep the bad spirits away and call home the good with the candle inside them. That is when the dancing and fun really begin. The loud music, dancing, and our guises will ward off the evil and honor the good while the veil between the living and the dead is at its thinnest."

Grandma's voice rang out with magic over the crowd. "Blessed Samhain!"

All around us, masks were donned, and, *"Blessed Samhain"* echoed through the trees before a hush fell, all of us basking in the glow of the moon and the anticipation of the night.

"On this night of great remembrance," Grandma began, her arms wide and her velvet cloak billowing, "of power and hope, we gather together to embark upon a new path." She looked up to the moon and breathed in deeply. "As you silently sup and remember your loved ones gone on from this Mortal Plane, look to your left and to your right and know that you are never alone. Though seats may be empty, hearts never are, no matter how lonely we might feel. Spirits surround us. They lead us, guide us, and move through us. Tonight, we banish the dark, and bring in the light!" As her last words rang out, the bonfire roared to life in a show of magical pyrotechnics, sparks flying high up into the night. The crowd went wild, cheering, stomping, clapping.

Aramis's face split into a wide grin, lit warmly by the fire. "I think I like Samhain!" he shouted over the noise, leaning down so I could hear him.

"Come on!" I shouted back, pulling at his arm. "We'd better find a seat!"

"Let us eat!" Grandma called out, and the cheering instantly fell eerily silent, the only sounds to be heard that of the night creatures and the shuffling of feet on cool grass.

Chairs groaned and dishes clinked, but everyone kept silent as they ate. Several times, I caught Aramis looking at me, but then we would both return to our feast and to watching all who had gathered.

As always, Mom left the table to light a candle for her

childhood friend, who had passed away just before I was born. Corbin followed behind her, leaving what looked like a locket—perhaps his mother's—at the altar. Around the table, I saw Maggie, less forlorn than earlier, sitting next to Maeve, who had my Aunt Moira and Hamish on her other side. I had to stifle a laugh when I saw Hamish and Oscar clashing elbows every three seconds, trying to cut their food. Kenny and Cole sat on Oscar's other side, stuffing their faces with chicken and potatoes.

Grandma, Tina, and Andrew sat near the head of one of the tables and each of them rose to light a candle during the meal. Tom sat with his mother, Linda, and Anon, who never once looked up from his plate. Lacuna was distinctly absent. It wasn't like her to miss Samhain and I tried not to worry. There was no way she would have gone back up to the cave with it so heavily guarded. Although...she'd gone *into* it while it was so heavily guarded.

I blew a strand of hair out of my face and finished my roasted chicken.

When the meal was declared over, the sounds of everyone moving, talking, and laughing felt almost deafening after the hour of silence.

Aramis and I put on our masks and talked through them, our voices muffled as we scanned the grounds for our friends. "I think Kenny is over there with Oscar!" Aramis yelled over the din. "He has on the bat mask!"

"Okay, but there are at least twenty bats! Even Hamish is a bat tonight!"

Things were made pretty easy for us when I saw Maggie lift her beautiful owl mask to take a drink of cider, because the bat we were stalking ripped off his mask a few feet away from her, staring at my cousin.

"Uh oh," Aramis chuckled as he saw precisely what I was looking at. "I know that look."

I almost blushed *for* Maggie. It was warm enough with the bonfire and plethora of bodies milling about, we didn't need Kenny starting any other fires. "Hey, what is Kenny's ethnicity?" I asked Aramis as we made our way over, realizing I'd never asked.

"Orc," he answered.

"Ha! Bet he got a real kick out of you tackling the Orc at the racetrack, huh?"

Aramis laughed, full-bellied and rife with the euphoria of a wonderful evening. "On the contrary." We made it to Kenny then. "This oaf was livid I got to the perp first." Aramis pushed him in the shoulder. "Stop ogling Blair's cousin and we'll introduce you."

Kenny's cheeks reddened. "I wasn't ogling her, Dread. She's—" He immediately looked across the party at her again.

"Yeah, yeah." Aramis clapped him on the back. "We get it. Come on."

On our way over, Mags tipped her head back and laughed at something someone had said to her and Kenny paused. "This is a bad idea."

"Oh, no you don't." Aramis pulled him along. "You're a veritable ox. You can't be scared of a little Witch."

Kenny pulled a face and groaned.

"He has a thing for Witches," Aramis whispered to me, but it was more like a shout due to all the noise, and Kenny snorted.

"A Witch doesn't need more than her pinky nail to destroy an ox," he mumbled.

"Got a point there," Aramis agreed.

I couldn't stop smiling, because the moment Maggie saw me, she smiled too, and the moment her eyes landed on Kenny, they turned into cartoon hearts. "Mags," I tried to keep the glee from my voice, "I don't think you've met Aramis's friend, Kenny. Kenny, this is my cousin, Margaret."

"Maggie." My cousin stuck out her hand, her chin high, and I thought I'd burst with pride.

Kenny took her outstretched hand and shook it. "It's a pleasure, Maggie."

"I think our job here is done," Aramis murmured against my ear and pulled me away. "Next up is pumpkin carving?"

I laughed. "I thought you'd try to get out of the pumpkin carving," I teased. "It doesn't strike me as your kind of thing."

"It isn't." He stopped walking and gave my hand a little pull, spinning me into him until there wasn't any space between us. "But *you* like that kind of thing."

"You're wonderful, you know that?" I looked up into those green eyes dancing with the light of the bonfire.

Aramis didn't answer me, not with words. Slowly, he bent in, bruising his lips against mine once before pulling back to look into my eyes. "I'm going to do that again, if that's okay," he said, his voice husky, and I nodded emphatically.

His lips met mine again, but this time he deepened the kiss, holding me close to him. There were internal fireworks, a marching band, and confetti canons, all topped with a deep sense of *rightness*. It was perfect. It was a perfect kiss on a perfect night.

When we pulled apart, Aramis looked at me with such warmth I felt my throat tighten. He wore a smile I'd never seen on him, one that I instantly knew was reserved for me.

"Let's carve, shall we?" he said without releasing his grip on my waist. "Before the evil spirits come and invade us."

It was a joke, and I smiled, but I couldn't help but think there was some truth to his words, even on this perfect night, and I tried not to let it sour the moment.

We found a free place at the carving table next to Tom and Maeve. The two exes were looking not-so-ex-like, laughing and working together on a Jack-o'-Lantern.

"Hey, guysssss." There was no way I could keep the suggestive tone out of my voice. "How's it going?"

Maeve beamed at me, her grisly monster mask balanced on her head and her fangs almost as purple as her lips.

"Enjoying the wine, I see," I teased and Maeve preened.

"It's been a lovely night."

Tom smiled brightly, too. "Hey, your tattoos are glowing a bit!" He pointed his carving knife at my hand.

"Oh, hey, they are!" The little stars and crescent moon he'd inked onto my fingers were twinkling just a bit more the darker it became with midnight's approach.

Mom came over, breathless and carrying two pumpkins, four more floating behind her next to Corbin who was also juggling a few, and he had gourds trailing by magic behind him.

"More pumpkins!" Mom called out, dumping them unceremoniously on the table.

A few people crowded in, going for the tools and pumpkins. One of the masked men bumped into us and Aramis grumbled, "This seems like an accident waiting to happen." Deftly, he pulled me out of the fray and snagged a giant pumpkin out from under someone's nose.

He carried our pumpkin over to a soft patch of grass

near the tree line. It was a little damp with dew, so I conjured a blanket and possibly a bottle of wine.

"Now that's handy," Aramis said as he set the pumpkin down on the blanket and discarded his mask, careful not to disturb the wrap over his viper dreads.

"It's a little far from the bonfire, though," I chattered, rubbing my hands together and curling up on the blanket.

Aramis was on his knees, about to sit next to me, but he paused to remove his cloak and slip it over my head, knocking my mask off in the process. "Better?"

Oh, Goddess, yes. It smelled like him. It was thick and soft and cozy and did I mention it smelled like him? *Swoon.* "Much better." I grinned at him, peeling off my boots. My feet were *killing* me. "Thank you. Oh, *peanuts!*" I snapped my fingers. "Did you grab any of the carving supplies?"

Aramis held up a pocket knife. "I think we can make due between this and your magic."

"That's cheating!" I scoffed.

"Yeah, yeah, yeah. Like you ever play by the rules."

I watched as he expertly sliced into the top of the pumpkin and pulled off what would become the lid to our Jack-o'-Lantern. I just caught the glint of mischief in his eye before he shoved his hand inside the pumpkin and threw a glob of pumpkin guts at me.

"Sir!" I admonished him, reaching in to grab a fistful of the slimy orange goop and throw it right back. "Very rude!"

But Aramis was laughing so hard I thought I would get those cartoon heart eyes like Mags had with Kenny. (Who, by the way, had been spotted carving gourds together.)

Once the entire bottle of wine was gone and we had a very poorly carved Jack-o'-Lantern and aching stomachs from laughing so much, Aramis went to get us some cider.

I sat curled in his cloak, looking up at the stars and contemplating the thinning veil. The loud hooting of an owl stirred me from my thoughts, and I looked out over the crowd of Gloam Hollow residents and more than a few tourists. Soon, the dancing would begin and the musicians were already setting up on the back porch of the inn.

Aramis was weaving through the crowd, stopping every little bit to talk with someone he knew, most of them maskless for a while until the music would begin. Except for the person behind him. I narrowed my eyes, cursing my not-so-great vision and the starburst glare of the bonfire on my glasses lenses. Was that person following him? Surely not. I could have sworn the masked man looked past Aramis then, attention landing directly on me before they veered off abruptly, lost to the crowd.

Someone is a traitor. Beware. A ll the mystic warnings came back to me.

No. No, no, no. It was the same kind of mask worn by the person who bumped into us at the carving table. The carving table full of knives and other sharp objects...

I shot to my feet just as Aramis approached, his smile faltering when he saw the alarm that was surely on my face.

Lacuna

Samhain. When the veil between worlds is thinnest.

All shadows and star-speckled night, I slipped past the guards of my sacred place and into the fog. I already knew Oliver would be waiting, I could sense it. Sense *him*.

This time, I barely had off my dark outer clothing that

concealed my tattoos before he was there, grabbing my hand.

"You came," he said, surprised.

"Of course I did."

"Come with me."

He began to pull me toward the Mortal Lands, toward daylight. But I wasn't ready to go there. Not yet. Maybe not ever.

"Stay with me," I said as I pulled him around to face me. "Here."

His eyes searched my face, almost like he was memorizing every part of it. "We'll sit a while in the dark, then—together."

We huddled against a cave wall, both of us spitting out question after question. I couldn't wait to learn more about this Mortal that had been in my head. The one I thought was a dream. Perhaps he still was.

Oliver's smile dropped as he peered at something over my head. "What is that?"

I turned just in time to see the faint outline of a person, coming through the fog just as Oliver had. "Oh, my Goddess..."

Blair

"What is it?" Aramis asked me, setting the cups of cider on a tree stump next to our blanket. "You look like you've seen a ghost."

Nope. Just a possible assassin in a Samhain mask. I could find Sheriff. I could have Aramis leave...

"Attention!" Grandma's voice rained down on us from where she floated in front of the band, looking ethereal and spooky all at once. "The Witching Hour is nigh, the veil is thin, and the spirits must know their place!"

A raucous applause shot across the grounds, chased by the gonging of midnight bells and the band kicking off with a lively song.

That masked man flashed in my mind's eye and I caught the faint hoot of an owl behind me.

I knew what I had to do.

I bent to pick up both of our masks, casting a silent spell over them that only Aramis couldn't see. "Here." I pasted on my best smile and handed him his mask. "Let's dance!"

He eyed me warily for a moment before I pulled him into the fray.

We swayed and moved with the crowd, masks on, faces concealed. There were so many people, all in various guises, and I couldn't find the one I needed eyes on.

"Are you alright?" Aramis shouted over the music, his hand on the small of my back.

"Yes!" I lied, eyes scanning the crowd.

There. Headed straight for us, shoulders slamming into dancing guests as he stalked toward Aramis. Something glinted in his hand. A knife. One most likely from the carving table. I tried not to gasp when I realized exactly who this left-handed assassin was.

A starling flew behind Aramis's back and I shook myself back to reality. To the here and the now and the *'hurry'* I felt whispered in the hoot of an owl and a starling trill.

Adder-fast, I cast a silent spell over Aramis. A glamor that fell over him, then me.

"I'm going for some water!" I shouted, rushing away

before he could follow me, knowing the other masked man would.

I pushed and weaved through the crowd, headed for the side of the inn until I knew Aramis wasn't behind me, couldn't see me. When a tingle shot up my neck, I darted for the dark forest, knowing my glamor wouldn't hold much longer.

CHAPTER 27

I can't hear anything over the roar of blood in my ears and my heavy breaths rushing out like bellows blowing into a hearth.

If I could think clearly, I would cast a spell to discern if they were still behind me. But I can't think beyond: *run*.

Tree branches slice at my face, my arms, bramble cutting at my bare feet as I rush through the woods, slipping and sliding on the slick leaves.

I risk a look backward—just one. I can still see the glow of the Samhain bonfire between the naked trees, but nothing else. Only dark shadows looming.

I don't see anyone, hear anyone, but I can't trust my ears.

And I've made a fatal error.

At my glance backward, I missed seeing the branch hanging low ahead of me.

With a slap, my face crashes into it. I fall to the forest floor, realizing with blood-chilling terror that my glasses have fallen off in the mayhem. On my knees, I scramble for them through the leaves. But it's no use. My hands are too cold. Trembling too much. I can't find them.

Maybe this was a mistake.

No. I can't think like that. Forward. I have to keep going.

I stand, but then I sense someone behind me.

Instantly, I freeze.

I have to keep moving. But now I can't trust my eyes, either.

My magic won't fail me. Quickly as possible, I rise and pump my legs as hard as I can, casting two tangled, frenzied spells.

A spare pair of glasses lands on my face and the path before me lights up, a wispy purple only I can see. Leading me. Lighting my way. I hear the hoot of an owl overhead and the trill of starlings overhead.

I know he's back there, behind me. Stalking me.

I pull the hood of Aramis's cloak lower over my face. If my stalker could see, he'd know the glamour is gone, that my silhouette is too short to be who he's after. But now it's too late.

For him.

My lungs burn, but I'm almost there. So close.

I break through the trees, skidding to a halt. "*Auntie!*" I bellow, my voice cracking. "Millie, *HELP!*"

My aunt comes rushing out of the portal cave, three dark figures looming behind her. For a frozen second in time, I'm terrified. Where are the guards? Is Millie in danger? Who is behind her?

But then I see the panic on her face turn to boiling rage, and I spin, magic poised. The masked man chasing me has a knife raised at my back. There's a small moment of hesitation when he sees my face. Sees that I'm not who he thought was his prey.

A bolt of my magic, lightning-hot because of my fear and intent to stop this man from ever harming Aramis or anyone else again, slams into the assassin's chest, Millie's spell rushing out to tie him like a hog.

His dagger falls to the ground and he's yowling, squirming. I stomp forward and rip off his mask to find I was right. Completely, sickeningly right about who this was. The traitor friend.

Millie is by my side in an instant, flanked on her other side by Lacuna and who I can only guess is Oliver. Behind this Mortal I don't have the mental fortitude to consider is the fourth person...

A gasp tears through me.

"Uncle Phillip?"

The woods were lit up like a football field.

Aramis was barking at absolutely anyone who would listen to get me water and a blanket. He had not, however, said a word to me after confirming proof of life. Never mind that I already had three blankets and two bottles of water thanks to his demands.

He'd been the first to arrive, Kenny on his heels and murder in both their eyes.

Sheriff Oliphant hadn't stopped shouting at me, Mom pacing behind him and punctuating his lecture with such staples as: *What were you thinking?* and *Dangerous!* and *Never again!*

Millie was explaining the whole encounter to Deputy Pete, while Uncle Phillip had been all but tackled by Maggie when she and Maeve rode up the mountain trails on Maeve's motorcycle.

Oliver had slunk back into the cave and through the portal just after Aramis and Kenny arrived. Sheriff hadn't stopped yelling at me long enough for me to ask Lacuna any questions yet, but she was dutifully steady by my side.

Finally, Corbin heaved a sigh and centered himself enough to walk away.

Mom crouched in front of me. "This wasn't what I had in mind, Pumpkin." The tears in her eyes pulled at my heartstrings.

"I'm sorry, Mama. But it worked."

"It could have ended so many other ways." She reached up and brushed the hair from my face. "You're lucky Grandma thought to use her locating device to find you when Aramis figured out you were missing."

I gave Mom a pitiful quirk of my lips. "I know. But I think Millie might need you more than I do." I gestured to where Millie was wrapped in a sandwich-hug with her long-lost husband and Maggie, all of them trembling with sobs.

Mom squeezed my knee, offered Lacuna a grateful smile for sitting with me, and went with Aunt Moira to support their sister.

Hamish sank onto the rock on my other side and elbowed me in the ribs. "You're an idiot."

I laughed. "Sometimes."

Lacuna leaned into me. "You are very loved, babe. Look around you. You had this entire town worried sick about you."

Aramis was having a heated conversation with Corbin, but I saw his attention dart to me more than once, then go dark when it landed back on the still-magic-wrapped assassin off to the side of the cave.

"You have a lot to tell me," I told Lacuna.

She took a deep breath and said, "Yeah..." on the exhale.

"It turns out that Anon's mysterious friend was Oliver." She smiled, her eyes watery. "But they never met. Oliver was leaving gifts for me, and Anon was unwittingly intercepting them in the cave." She shrugged. "I think he wanted to take credit for them."

Yipes. I worried for what that meant about his true feelings for Lac.

"He finally admitted to everything." She pointed to where Anon was off by himself next to a tree, scuffing the toe of his shoe in the dirt.

"He came up here on his own?" That surprised me.

"I guess so. He's been wigging out so easily lately that I guess his Wendigo was coming out more and more. He needed space to breathe."

That made sense. "Wait. What about the Mortal Lands books? How did he check those out of the library and disguise them?"

"Oh!" Lacuna laughed. "Apparently, that was just Ms. Lilly. She was bored."

I snorted and shook my head. "Sounds like her." But then I remembered what Hamish had noticed about the magic used to lift those books. "That's strange, though," I commented. "The signature on that spell wasn't Tuttle."

Lacuna cocked her head to one side. "That is strange... I did hear Ms. Lilly mention to Ms. Cooper that her magic has been wonky for a while."

That was too much for my tired brain to contemplate, quite frankly.

After a few moments of silence, I asked, "Will you see him again? Oliver, I mean?"

"I hope so." Lacuna turned to look over her shoulder at

the portal cave crawling with people. "Millie is the one who hired the guards. I don't know what will happen now that everyone knows about the portal."

"I suppose that's my fault, isn't it?" I grimaced.

Lacuna only smiled. "No. It's not." Her smile fell into a wince. "Incoming..."

I looked up to see Aramis and Oliphant headed for us, twin scowls in place.

"You started this, Wardwell," Aramis said smoothly. "You want to finish it?" Oh, he thought he was *so* slick, thinking I couldn't hear that undercurrent of pride in his tone.

So I gave him my haughtiest grin. "I was only waiting for you jabronies."

Aramis tried to fight a smirk but failed. Even Oliphant's mustache twitched.

"Let's go, then," Corbin said, helping me and my mound of blankets up. "Better get this over with before Bill waddles up the mountain to get involved."

Corbin walked off and I made to follow, but Aramis stopped me with a hand clasping mine. "I'm sorry," he said, looking stricken. "You–" He sighed and ran a hand down his beard. "You scare the daylights out of me, Wardwell."

I looked up at him for a long moment, studying the little flecks of amber in his eyes and all the myriad emotions crossing his features. "I'm not going to apologize. For doing what I felt was right. For keeping you safe." I shook my head and shrugged. "I'm not going to apologize for caring about you."

Aramis gently took my chin in his fingers and tipped my face up. "Please, never apologize for that." He crushed my lips with his, sufficiently saying anything else that was left unsaid.

The kiss ended all too soon, and he asked, "How did you figure it all out?"

As we strode over to where Corbin was standing over a very irritated captured assassin, I explained, "It started with dinner tonight. Hamish kept bumping arms with him and I realized it was because he was left-handed and Hamish is not. Now, there are a lot of left-handed people in the realm, but for some reason, it stuck with me. Later, I noticed someone in a mask bumped into you at the pumpkin carving table, then was following you through the crowd, and hid when I noticed him. Once I figured out what was happening, I had my suspicions confirmed about who it was because I saw a scar on his left hand. So, I glamored our masks and our appearances to make it look like he was following *you* into the woods."

"And you were right," Aramis said, but he was looking down at his would-be assassin, hands in his pockets. "Hello, Oscar."

Oliphant stepped back, and I did the same as Aramis crouched in front of the man who had been working for him for moons. "How about you explain yourself?"

Oscar's face contorted to the point I thought he'd convulse or start foaming at the mouth. "It was all your fault," he spat at Aramis, who didn't so much as flinch. Nope, he was stone-cold, unmoved.

"And what was all my fault, hm?"

"You're the reason my bird sanctuary closed down. Decades of hard work and all those endangered birds just *gone!*"

I'd never seen a grown man cry over birds before...

"Come again?" Aramis asked, his brows furrowed.

Oliphant looked equally as stumped.

"Oh, my Goddess," I whispered. "You owned the Starling Bird Sanctuary whose principal donor was Arnold Comfrey."

Realization dawned on Aramis. "I put away your biggest donor. So you wanted to kill me?" He whistled. "That sounds about even. Don't you think, Sheriff?"

Sheriff Oliphant had his thumbs hanging in his front belt loops. "I know you're not a cop anymore, but it sounds like *fair* is you making a citizen's arrest, my friend."

Aramis stood. "Nothing would make me happier."

Back at the station, Oscar admitted to hiring the assassins to kill Aramis and admitted to coming to Gloam Hollow to ensure the job was done. When it wasn't, he took matters into his own hands.

"Why did you kill Steven Littlebottom?" Aramis grilled Oscar. "Did he catch you on camera?"

He hadn't quite admitted to that one yet, but I had a feeling Aramis's ploy was about to work.

Oscar's lip curled and his handcuffs clanked against the table. "That idiot Troll always had a camera in my face. He was bound to ruin everything."

Aramis huffed a laugh. "Thought I was the one who ruined everything."

Oscar wrinkled his nose at Aramis.

"So you just decided to do away with the potential problem?" Sheriff Oliphant added, leaning over the table, his chair protesting.

"He already had the photo of you when you sliced your hand open," I pointed out, gesturing to the long cut on his left thumb. "That's how I figured out you did it."

"You think you're so clever, Witch," he snarled at me and

I felt Aramis go rigid beside me. "Steven was less of a menace than you. I should've done you in the same way."

Slowly, Aramis began to clap, looking at me. "Well, well, well. I think you just got yourself a confession, Wardwell."

Sheriff began working up a statement of confession and the questioning was coming to an end.

"There's one thing I don't understand," I said. "Why the bird tattoos? You made your assassins get them."

Oscar nodded, sneering at me. He looked a lot different across an interrogation table than he did flipping omelets. "Everyone at the sanctuary had a bird tattoo." His face fell and he looked at his handcuffed wrists, sounding like the Oscar Aramis had befriended for the first time since the woods. "Nostalgia, I guess."

Hm. If he hadn't tried to kill my Dread Monster, I might just feel bad for the guy. "Next time, maybe think about looking for new donors before you throw your entire life away and try to take someone else's."

I'd had enough of him, so I stood and left the room and the Sheriff's Office. It was nearly 3 A.M. but I had an inn full of family that I needed to be there for.

"PHILLIP." Grandma's voice wavered and I watched her throat bob. "I think the floor is yours."

There wasn't a dry eye in the place. All the Samhain guests had gone into the woods looking for me or headed home. By the time I arrived after taking in Oscar, the place was deserted and my family had gathered around Grandma's living area in her sector of the inn.

Mom had her arm tight around me, the other wrapped around Moira who was squeezing Hamish's arm. Mags was next to Millie, rubbing small circles on her back.

Phillip stood at the front of the room where Grandma had just vacated to sit on Millie's other side. My long-missing uncle cleared his throat. "Several years ago on Samhain night, I went into the woods for a hike, and I never came back. I found a cave that Mills and I had never seen before." He offered his wife a wan smile, his eyes misty. "I couldn't wait to tell you about it, but I wanted to see more of it before I brought you." Millie hiccupped a sob. "As I believe you all have gathered by now, it was not just a cave, but a portal into another world. The Mortal Lands."

He shuffled on his feet, the same man I'd known when I was younger, and yet very different now, too.

"I couldn't get back through." His voice broke, eyes on Millie and Mags alone. "I tried. Goddess, I tried so many times... It wasn't until recently that I noticed a boy kept coming to the portal on the Mortal side and studying it. Like he knew something about it. I started coming every day, thinking maybe I'd see him until I finally worked long enough to buy the house across from the gaslight that marks the portal." He tried for a laugh, but it came out strained and huffed. "I even sent my magic through one day when I saw you there, Mills, with that boy with the camera."

I let out a little gasp. "The hex!" Everyone looked at me. "It was making things in Wardwell Cottage and Andrew's house try to go through other things, like they wanted to escape."

Everyone *hmm'd*, another mystery solved, and turned back to Phillip.

"Go on, honey," Millie sniffled.

Uncle Phillip nodded several times, still off-kilter. "When I saw the Mortal boy begin to leave gifts and they would disappear, I never stopped watching. I knew he was my ticket through. And tonight, I followed that boy through. I followed him home."

Snow fell in a hush, the Gloam Hollow Square aglow with warm, twinkling lights as Aramis and I strolled hand in hand past carolers singing outside *Goodman's Grocery.*

"You were right about winter following autumn this year," Aramis mused.

I breathed in the scent of Lacuna's peppermint cocoa as we passed the stand outside her shop, there to cater to the townsfolk who wanted to be outdoors in the snow. "Mm. It's wonderful. I hope it lasts long enough to have Yule. It's been a couple of years."

Aramis looked up toward the mountains beyond the square, dotted with evergreens. "We're still on for skiing tomorrow?"

"You bet we are."

I wasn't big on physical activity, but I could get down with skiing—if only because after one pass down the mountain, I could sit in the lodge way up on Draak Summit and *read.* The mountains were finally open up there now that our resident Dragon had gone to slumber in her cave.

Life had been *good* since putting away Aramis's would-be assassin and my Uncle Phillip returning from the Mortal Lands. Aramis and I had finally gone on our first date, frequented the record shop for him and the new bookshop for me, and spent many other dates together since.

Mags and Millie, as well as the rest of our family, were over the moon to have my uncle back. It had taken some time, but everyone was falling into a new rhythm.

Lacuna, however, was more glum than I'd ever seen her.

She and Anon were hardly speaking still, and I suspected it was because of his unrequited feelings for Lac. She, on the other hand, was struggling with the new mandate on the Mortal Lands Portal. No one in, no one out.

Aramis and I had snuck her past the guards twice to see Oliver, but each time had just made them both so sad. I wondered if, one day, Lac would slip through and never come back.

"Hey, there's Ken and Mags," Aramis's voice broke through my thoughts as he pointed over by the gazebo twinkling with Yule lights.

Kenny quite obviously had a crush on my cousin, but this was the first time I'd seen them actually hang out together. The closer we got, though, the more I realized she looked...distraught.

Mags caught sight of us and took off at a run through the snow, meeting us in the middle of the square. "Guys," she huffed, the cold coloring the tip of her nose, "we've been looking everywhere for you."

"What's going on, Mags?" I asked, looking between her and Kenny.

"It's Ms. Lilly," my cousin breathed. "She's missing."

"4592681."

Oliver recited the number over and over again. "4592681. 4592681."

He spun in a small circle on the pathway lined with pretty trees all dressed up in lights and pink flowers, one hand running through his carob curls.

"This is ridiculous."

None of the lamp posts had the serial number he'd been sent to find. It seemed to him that the city planner should have *planned* things a lot more thoroughly. Who just jots a bunch of long serial numbers down in a row on a map that spans 35 gas lamp posts? The genius who designed the parks and trails of Billings, Ohio, that's who. And who sends the new City Planner to fix it? Rob Knopf, that's who. City Manager and a royal thorn in Oliver's side.

Working his jaw back and forth, Oliver snatched the wrinkled list of lamp post serial numbers out of his pocket. Running a finger down the list and mumbling the numeric figures as he went, he failed to see the two small children hurtling toward him. They ran, giggling, eyes on each other and not on Oliver. A woman off in the grass shouted a warning, but it was too late. The children bowled into him and Oliver fumbled to the ground in a heap of lanky limbs.

The children fell into further fits of laughter, and ran back toward the attractive brunette he assumed was their mother.

Oliver's list of offensive numerals lifted up on the breeze and he reached out to grab it before it flew away to be crushed up and thrown in the garbage by someone with more sense than him. Someone with the sense to realize that the list of numbers was pointless.

Still on the ground, the cobblestone path digging into him, Oliver flipped the paper over and studied the peculiar symbols he'd scrawled on the back. The ones he'd seen the day his roommate slipped something into his tea, all because he'd wanted to read in his room instead of rubbing up against all of Keith's *upstanding* party guests on their living room dance floor.

Since that night, Oliver hadn't been able to stop drawing the symbols on every spare piece of paper, receipt, or ticket stub he found lying around. They haunted his dreams, those symbols. It was why he'd quit his job writing for the Billings Gazette and become the stupid City Planner.

When he was tripping off whatever godforsaken thing Keith slipped into his tea that night, Oliver had seen things. It had all been a chaotic kaleidoscope of madness, except for two elements. A vague outline of a woman that was more a blur of midnight littered with strange symbols glittering through the dark, and a lamp post.

When he'd thrown up the contents of his stomach and sobered up, Oliver had felt compelled to make the symbols. It felt like the future calling to him through some fog. He searched the library for anything he could find on city lamps and bioluminescence. Three months later, he had a job as City Planner, one vial of glowing ink thanks to his MIT days paying off, and three calls to a psych ward. (He'd hung up all three times)

Oliver shook his head and stood, brushing off his ugly khaki slacks—the uniform for the Great City Planner. *'Called to'* was the best term he could come up with for his insanity toward the imaginary lamp post. It pulled at him, whatever it was he'd seen.

Alas, *six* months later, Oliver's vial of glowing ink still sat gathering dust in his room, and he was facing a depression flair-up at his office job because Rob Knopf was perpetually sending him off to chase a Purple Pony.

That was what Oliver called all the nonsensical, impossible tasks Rob came up with to send him trotting after, day in and day out. Case in point: Gas Lamp 4592681. Its sensor had gone out. The one that told it to keep feeding gas to the flame from sundown to sun up. But, it was in the middle of the stupid day. They were all off and he had a list of numbers, in no specific order, for lamps spanning a three-mile radius.

"Maybe you can, uh, figure out a better system for the lamps, too, kid."

"Forget this." Oliver shoved the paper into his pocket and ambled toward his duplex on Locust Street.

Maybe this was his wake-up call. He'd graduated from MIT a year ago and here he was chasing some weird tea-induced dream. He'd even been asked to join three separate tech teams that actually did something to benefit society after his graduation, but he'd turned them all down.

In truth, it all got rocky before the tainted tea incident.

Life just felt so *heavy* after his mom died... Then, her old buddy at the Gazette said he could have her old position if he wanted it, and Oliver had taken it to just feel a little closer to her.

He didn't.

Keith then gives him the crazy tea and suddenly he's not only depressed but planning to find a way to light up a mystical land of symbols, all because he has a *feeling* it means something. Maybe he was just chasing the idea that he actually *could* feel anything at all.

Oliver kicked a piece of trash against the curb on his way to the duplex. Maybe he should take his aunt up on her offer to live on her farm for a bit. Clear his head. It couldn't be any worse than completing meaningless tasks under the direction of Rob Useless Knopf.

Oliver fished his keys out of his pocket and unlocked the door. Keith was passed out on the couch, a pizza box turned upside down over his chest like a blanket. Knowing Keith, he was probably using it for just such an item.

He half woke up when the door shut, eyes bleary and the pizza box sliding to the floor. "Oh, hey, Oliver." Keith ran the back of his hand along his jaw collecting spittle. "5 o'clock already?"

"Nope."

Oliver kept walking, feet sliding against the worn carpet, drawing his attention to his brown loafers and making him hate his life even more. He took them off and shut himself into his room. The first thing he did was strip off his blasphemous khaki pants and collared polo shirt, slipping on his favorite pair of jeans and a Nirvana tee. He made to lay on his bed, but his first sketch of the symbols mocked him from above his desk. So did his khaki pants and ugly loafers from the floor.

Wordlessly, he gathered the khakis and ripped off the drawing from its tack on the wall. He walked back through the living room, startling Keith again, and went out the door barefoot. He stood in front of the metal trash can for a minute, really contemplating his mental state.

He couldn't be that crazy if he worried that he was crazy. Right?

Oliver threw his pants and the drawing into the bin and pulled out his lighter. He vaguely thought he should've doused it all in lighter fluid first, but that seemed a little too imbalanced. He flicked the lighter to stay on and threw it in the bin with the sources of his madness.

When his cell vibrated in his pocket, jarring Oliver from his flame-induced stupor, he came to his senses.

ROB USELESS KNOPF.

"Hello?"

"Oliver. Where the hell are you? You were supposed to come back to the office after you changed the light bulb."

"That isn't how gas lights work." Oliver threw his phone into the flaming bin, too.

"OLLIE."

Oliver sat staring, not even hearing his name. Their duplex was full of people Keith had invited over on a

Wednesday night, and he had a drink in his hand, but he hadn't taken a sip yet. Keith had been the one to find the garbage can fire. He'd put it out but the khakis and paper were long dead by then.

"Oliver."

He kept looking at the liquid in the red solo cup because it was definitely clear, but it distinctly smelled like coffee. It was driving him crazy. Crazi*er*. The ghost-girl liked coffee instead of tea, while he was the opposite. It freaked him out that he knew it.

"*Oliver*."

He looked up. "What? Sorry." He thrust his cup in Katie's face, where she sat far too close to him. "Does this smell like coffee to you?"

Katie made a face like she'd just caught a whiff of vomit and pushed the cup back at him, sloshing the liquid onto his jeans. "It's vodka."

"Oh." Oliver inspected his cup. It definitely smelled like coffee. "Is someone making coffee?"

Katie sighed and crossed her arms, tanned face and blue eyes pinched. "You're doing it again."

"Doing what?" Being a lunatic.

"You're not *here*, Oliver." She twirled her blonde curls around a finger. "What happened to you at MIT? You're not the same anymore. You used to be Fun Ollie. Now you're..." She gestured to him with a grimace.

He and Katie had dated in high school. It was a wild, fun ride, sure. But Katie was... Katie. And she hadn't changed an iota since they were fifteen. He'd wager his life she didn't know what *iota* meant.

"I grew up, Katie. And my mom died, alright?"

"Geez, Ollie. I know that. But come on. I'm just trying to

talk to you." Her face slipped into that of a not-so-innocent school girl and he tried not to gag. She reached forward with a hand, sliding it up his chest.

Oliver pinched her fingers between his like they were dead fish and peeled her hand away. "Katie, you and I had a good run. We did. But that was over a decade ago and I'm not who I used to be."

"Clearly." She pouted, shoving a lock of hair out of her face. "So, you've met someone then?"

"No." Oliver cocked his head to the side. It suddenly felt like a lie. Which didn't make sense... Maybe he did need the fresh air at his aunt's. Maybe he should get away, or leave Billings and never come back.

"Ollie."

Maybe he should be in a straight jacket in a mental institution. He stared into his stupid cup. It still smelled like coffee. Lavender coffee, to be precise.

"*Oliver.*"

He looked up at Katie blearily, wondering why she was still sitting there. "Sorry."

She pouted. "I was asking you what you thought about me getting a puppy."

"Oh, uh... I'm more of a cat person, so..."

Katie stared at him blankly.

OLIVER KICKED a can down the road, ambling with his hands in his pockets and a disposition darker than the night sky.

Katie had tired of his half-there conversation and Oliver had said good riddance when she stormed off. He was fairly certain he'd only said it inwardly, but she did have an affronted look on her face and he was beginning to blur the fictional and non-fictional, anyway.

Who cared? He'd left the sorry excuse for a party and welcomed the cool air against his skin. The moon was bright and the riverwalk beckoned him. There was something about the water that could always clear his mind.

Normally, there were several people out on the walk, exercising or taking a stroll. Though, at the late hour, the coney stand was closed up, the canoes were all bobbing in a line, and the walk was devoid of human life. Just how Oliver liked things.

With a sigh as close to contentment as he could get while still grappling with his potential insanity, Oliver dropped down onto a cold bench overlooking the water. It was truly a beautiful night.

He tipped his head back, wanting to soak in the stars. The gas lamp, however, was glowing obnoxiously and obscuring his view. He rose and crouched in front of the panel, wondering if he could pry it open and disconnect the gas valve. Pocket knife out and flicked open, Oliver *hmmphed.*

Gas Lamp 4592681.

"Well, I'll be damned." The elusive lamp he'd spent days searching for wasn't even in the area he was told, and it was working just fine.

Oliver pried the panel open and cut the valve. Now he'd have something to do on Monday morning that would shut Rob Useless Knopf up.

He returned back to his spot on the bench and shoved his hands into his pockets, watching the stars dance on the dark water.

Oliver scrubbed his hand over his face. One moment, he was watching the stars on the water, the next he saw a glimmering fog seep out from the lamp post base he'd pried open and someone materialize out of thin air.

A girl. The most beautiful woman he'd ever seen with dark skin and icy purple hair. She was leaning over a counter he thought, but everything was hazy. She had her chin in her hand and he could almost swear he could hear her... Then it all dissipated over the water.

What had just happened? Oliver stood, panting, his hand on his forehead. He was well and truly losing his mind, that's what. Unless... No. it couldn't be her. The one he'd made the ink for. The one who haunted his every waking moment in a beautiful daydream. his ghost-girl.

Reaching for his cell, Oliver came up empty, realizing it was a half-melted mess sitting in the garbage bin outside his duplex. Cursing, he made his way back home, replaying the strange moment with... With what? A ghost? Was it truly a ghost he'd felt a peculiar connection to since the tainted tea incident?

He stumbled through the front door of the duplex, shoving drunk acquaintances out of the way and rushing to his room. He slammed the door behind him and dropped into his desk chair. Heart racing, Oliver pulled out the glowing ink from his drawer, twirling the vial in his fingers.

A mad, unhinged thought was unfurling itself in his brain. Something told him to make an experiment out of this gas lamp.

Oliver looked around his room, trying to conjure a plan,

when his gaze landed on his worn copy of *The Catcher in the Rye*. It was perfect. His fever ghost loved books.

Did she? God, how did he know that?

Before he could talk himself out of it, Oliver shoved the ink back in his drawer and snatched up his old book, headed back for Gas Lamp 4592681.

Gloam HOLLOW

RECIPES

Moonrise Manor
Beef & Vegetable Stew

***The Moonrise Manor chef, on principle,
does not use exact measurements.**

Ingredients:

1.5-2lb stew meat, browned

Beef Bouillon (enough to fill a soup pot)

1 white or yellow onion, diced

1 can of tomato sauce

5-6 Potatoes, peeled and diced

A few handfuls of baby or sliced carrots

2-3 cups or snapped green beans (or one large can)

Salt & pepper to taste

Instructions:

- Brown meat
- Prepare vegetables
- Bring all ingredients to a boil in a large soup pot
- Lower stove to low-medium heat and simmer 4-6 hours

Aramis's
'Bat's Brew'
Mulled Wine

Ingredients:

- 4L Red Wine (dry, full-bodied)
- 1 Cup Brown Sugar
- 4 Oranges
- 1 Cup Cranberries
- 15-20 Whole Cloves.
- 10-12 Cinnamon Sticks
- Extra fruit and cinnamon sticks for garnish

*Makes 16 cups

Instructions:

1. Place a large pot over medium-high heat.
2. Add the orange slices, wine, and brown sugar, stir until the sugar is dissolved.
3. Then, add in the spices and fruits. Do not use ground spices.
4. Reduce the heat to low and simmer the mulled wine for 30 minutes.

Serve the mulled wine garnished with cinnamon sticks, orange slices, and cranberries

Leftover mulled wine will keep in the refrigerator for 3-4 days.

Mama Wardwell's
Chocolate Espresso Muffins

INGREDIENTS

1 1/2 cups all purpose flour, spooned and leveled
1/2 cup unsweetened cocoa powder
3/4 tsp baking soda
1 tsp baking powder
1/2 tsp salt
3 Tbsp freshly brewed espresso, cooled
1 1/2 tsp vanilla extract
3/4 cup granulated sugar
2 large eggs
1 cup low-fat buttermilk
8 Tbsp {1 stick} unsalted butter, melted
3/4 cup semisweet or dark chocolate chips

INSTRUCTIONS

- Preheat oven to 425 degrees
- Line 2 muffin tins with foil or tulip paper liners
- In a medium bowl, whisk together flour, cocoa powder, baking soda, baking powder, and salt
- In a separate bowl, mix together cooled espresso, vanilla, sugar, eggs, butter, and buttermilk
- Add the dry ingredients, stirring until barely combined and a few streaks of flour remain
- Gently fold in the chocolate chips
- Divide the batter evenly amongst the muffin cups, filling each nearly to the top
- Bake for 5 minutes at 425 degrees. Then reduce the temperature to 350 degrees and bake for an additional 10-12 minutes, use a toothpick to check, ensure it come out clean
- Cool for 5-10 minutes, then remove muffins from pan to cool completely on a wire rack

STONEWOOD
Coffee Shop On The Square

LACUNA'S
BROWN SUGAR
PECAN LATTÉ

Ingredients:

- 4 pumps butter pecan syrup
- 1 pump brown sugar syrup
- 1/2 cup heavy cream
- 1/2 tsp vanilla extract
- 1 cup strong coffee or 2 shots of espresso
- Milk (your choice)
- 1 Tbsp toasted pecans (for garnish)
- Whipped cream (for topping)

Instructions:

1. Pump syrups into desired mug
2. Steam heavy cream using a frother or steamer and pour into mug
3. Brew your coffee or espresso, pour over heavy cream and syrup
4. Steam milk, pour over the coffee syrup mixture
5. Top with whipped cream and toasted pecans

Blair ☾ Wardwell's

FASHION BOARD

*The only thing she enjoys
about the magical Interweb

J.L. VAMPA

Jane Lenore (J.L.) Vampa is an author of Fantasy and Victorian Gothic fiction. She lives in the south with her musician husband and their littles who are just as peculiar as they are.

Be sure to follow JL on TikTok - @JLVampa